ELAGABALUS

A GAY NOVEL OF SEX, EXCESS, AND DECADENCE

GAY ROME SERIES BOOK 1

EVAN D. BERG

DISCLAIMER

Elagabalus: A gay novel of sex, excess, and decadence is a work of fiction. All incidents and dialogue, and all characters and events, with the exception of some well-known historical figures and facts, are products of the author's imagination and are not to be construed as real. Where real-life historical figures appear, the situations, incidents, and dialogues concerning those persons are entirely fictional and are not intended to depict actual events or to change the fictional nature of the work. In all other respects, any resemblance to actual persons, living or dead, events, or locales is entirely coincidental.

WARNING

Gay erotic romance. The material in this book contains explicit sexual content that is intended for mature audiences only. All characters involved are adults capable of consent, are over the age of eighteen, and are willing participants.

Published by Faliscan Publishing.
Copyright © 2023 Evan D. Berg.
ISBN Paperback: 979-8-39-619143-3.

PROOEMIUM

Varius Avitus Bassianus was but a young man—a horny young man—when he was proclaimed emperor of the mightiest empire the Earth had ever seen...

Although history knows him by the name of Elagabalus, our protagonist went by different names throughout his life: Varius, at birth; Bassianus, as a cognomen; and Antoninus, as emperor. Elagabal was the name of his god, which was later used by historians to identify the emperor as well.

He was never cruel or evil, but his extravagant lifestyle earned him a scandalous reputation throughout history: if there was one thing pagans and Christians could agree on, it was the moral condemnation of the priest of the sun.

The time has come, if not to redeem him, to celebrate him. Elagabalus's acts appear to the modern eye more as those of an ancient, troubled celebrity, a sensual hedonist, and an aesthete, than as those of a pervert or lunatic. Like it often happens to people who rise to fame overnight, the delirium produced by the exaltation of having been taken suddenly to a summit that reached the heavens must have turned the real world into only a mirage. The horizon before him could have never constituted a limit to his passionate dreams of loving, first a god, then a man.

You offer yourself for sale; mercenaries do the like. You belong to anyone who pays your price; so do pilots.

We drink of you as of the streams; we feel of you as of the roses. Your lovers like you because you stand naked and offer yourself for admiration—something that is a peculiar right of beauty alone—beauty fortunate in its freedom of action.

Pray, do not be ashamed of your compliance, but be proud of your readiness; for water too is public property, and fire belongs to no individual, and the stars belong to all, and the sun is a common god.

Your house is a citadel of beauty, those who enter are priests, those who are garlanded are sacred envoys, their silver is tribute money.

Rule graciously over your subjects, and receive what they offer, and furthermore, accept their adoration.

Erotic Letter No. 19 by *Philostratus*, thought to have been written about Emperor Elagabalus.

CHAPTER 1

THE DANCE

"Come on in, the temple is almost full. Find a place to sit if you can."

The soldiers of the *Legio III Gallica*, sweaty from the long walk in the sun from the Roman camp at Raphanea, followed the hostess's instructions and made their way across the carpeted floor to the dimly lit *cella*, amid the sweet incense smoke wafting in the air and the sullen stare and murmur of the religious attendees. The straitened seating space near the altar was already taken, so they settled for a slightly distant spot with an unobstructed view.

The reason for the Romans' interest in the ceremony was not religion, but entertainment. Their peers had told them of the exuberant dance of the chief priest Bassianus, a young man of extraordinary beauty, and they wanted to delight their eyes before heading back to the camp for an early drunken revelry. Recreation was not plentiful in Emesa, and they had to make the most of their time before being sent on a mission to the Parthian frontier or elsewhere.

As the doors closed and all the attendees were seated, four young women wearing loose red tunics and long pearl necklaces extinguished the aisle lighting, leaving only the altar candles lit, plunging the *cella* into almost complete darkness. The chatter turned into a deferential silence, giving the Romans the feeling of being in a theater.

From behind the altar emanated the leisurely rhythm of a solitary drum. The drummer appeared soon after, followed by his companions, increasing the tempo of the beat. Other musicians joined in playing flutes, pipes—and pear-shaped, stringed instruments that the Romans could not identify—taking up positions on either side of the altar, which was lavishly decorated with gold, silver, and gems of incalculable value.

Those treasures proceeded not only from Emesa and its countryside, but from kingdoms and satrapies throughout the Eastern Roman Empire. The luxury was such that the Temple of Elagabal surpassed even the Temple of Solomon—often regarded as the last word in barbaric ostentation—in taste, wealth, and splendor.

The young women in the red tunics announced the entrance of the chief priest with a ceremonial bow.

Bassianus emerged through the darkness solemnly amid the music and took up a central position in front of the female dancers. He was a tall, slender young man, dressed in what the Romans considered barbarian attire: a long-sleeved purple tunic and a shawl of a darker shade tied around his neck, draping over his chest down to the hips. The reflection of the candlelight on the gold of his numerous bracelets and necklaces and on the embroidery of his clothes dazzled the attendees seated in the front rows, who had to cover their eyes as if they were staring at the sun. The young priest also wore a diadem of the same metal inlaid with various precious stones. His attire was designed not only to please his god, but to remind those in attendance of his noble origin, something that since his exile from Rome some carefree plebeians tended to forget.

Arms drooping, he gazed at the audience with his dreamy hazel eyes. He wore his short, wavy light brown hair combed forward and his pale oval face was framed by jaw-length sideburns. A wispy mustache showed above his full, rosy lips. His expression betrayed no emotion of any kind, and his posture revealed the glamour of royal grandeur, something that had vanished in those Phoenician lands since the emperor Domitian had abolished the monarchy of his ancestors five generations before.

"Beautiful boy, isn't he?" an excited young blond soldier said to his superior sitting beside him.

"Yes, he looks like Bacchus himself," the officer replied in his husky voice.

The priest turned around, climbed the wide marble steps leading up to the altar and split open a pair of thick black velvet curtains, securing them at the sides. Thus appeared a conical stone, black and porous, half the size of a man, with curious reliefs, not carved by human hands—the rock sent to Earth by the sun god Elagabal himself. An engraved golden Syrian eagle in a descending posture watched over it.

When Bassianus exposed the meteorite, the music ceased, and the musicians and dancers kneeled with him before the altar for a seemingly endless time. Just as the soldiers were losing their patience, the young priest raised his left hand with a slow and delicate flick of the wrist, to which the flute players started a melody with a soft and subtle cadence. The other musicians followed the rhythm. Bassianus rose with his dancers, and through a variety of silky moves, always facing his god and with his back to the audience, he allowed them to peck through the slits in his robe at his white, perfectly toned, hairless arms and thighs.

After this sultry dance had continued for some time, Bassianus knelt down on one knee and, looking to one side, remained motionless for a few moments, the music stopping with him. Then he leaped with great impetus, executing a spin, his garments swirling in the air. At the same instant, the drummers set a faster tempo, alluring and seductive, and by the time his feet touched the floor again, his dancers swayed back and forth to the throb of the sound of the full ensemble, their bodies bronzing in the liquid glow of the candlelight. The heady drumbeat had been enriched by the peculiar sound of nimble fingers drumming on the taut goatskins. The sinewy, tall young man dominated the scene with jumps, twists, the swooshing of hands, and the billow of his attire, causing a frenzy far greater than the soldiers had expected.

The two military men, sitting close to one another, their hairy legs touching, gazed into each other's eyes, and exchanged smiles. Their physical proximity increased their already sweltering body heat and quickened their heartbeat. The lower-ranking soldier lightly pawed at his superior's bulge.

"Excuse me, *domine*; I couldn't help but notice your hard on."

"Who would not have one with this fine spectacle?"

"Agreed," the young legionary said, as his superior reciprocated his gesture, grabbing him by his privates. "But I bet this would be more appropriate for the worship of *Fascinus*, wouldn't it, *domine*?"

The two men were trying to stifle their laughter when a woman of a certain age, with large protruding eyes, sunken cheeks, and dyed black hair combed in a middle parting, approached them from behind and patted the older of the two on the shoulder.

"Excuse me," she said with a stern face, as the candlelight highlighted her large nose and jutting chin. "You *domini* don't seem to be paying due respect to our god."

The officer turned around, startled. By the clothes she was wearing—an amaranth red silk tunic, richly decorated around the neckline and hem with golden embroidery, and a dark red lace-knit stola tied with a peacock-shaped brooch—she had to be an important woman, maybe the wife of some city official. He bowed his head, quickly suppressing his smile, like a child scolded by a tutor.

"May I ask your name?"

"I am General Publius Valerius Comazon, *domina*."

His eyes, radiant with the deep blue of a lake before a waterfall, brightened his light olive-toned skin. Short, kinky black hair, poised to unleash its wild nature if left ungroomed, framed the strong profile of a full-blooded Roman. His slightly weathered—but handsome—face revealed the virile expression of an experienced legionary. A heavy stubble, not grown enough to obscure his deep cleft chin and his chiseled jaw, darkened the thick skin of his face.

"I am Julia Maesa."

"Julia Maesa, the aunt of…"

"Yes, the aunt of our beloved late emperor Caracalla herself."

Comazon was about to get up when she motioned for him to follow her to the back of the temple. They slipped through the sitting crowd while the priest busied himself with food offerings and libations, the smell of which overpowered that of the incense. They walked through a thick velvet curtain that led to a hidden room where the sound of the music came only muffled.

"There's no need for formalities, *domine*." She held him with her bracelet-heavy arm. "I respect your service to our fatherland."

"I appreciate it." Comazon was unable to offer a more substantial reply.

"You must be aware of the gravity of the situation, with the usurper Macrinus controlling the empire… I am convinced that he was behind the murder of my nephew." Her grasp on him tightened. "But that is of course, talk for another day." She released his arm. "There is something of greater importance that I would like to confide to you right now, my dear General."

"Yes…?"

"I'm not only Caracalla's aunt; I'm also the grandmother of this adorable boy," she said, as she opened the curtains slightly and looked at the altar. "I've noticed that you've taken a liking to him... am I right?"

"His priestly worship of the sun god is something we had never witnessed before, *domina*." Comazon wondered what exactly the woman had seen.

"That class and elegance have a reason to be. He is the secret son of our beloved emperor."

"You mean... son of Caracalla? But... how can that be?"

"My daughter Soaemias was very dear to him and bore him a son." She chuckled. "We have kept it a secret all along. It was not convenient to reveal the truth at the time, for she was a married woman, but now things have changed." She paused slightly and pierced his eyes with hers. "You know what this means for the empire, don't you?"

The general remained silent, shivers running down his spine.

"I know you do; I can tell you're a smart man." She relaxed her expression, giving her face a chance to evoke the beauty of former times. "In any case, all I need from you is something very simple." She laid a hand on his shoulder. "Would you be so kind as to share with your legion what you now know about dear Bassianus?"

"But *domina*." Comazon looked behind the curtain. "Such an action would be considered treason... You know that!"

"Would this entice you?" Maesa handed him a red velvet purse tied with a yellow cord.

Comazon untied it and when he looked inside his jaw dropped. He looked at her, his eyes wide. The bag contained at least forty *aurei*.

"I can give you much more. That's not a problem. All you have to do is help me spread the truth about my grandson." She smiled as she saw the spark in the officer's eyes. "Don't do it just for the money. It would be a great service to your fatherland."

Δ

After the ceremony, the legionaries walked the long road back to their base commenting on the way about the exotic—but arousing—performance they had witnessed, and how thrilling it had been to admire in real life someone so dissolute, yet so divine. The march passed quickly, and upon arrival they lit campfires to roast the fine game meat from the morning's hunt and brought out the amphorae with *posca*, a fermented drink they used as an aperitif.

Comazon entered his headquarters, lit a small candle, and threw himself on the bed. He remained there for a while, his gaze fixed on an undefined point. Maesa must have seen him and the soldier playing around. Fuck. The bag of money was still in his hand; he tossed it in the air a few times. Was that boy the rightful heir of Caracalla? He shook his head. But wouldn't it be nice to have such beauty to admire on the throne? He chortled. How bad a ruler could he be? Certainly not worse than Macrinus, who—he agreed with Maesa—was responsible for Caracalla's death, and who definitely did not treat the troops with the respect of his predecessor. He had denied them privileges and a pay raise, while he lived in luxury in Antioch, grooming his beard and organizing "philosophical" debates. Yes, it would be a good thing to get rid of Macrinus. However, was it lawful to install this boy in his place? If what his grandmother claimed about his ancestry was true, it would all be perfectly legal. But, if not? He looked at the bag again. He sighed. That woman was not someone he wanted as an enemy, especially if she had seen what he thought she had seen. Upon hearing the loud blaring of horns, trumpets and *buccinae*, he stood up and placed the bag on the bedside table.

Outside, some legionaries were already engaged in the singing of old war songs, while others were attempting, to the laughter of their peers, to recreate the dance steps they had seen in the temple. The men drank, sang, danced, and laughed, arm in arm in a camaraderie that couldn't make Comazon prouder. It was the personal sign of his leadership: bravery on the battlefield and levity in the camp. That was why his men loved him.

After a few hours, Comazon stood up and stretched his arms with a yawn. He stumbled a few steps toward his room, then turned around and stared at the young blond soldier who had been sitting next to him in the temple. When the boy returned his gaze, he jerked his head, motioning for him to follow. They walked in an embrace, away from the firelights.

Once inside the lair, the two men merged in a passionate kiss, Comazon masterfully stripping the soldier of his tunic and *subligaculum*, rubbing his rough hands over the legionary's white skin. His mate undressed him in return. They fell on the bed kissing, tasting the wine on their tongues, caressing each other with desperation. Comazon blew out the only candle that illuminated the room, and both men, completely naked, crawled under a thick fur blanket to protect themselves from the autumn chill. They embraced tightly and continued to kiss and touch each other's bodies at will. The soldier could not get enough of Comazon's furry chest and brushed his nose rashly against the thick-haired, man-scented armpits of the general. Comazon rubbed one of the soldier's white, delicate cheeks with his rough stubble before kissing some more, while touching and fingering the hungry hole behind. He turned his boy around to lay his back against him and spat on his own hand to lubricate his growing cock. He gently inserted the head of his member into the young soldier's asshole, while holding him by the chest with one of his strong, hairy arms. He used his other hand to hold the legionary's fully erect cock, at the same time as he entered him. Comazon let out a grunt and the boy moaned, a victim of unfamiliar pleasure, having never before tried the general's weapon of choice. Comazon kept thrusting until he was completely inside the legionary's tight hole, his cock enjoying the cozy warmth inside. He moved slowly, savoring every thrust as the slides of his log became slicker. The movement of his body caused his chest hair to pleasantly scrub the boy's back. He kissed the soldier's neck and inserted his tongue into his ear as he jerked him off, which made the young man shiver and yelp.

The men outside noticed the absence of the general and the recruit. They knew that their leader liked to have a different young man in his lair most nights when they were encamped. It was a matter of no consequence to them, for he was the best and bravest commander in the world and had led them to countless victories at both ends of the frontier.

Inside the room, the boy was now lying on his back, while Comazon topped him mercilessly. In this position, the general had been able to go even deeper inside his male cavity and inserted his impossibly erect penis in rhythmic thrusts, coordinated with the ever louder moans of his boy.

"Yes, General Comazon, take me, make me yours, ahh!"

It was time to release his load. He took out his cock and jerked it off violently until the thick white substance fell onto the young man's chiseled abs. He kissed his lover deeply as he smeared his cum on the boy's cock and balls and helped him blow his own load.

When they finished, the two men lay down, cuddling in the warmth of the sex-smelling den: the sweet smell that gave Comazon incredible bravery before a battle, and also great comfort after winning it. However, sex on a regular day, especially on a drinking day, was not an uncommon demand of his insatiable masculinity. Comazon embraced his boy, protecting him with his body heat like a bear would his cub, and both slept soundly.

Δ

The lovers awoke before dawn—discipline was for Comazon the only thing as sacred as sex. Despite his nocturnal amusements, the general cared deeply about maintaining the morale of his legion. The boy rested his head on the commander's powerful chest, running his fingers through the thick black fur.

"Did you have a good time last night?" Comazon whispered in his deep voice, his arm draped around the young man.

"Yes, I did, my general. And it was an honor to finally serve you as every good soldier of this legion should."

"You did well, my boy, you did well," Comazon said, running his fingers through the young man's blond hair.

"Would you like me to prepare you a drink?" the soldier said, rising slightly.

"No, stay here a little longer." Comazon got up and leaned on his side. "There's something I want to talk to you about. Do you remember that woman who approached me in the temple?"

"Of course. She seemed of the scary type."

Comazon nodded. "She's indeed a respectable matron. Did you see what she gave me?"

The boy shrugged his shoulders.

"Hand me that bag on the bedside table."

The boy reached for the heavy purse. Comazon untied it.

"What is this?" the boy said, his eyes sparkling. "Did she owe you this money?"

Comazon smiled. "No. I will not lie to you, Son. It is a bribe."

"A bribe?"

"Yes, a bribe. I presume she wants us to proclaim her grandson... that cute little priest... emperor of Rome."

The boy burst out laughing. "You don't think she's serious, right, General?"

"I am completely sure she is."

"But, you couldn't consider it, right? That would be treason! We would be crucified."

"If we fail. Besides, she gave me an even more powerful reason to help her."

"What is it?"

"She claims that the youth is Caracalla's son."

The boy put his hand to his chin. "Does she have any proof?"

"His resemblance to the emperor." Comazon paused briefly. "And her word," he said winking.

"Why are you telling me this, General?"

"I want your advice on what to do."

"My advice? But the wise man in this bed is you, not me. How can I, a simple *miles*, advise the greatest general of our times on what to do?"

"Sometimes good advice comes from the most unexpected places."

Comazon laid his back on the bed and the boy rested his head on the immense chest again.

"I'm flattered by your confidence, *domine*," he said while caressing him. "And I'm sorry that I cannot offer you any advice, but..."

"But?"

"All I can say is that your men and I will follow you to glory or death in battle, if necessary."

Comazon smiled and kissed the boy passionately. Then he looked him in the eye. "That is all I needed to hear. The men of this legion make me so proud." He gave him a peck on the lips. "Not only do I believe the old lady's account of her grandson's lineage, but…"

"But?"

"It would not hurt if we all suddenly became very rich."

The boy burst in laughter and tongue-kissed his man again. Nothing in the world could top being a legionary of the *Legio III Gallica.*

Δ

Dinner had been served in Julia Maesa's *domus*. She lay on the central divan of the *triclinium*, accompanied by her family, consisting of her eldest daughter, Julia Soaemias, and her son, Bassianus—the high priest of Elagabal—plus her youngest daughter, Julia Mamaea, and her son Alexianus, four years younger than his cousin. There were no older men, as all the women were widows.

The family enjoyed in silence a dinner consisting of bread, legume soup, herb chicken with asparagus, dates, plums, and wine when they were interrupted by a slave boy.

"Excuse me, *domina*." He addressed Maesa, who gave him an annoyed look. "The man who gave me this notice said it was of the utmost importance."

She gestured for him to come closer and wiped the crumbs from her hands with a napkin. With a bow, he handed over the sealed roll. She waved him away and broke the seal briskly.

"What is it, Mother?" Soaemias said, gnawing on a plum. She was a woman in her forties, with green eyes and just a few grays among her lush blond hair. In spite of her noticeable weight gain, she had not lost much of the beauty and charm of her younger years.

Maesa read the notice and almost choked on her bread. She stared at her daughter. "Soaemias! It's a letter from Comazon, the commander of the *Legio III Gallica*!"

Soaemias frowned. Her sister looked at her in confusion. The two boys seemed disinterested.

"My dear child! Your son will be emperor!"

"What are you talking about, Mother? Is this a joke!"

"No, this is not a joke. I knew it would work!" She clapped feverishly. "We'll be back in Rome very soon!"

"All of us?" Mamaea asked.

Mamaea didn't seem thrilled with the news, as it made no reference to her son. Eight years younger than her sister, and still somewhat in her prime, she had always been jealous of Soaemias's splendor—and ability to attract suitors. She resented lacking both the charisma and the looks to have given her competition. Her strong, austere facial features and amber-black hair betrayed the temperament of a strong woman whom men feared like the plague. In neither of her two marriages had she been as fortunate as her sister, though that hardly mattered now.

"You still haven't explained to me what's going on," Soaemias said to her mother.

Maesa handed her the letter.

Soaemias read it quickly and gazed back at her. "But... why would they do such a thing?"

"Didn't you see me talking to the man during the worship?"

"I saw you talking to an officer, yes... but I didn't suspect that my son was the subject of your conversation. What did you tell him?"

"Simply the truth."

"What truth?" Soaemias said in a trembling voice.

"That your son is also Caracalla's son."

The two boys looked at each other in astonishment.

"Mother!" Soaemias rose frantically to her feet. "How could you disgrace my late husband's honor this way?"

"The dead don't care about honor, darling."

"But this is dangerous... what will Macrinus think if he finds out what you've done?"

"Don't mention that vile name. Least of all in front of your sister."

Mamaea sobbed as she remembered how Macrinus had had her husband killed.

Not only had he done that, but he had exiled the entire family to Emesa, where—he thought—they couldn't conspire against his reign. The two daughters had accepted their fate, but not Maesa, who could never resign herself to spending her last years in a remote corner of the world.

Fortune had always favored her sister, Julia Domna. As the eldest daughter, Domna had enjoyed the privilege of the finest education and of being introduced to more desirable suitors, among them one who would become emperor. In due course, she bore him a son—the future Caracalla.

As for Maesa, she had wedded a nobleman without any prospect of ascending the throne, and jealousy had consumed her as she witnessed her sister at the pinnacle of the world.

Caracalla lusted after her beautiful daughter Soaemias, and Maesa spurred his appetites. However, she could never compel Soaemias to betray her husband for a man she didn't love—not even for the emperor. Unfortunately, Caracalla didn't go as far as having her husband murdered to wed her; he didn't even force her to lie with him.

But those were bygone days and now life had granted her another chance: Caracalla was dead and Macrinus had usurped the throne. She didn't need an oracle to know her time had come. All she needed was a lie and the right moment. That moment had come in the temple, when she saw a high-ranked officer caressing his subordinate. She had found her tool.

The plan was simple: offer the man a bribe, and if he refused, threaten to expose him as the homophile he was and destroy his career and his life.

Once back in Rome, she would not make her sister's mistake by becoming a mere piece of palace furniture. She would not rest until becoming the *de facto* ruler of the world. The most powerful woman in history.

"Don't cry, dear." Maesa reached out to Mamaea. "Soon he will be dethroned and sent back where he belongs."

Soaemias was leaving the room when Maesa ran up to her and grabbed her by the shoulders. "Listen to me!" She made her turn around to face her. "Don't you want to return to the palace?"

"No, Mother, life is good here. We have made new friends and there are people who love us. Why do we need to go back to Rome? Here we can all be happy together."

"Rome is the place where things happen, dear child. That's what I always told your father. He listened to my advice and made us very rich." She looked at her daughter sternly. "You may have gotten used to this filthy place again, but I never will. Besides, I can't suffer a traitor to get away with murdering the emperor. That man does not deserve to be in office. He's a usurper! The only rightful heir to the throne is your son. Do you understand?"

Soaemias stood speechless, shaking her head, and holding a hand to her cheek.

"Cousin, you're going to be emperor. Congratulations!" Alexianus said.

Bassianus jumped up from his divan and danced around the room as Mamaea rolled her eyes.

"The letter says to be at the camp in three days' time," Maesa said. "There's no time to lose. We must get new clothes. And a carriage!"

Δ

The night before the big day, close to midnight, Maesa, Soaemias, and Bassianus boarded the carriage that would cross the city walls and take them across the desert, amid rolling hills and olive groves, to their appointment with destiny. It would take several hours to reach the camp of Raphanea, located about twenty miles west of Emesa, at the end of a long and dusty *via Romana*. The fortress was the pride of the *Legio III Gallica*, a legion with a long and glorious history. Founded by Julius Caesar himself with veterans of the conquest of Gaul—hence its name—it had taken part since its creation in important battles in places as far away as Hispania or Mesopotamia, and due to constant conflicts with the Parthians, it had remained stationed in the East for more than a century.

The family wore their most dazzling finery: Maesa and Soaemias, silk *stolas*—with ornaments at the neckline and hem—topped with colorful *pallas* fastened by gold brooches, worn as hooded cloaks, and Bassianus the characteristic purple silk tunic that he loved above all other garments.

The members of the soon-to-be imperial family lay on the velvet-upholstered beds and cushions inside the spacious and nicely decorated *carpentum* that Maesa had been able to procure at the last minute from a very happy seller. Bassianus lay in the center, and his mother and grandmother occupied the sides.

The family traveled amid the creaking and grinding noise of the iron-shod wheels that, if it weren't for the leather straps that helped to muffle it, would have made the journey unbearable. When enough sunlight peeked over the horizon,

Soaemias opened the curtains and silently contemplated the desolate landscape around them. Worry, however, had begun to grow in her mind.

"Mother, are you sure we're doing the right thing?"

"Darling, not again, please. It's the only thing to do."

Bassianus looked out of the window, resting his head and hand on his mother's shoulder. Maesa gazed at his robe, irritated that she couldn't make him wear the *toga virilis*, as it befitted a Roman citizen—especially one who was about to be proclaimed emperor. "Maybe in Rome," he had told her. Sleep deprivation took its toll on the boy, who yawned and stretched his arms until a gust of sandy wind forced him to shut the curtains.

"When will we arrive?" he asked, squinting his eyes.

Maesa remained expressionless. Oh, how she hated his whiny, effeminate voice. Although he had already turned eighteen, his demeanor had not yet evolved into one worthy of a young man his age. She sighed. It never would. How depressing to be the only one in the family who understood the magnitude of the moment. Or maybe the only one who cared. "We're almost there, dear."

A little after the *hora prima*, the carriage came to an abrupt halt in a valley dominated by a sanctuary. On one side stood a large quarry of black stone, and on the other, the imposing camp of the legion. A cloud of dust inundated the cabin through the chinks of the curtains, making the family cough. They stepped out of the carriage, vigorously dusting off their once pristine garments.

A guard approached the vehicle. After the protocolary greetings, he signaled a fellow soldier to open the main gate of the fortress and led the family down the *via praetoria*, which ran between not yet extinct campfires in front of the wooden barracks of the legionaries. They stopped at the forum, where a prominent *aquila* stood, and the visitors were able to admire the austere but sturdy brick buildings, which included the commander's headquarters, residences of centurions, chapels for the various gods, workshops, and even rudimentary baths. A radiant Comazon approached the visitors dressed in impeccable *legatus* attire, which included a helmet with a longitudinal crest of red feathers, a scarlet cloak, and a muscle cuirass—wide enough to cover his massive chest. His soldiers waited behind him.

"*Salve*, Highness," he said, bowing his head slightly, "we are honored by your presence, and that of your mother and grandmother."

Bassianus looked the officer up and down. "Is this the man you told me about, Grandma?"

Maesa nodded with a slight smile. She scrutinized the general. He looked different in full uniform: more striking, more attractive. His blue eyes shone brighter in the incipient sunlight. He was by far the tallest and best-built man in the camp. Even the heavy armor could not hide his solid body features. What lay beneath was surely more impressive than the iron breastplate itself. He was also remarkably young for his position as commander; he looked no more than thirty-five years old.

"Let's get this over with," Bassianus said, approaching Comazon with a haughty look.

Comazon was pleasantly surprised by the boy's attitude. Lack of servility is the unmistakable mark of a born sovereign.

A soldier handed Comazon a purple military cloak. Maesa recognized it. It was the famous cloak that had belonged to Caracalla, and from which he got his nickname. Comazon walked behind the boy and carefully wrapped him in it. As he did so, he made sure to gently brush his dark, hairy forearms over the creamy white arms and shoulders of the soon-to-be emperor. The contact made Bassianus shiver in pleasure. He opened his mouth to protest, but in the end said nothing. In truth, he wished the touch had lasted longer.

Comazon fastened the cloak with a gold brooch. Finally, he placed around his waist a *cingulum* with a *gladius*, forged especially for the boy. Then he walked in front of Bassianus and gave him the military salute.

"*Ave* Caesar!" he exclaimed in unison with his men.

"We, the soldiers of the *Legio III Gallica*," the general announced, "proclaim you, *Domine Excellentissime*, the only legitimate emperor of Rome, by acknowledging your noble birth in the House of Antoninus, to which we have sworn allegiance, as son and heir of the late emperor Caracalla and grandson of Severus, Pius, Felix and Augustus."

He unsheathed his sword and swung it in the air before holding it firmly at an angle.

"We will defend you in battle against the forces of any who dare defy your authority! *Roma et Imperator! Roma Victrix!*"

"*Roma et Imperator! Roma Victrix!*" the soldiers exclaimed.

Bassianus was astounded by the effusiveness of the men but tried hard not to show it. His stomach shrank amid butterflies and worms. He strolled among his new subjects, clutching his garments, and holding his head high like a peacock, surveying them, but being careful not to look them in the eye, lest a nervous smile betray his feminine lips and ruin the impression. Drawing his gladius and wielding it in front of the soldiers would be risky, considering that he had never held a sword before. Since his religious services were attended mostly by women, he was not accustomed to the praise of young men. Having been raised by his mother alone, he still felt intimidated in an environment of total virility. He took a deep breath, disguising it with a cough, before returning to his front position to deliver his first official speech, which he had rehearsed extensively with his grandmother the night before.

"Romans," he said in a contrived tone of command, "the time has come to restore legitimacy to the government of our fatherland. The usurper Macrinus has tried to take away by brute force what belongs to me only; he has tried to deprive me of my right to lead my people to their destiny. Know, dear friends, that I, like the divine Augustus, will bring Rome the glory she has long awaited. I, young and wise, will emulate in all things the actions of the *Pater Patriae*, the most glorious man Rome has given birth to. I, emperor and Caesar, the child of Venus and Apollo, declare at this moment that I also hold the office of proconsul, and exercise tribunician power, for I am *Pontifex Maximus* and will hold authority in all matters, before the Senate, for the good of the people."

A burst of *aves* and cheers erupted from the ranks.

"Therefore," he continued, "I declare that my name will henceforth be Antoninus; for the name of my father must be restored and will continue to represent a legacy of virtue and honor. And you, my loyal legion, will receive the reward you deserve. As a first ruling act to take place immediately upon my arrival in Rome, I will restore to the frontier legions the privileges and conditions that existed under my father, and not only that: I will distribute the treasuries among all of you, as just pay for your bravery and devotion."

A plethora of even more enthusiastic cheers emerged from the legion, now in unbridled ecstasy.

"This face you see," he improvised, pointing to himself, "will not lie to you nor disappoint you. Know very well, my dear soldiers, that my beauty equals my wisdom, and my glory will equal my beauty. And you, sons of Rome, will share in that glory, because I am one of you, and it is because of you alone that I care to live."

"*Roma et Antoninus! Roma Victrix!*" one of the soldiers exclaimed. The rest followed in unison, wielding their swords.

Maesa, breathing hard with one hand on her bosom, opened her eyes after her grandson finished his improvisation and gazed nervously at Comazon. He smiled slightly, causing a dimple to appear on his cheek, and winked at her. She winked back.

Δ

News of the proclamation broke out to the provinces only days after the boy's departure from the Raphanea camp. Macrinus, a man shameless in spirit and in looks, and holder of the supreme office of emperor of Rome, hastened to dispatch a cavalry unit to put down what he thought was just the insignificant rebellion of a Roman legion, instigated to install an unknown boy on the throne. He had ordered his men to crucify any survivors among the insurgents, after their camp had been burned to the ground.

One evening, while Comazon was dining with his general staff, an agitated sentry arrived at the *praetorium*. "Commander," he said as he caught his breath, "an imperial cavalry unit is approaching!"

Comazon stood up abruptly, grabbed his sword and shield, hastily put on his helmet, and ran down the *via praetoria* in the dimming light of dusk, alerting his men along the way. His staff followed him to one of the watchtowers. A whole cavalry unit galloped in the distance amid a massive cloud of dust.

"Bar the gates!" Comazon ordered one of his officers.

"How are we going to confront them, commander? Our cavalry unit is much smaller than theirs," an officer said, standing next to Comazon on the watchtower. "Shall I order our men to face them in the field?"

"I have a better idea." The general descended from the tower. "Do not respond! Shoot only those who try to jump the walls!"

The enemy cavalry had approached the gates and aimed their bows at the camp. A few legionaries fell dead with arrows through their necks and chests. The enemy dismounted, and some of the attackers threw grappling hooks with ropes against the walls, while others improvised battering rams. Comazon returned to the watchtower a few moments later, with a bag brought from his headquarters by a legionary. He walked to a visible spot on the front wall.

"Commander!" a soldier shouted, "be careful!"

Comazon ignored the warning, even though beneath him stood one of the mightiest cavalry units of the Roman empire.

"Soldiers of Rome! If you would allow me a word with you!"

"Don't listen to him!" the unit's commander shouted, a man by the name of Ulpius Julianus. "Maintain the attack!"

Comazon, seeing his words ignored, made use of his magic trick. He opened the bag that his envoy had brought him and tossed its precious contents on the soldiers.

"Look!" one of the cavalrymen shouted, "this fool is giving us gold!"

The other soldiers stopped in amazement to pick up the coins.

"Listen to me, brothers!" Comazon said. "I know Macrinus has been greedy and withheld your rightful pay. That's a dishonorable attitude for a man who has sworn to support the army and take care of its men. Look at the effigy in the coins, my comrades! Behold the image of your benefactor!"

The soldiers did as indicated.

"This young man you see on the coins is Emperor Antoninus. He is the rightful heir of our late emperor Caracalla, by virtue of birth. How can you fight him and us, who stand by him out of love for his father?"

"Shut up, you fool!" one of the soldiers shouted. "Shut up and fight!"

A second and larger set of coins rained over the soldiers.

"There is much more inside and it is all yours! All you have to do is join us in the fight for our Emperor Antoninus!"

The soldiers looked at each other in confusion. Then they all raised their swords in the air and hollered, "Antoninus! Antoninus!"

"What are you doing, idiots?" Julianus shouted. "He's trying to deceive you! If you stop fighting he'll have you killed!"

His soldiers, however, not only did not listen to him, but charged back to capture him. Julianus fled, but several cavalrymen persecuted him. They caught up with him, knocked him off his horse and forced him to walk, hands bound, back to the camp. With a kick in the back, he was pushed to his knees before Comazon, who was still standing on the wall, arms folded and cloak billowing in the air.

One crazed soldier grabbed the disgraced Julianus by the hair, while another pointed his sword at his neck. With a swift sawing motion, the latter cut Julianus's neck until the head came off and the body fell to the ground in a spring of blood.

The soldier now held the disembodied head in front of Comazon and shouted: "Here's the proof of our allegiance!"

Comazon ordered his men to open the gate, and they greeted the cavalrymen like brothers. They exchanged hugs and kisses, opened amphorae of wine, and blew trumpets. The fallen were buried outside the camp with the necessary honors. In spite of the misfortune of a few, a new bond emerged among these men, partly due to the enthusiasm for a new Rome under the young Antoninus and partly due to excitement sparked by the lust for gold. The men indulged in drink and food, sang songs by the campfires, and finally passed out, cuddling, in the middle of the cold Syrian night.

Δ

It didn't help that Macrinus received Julianus's head wrapped in linen cloths—tied with many intricate knots and Julianus's own signet ring—and an insolent greeting from "the victorious general Comazon" during a fundraising dinner, where, speaking laboriously with his low voice, he was trying to cajole some of the wealthiest men of Anatolia to support his cause of reinforcing the frontier after the destruction of the rebellious *Legio III Gallica*. Confident that it was Comazon's head he was receiving, he had the bundle opened without inspection in front of his guests, and left them paralyzed with shock, terror, and disgust when the grisly mass was held aloft by the hair in front of them. Needless to say, he failed to raise the funding and troops he sought.

A few weeks later, the Roman Senate met in an extraordinary assembly at the *curia Iulia*. Their amicable chat ended when Consul Quintus Tineius Sacerdos arrived to preside over the meeting. As they rose, the old, clean-shaven man gestured for them to return to their seats.

"Honorable Fathers of the Roman Senate," he said in his sonorous, oratorical voice, "I have called his meeting to inform you of the latest news from the Syrian frontier."

Murmuring echoed through the ranks. The consul held out his hand with a scroll bearing the imperial seal.

"I have received a letter from the emperor, which I presume relates the status of the insurrection."

He opened the scroll and spread it out, holding it away from his tired eyes.

"*Imperator* Caesar Marcus Opellius Severus Macrinus Pius Felix Augustus to the sacred Senate of Rome, *salvete*! It is my duty to inform you of the latest developments concerning the rebellion initiated by the *Legio III Gallica* with the seditious intention of deposing me as emperor and installing a delusional Syrian boy in my place."

The letter continued to recount the events of the attempted assault on the legion's camp.

"I attribute the defeat to the greed of the new recruits, who joined the rebellion lured by the promise of wealth. I am aware that some among the troops hold a grudge against me for not having increased their salaries, but I refuse to continue the policy of my predecessor, who, in the desire to win the loyalty of the soldiers, drained the imperial coffers by paying them benefits the financial situation of the empire did not allow."

A few more lines of self-exaltation followed.

"I know how highly esteemed I am among you, dear Fathers, and I know that you all wish me to have a long reign, and not to die at the hands of a stranger—"

"We have all prayed for it," Senator Fulvius Diogenianus interrupted, to the laughter of his peers.

"...therefore, I request your support to crush this insolent rebellion once and for all, and the dispatch of at least three, but preferably five legions, in case the boy is able to get more recruits using his grandmother's money. I have also sent letters to the governors of the nearby provinces, and I count on their loyal support."

There was silence after the consul finished reading the letter. "So what do we do now?" he asked.

A senator raised his hand. Sacerdos nodded. "As Senator Fulvius very neatly put it, the boy would do us a favor if he eliminates the man."

"However," another senator said, "we, the Senate, have approved Macrinus in his office. As much as some of us dislike him, not to support him during an insurrection would be tantamount to treason."

Some senators raised their voices at the same time.

"Order. Order!" Sacerdos shouted.

"I have a solution," another senator shouted. "He is requesting the support of three legions, correct? We don't have them."

Exclamations of confusion followed.

"Indeed," the senator said, rising to his feet. "All of our legions are located far away in the provinces. How long would it take them to reach Syria from, say, Brittania or Africa? Surely they wouldn't get there fast enough to deal with the rebels. Besides, we would leave parts of the empire unprotected from barbarian attack. His request is impossible to fulfill."

"But we must send something," another said, "we must at least pretend that we're assisting the emperor in his moment of need."

"Let us send the Praetorian Guard then," Sacerdos said. "It makes no sense to keep it in Rome if the emperor is in trouble in Syria."

"But the Praetorians won't be enough—surely not against a full legion and its allies. He won't stand a chance."

"They are more skilled," Sacerdos said. "Besides…"

The senators awaited in silence.

"Isn't that what we have all *prayed* for?" Sacerdos said, giving Fulvius a sideways glance.

The assembly burst out in laughter.

"I take that as unanimous approval," Sacerdos said.

"One question," a senator said, raising his hand. "What shall we do with the boy?"

"He is that, just a boy." Sacerdos smiled. "Let's not get too far ahead of ourselves. He must win his battle first. If he does… then we shall see what to do with him!"

Λ

After the meager support from the Senate arrived, Macrinus and his men rode into the depths of Syria in pursuit of the rogue stripling and his family. Not far from Emesa, the imperial troops encountered armed resistance, not only from the *Legio III Gallica* and Julianus's former cavalry unit, but also from the *Legio II Parthica*, which had joined the revolt. The combined rebel army was commanded by a peculiar man, or one might say, half-man: a eunuch by the name of Gannys, whom Maesa ordered to temporarily abandon his life of luxury and comfort in Emesa to assume command of the growing army. He may not have had enough military experience, but he was a loyal man, and that was what mattered the most to Maesa at the time.

Naturally, Comazon was still in command of his legion, and the battle was set to begin one morning in June, a month after the failed assault on the camp. Scorching heat punished the region where the two armies met. Although Gannys's troops were numerically superior, they were exhausted and thirsty from the early hours due to their heavy helmets and armor and were surprised by the bold charge of the men of Macrinus's army—whom he had ordered to remove their breastplates, to be lighter in battle—who broke through the close-packed, thick defense lines and caused most legionaries to flee.

Maesa, who had been watching the battle from behind the lines, was determined not to allow defeat. She spurred her horse to make it run at full speed, passing among the deserters, whom she reprimanded and shamed for their cowardice. Behind her rode her grandson, who, though he was on the verge of fainting from heat exhaustion and fear, did his best to remain gracious and look brave during the ordeal. The old woman and the boy continued galloping in the opposite direction to the fleeing men until they reached the heart of the battlefield, where the core of the rebel army stood.

Comazon looked back when he heard the loud neighing of approaching horses. The first rider rode past him like lightning, but the second stopped abruptly and stared at him. The image was so surreal, that for a moment he thought he had died, and Apollo had come to take him to the afterlife. He tried to see the rider's face, but the sunlight blinded his eyes. The horseman came a little closer and his head obscured the sun like an eclipse. Comazon could at last see his face; it was Antoninus. Even in darkness, the boy's face was still splendorous, perhaps more so than ever. Comazon fell to the ground and rubbed his eyes, trying to wake up from a dream. But when he looked up, the boy still stood there, motionless on his horse, with Caracalla's cloak fluttering on his back, wielding the sword he had taken during the proclamation. Comazon thought he heard his soft voice saying: "Fight for me, Comazon. Fight for me, my loyal general." Then the figure vanished in a cloud of dust.

It took a few moments for Comazon to recover. His eyes still hurt from the light and the rubbing of his dusty hands. Then he wielded his sword and raised it in the air, exclaiming: "For the emperor! For Antoninus!" and ran toward the enemy. The men, seeing the courage of their commander, turned and charged like lions with a fury they had not yet shown that morning. Macrinus, horrified by this counterattack, fled the scene, and abandoned his men to their fate.

By evening the soldiers were back in the camp, recovering from the horrible intimacy of the battle. Comazon was lying on his bed, when a young soldier entered his lair after a light knock on the door.

"Are you feeling alright, commander?"

"Yes, I am fine," Comazon replied in a quiet voice.

"We were surprised that you did not require the company of one of your men tonight to help you recharge your energy, *domine*."

Comazon smiled. Of course, he wanted the company of a boy. The problem was that that boy had already ridden back where he belonged. "I am just too tired tonight; I think I will try to get some sleep."

"Let me at least tend to your wounds, my general."

The boy took a clean white cloth and soaked it in water. Then he rubbed it on Comazon's bloody arms and legs.

"Ouch, gently."

The boy wrung out the bloody cloth over a pot and soaked it again in fresh water. He undressed the general and washed him gently, and when he was done, he was rewarded with a kiss on the lips.

"Good night, my boy. Tell my men they did good, and I am proud of them. But you must also realize that this might just be the beginning of a war."

When the legionary left, Comazon lay on his back, wearing only a loincloth, recalling the vision he had had during the battle. Or had it been real? Everything was fuzzy in his mind. He turned to one side and hugged a huge pillow. He was sure of only one thing. There was no one in the world he'd rather be with that night. No one but the sun boy.

Δ

Two days later, just after the sun began to radiate its yellow rays on the desert horizon, Comazon had already put on his uniform and was preparing himself a cup of *calda*. About to leave his headquarters to meet with his staff, he was approached by a legionary.

"My general," the young man said with the military salute, "you have received this letter in the mail."

Comazon took the roll and gazed at it. It was tied with a purple ribbon and sealed with the imperial emblem; it could only have come from… He hastily put his drink aside, almost spilling its contents, cracked the seal and unrolled the papyrus. His eyeballs moved rapidly from side to side as he read.

HIGHLY ESTEEMED GENERAL PUBLIUS VALERIUS COMAZON:

YOU HAVE BEEN SUMMONED TO THE CITY OF EMESA FOR AN AUDIENCE WITH THE EMPEROR.

YOU ARE EXPECTED TO ARRIVE NO LATER THAN THIS AFTERNOON.

HIS IMPERIAL MAJESTY, MARCUS AURELIUS ANTONINUS AUGUSTUS.

He jumped with excitement like a little boy and, without revealing the contents of the letter to the courier, kissed him on both cheeks and hugged him. Then he told him to advise his men to prepare him the best horse. He set out immediately for Emesa.

Comazon arrived at the court shortly after *prandium*. He had not expected to be offered a meal at the imperial house, so he ate something quickly at a food cart on the road. The last thing he wanted was for his stomach to growl during the meeting with the emperor. At least, not from hunger. Butterflies can be noisy sometimes.

The residence was luxurious by Syrian standards but lacked much of the luster of the patrician houses in Rome, to which Comazon was regularly invited, due to his military accomplishments, whenever he returned to the eternal city. He came from a poor background, and in his younger years had worked as a mime and street dancer to help support his family, which his father, an inveterate drunkard, took little care of. His handsome looks, and the occasional and discrete sexual favors he did to some men of high society, had always helped him earn extra coins. When he became a soldier, he had more than once been punished for petty crimes, and even once sentenced to be shackled and forced to row a war galley. On that occasion he had been demoted from legionary to marine, but had later recovered, and reached greater heights in his military career. In fact, it was those hard times that he had to thank for his impressive musculature. No one in the legion knew about his past; he was very careful to conceal it. He was not going to risk losing the respect of his men because of an unworthy background. Deep inside, however, he was aware of their love, and he had the feeling that he wouldn't lose their devotion, even over a matter like that. Regardless, he thought it better not to find out.

But of all the issues in his past, it was his relationship with his father that remained unresolved: he had loved him deeply and had wanted him to reciprocate but had gotten only violence in return. It was not his blows that had hurt him the most, but the coldness and indifference, the lack of an embrace or a kind word. The man had been unfaithful to his wife, negligent with his work, and absent from his children, and had left a void in Comazon's heart that he had not yet been able to fill. Deep down, he had always felt that he was not good enough, that it was his fault that his father had not loved him. Now he was a grown man, and he wanted to redeem himself by finding a boy, a young man to be the object of his immense love and affection. He was well aware that his affairs with the legionaries were temporary satisfactions: he wanted something true and for life.

After a few minutes, he was ushered by a slave into what he thought would be the young emperor's *tablinum*, but he was quite surprised to see that it was actually his *cubiculum*.

The slave announced him, and Comazon stood at the entrance with a firm posture, but trembling hands.

"Come in, General," a soft voice said.

Comazon stepped inside, his heart racing, not knowing exactly where the voice had come from. He was mesmerized by the ostentatious bed that dominated the room, which made imperceptible any other object than the soft and extremely clean oriental carpet. The thick mattress was lined with dark green silk sheets, covered by oversized pillows and fluffy bedding, and enclosed by a canopy of white and green fabric.

The boy finally emerged wearing only a light white sleeping robe. His wavy hair was in disarray, giving the impression that he had not yet gotten out of bed that morning. Comazon froze, standing awkwardly with hands clasped in front. He stared blankly at the canopy, straining not to rest his eyes on the beauty before him.

"So, here he is, the hero of my battle," the emperor said in a seductive tone.

Comazon blushed, finally daring a quick glance at the boy. "All the men fought with bravery, Excellency," he said, looking away.

"Not all of them. Most of them were fleeing like rats. Especially those cowards of the *Legio II Parthica*. My grandmother says I should have them flogged."

Comazon stood still, not knowing what to do or say. Antoninus sat on the edge of the bed, touching the floor with his feet.

"Come closer, sit down here, General," he said, patting the space beside him.

Comazon complied.

"The reason I have summoned you is so you can tell me the details of the battle."

"Sure, Majesty," Comazon said, trying to hide his disappointment. "Well, you saw the battle from the hill, I am not sure what details you want me to fill you in with."

"Mostly, I want explanations. I want you to tell me why the enemy was able to surprise us at the beginning of the fight. Such things should not happen to an experienced commander like you. I don't want it to happen again."

"I am not entirely sure, Excellency. But I did notice that the Praetorians were not wearing their traditional breastplates and grooved shields… I think that helped them have more mobility. Besides…"

"Besides?"

"I do not wish to be impertinent, but I must remind your Grace that I was not in command of the whole army… only of my legion."

Antoninus remained silent for a while. "What do you think about Gannys's leadership? I want your honest opinion," he said, resting his head on his hand.

Comazon pondered his words before speaking. He did not want to disparage an officer of a higher rank.

"Come on, say it, say it! Gannys… is a eunuch, a eunuch!" Antoninus said with a malicious laugh. "It was my grandmother who decided that that man should be in command of the composite army. Isn't it ridiculous!? Of course, I knew it would be much better if you were in full command. I told her so. Multiple times! A eunuch, by Elagabal, a eunuch!"

"A eunuch with something better than balls. A eunuch with brains. He did nothing more than what most commanding generals do during battle: stay behind the lines observing, giving orders according to the unfolding of events. As you have already seen, battles are grand, chaotic, terrifying events that often spiral out of control. It is difficult to get late orders implemented."

Antoninus reached over and touched the general's chin with his forefinger, rubbing the rough stubble. "I know you're trying to be kind, general. But I also know very well that this battle would have never been won, had it not been for you and your determined action."

Comazon listened but was distracted reeling on the feel of the emperor touching his face. He closed his eyes.

"Do you always wear this stubble? I don't think I've ever seen you with a clean-shaven face."

"It starts to grow as soon as I finish shaving, Auguste."

Antoninus smiled. "Now seriously, do tell. How is it that you defeated Macrinus's army so easily?"

Comazon was going to start speaking when Antoninus interrupted him.

"No, no, no. Come over here. This is much better," the boy said, pulling the man toward the headboard.

Comazon rested his calves on the side of the bed with his feet in the air. He didn't want to stain the sheets.

"Get comfortable, my General, take off your sandals."

Comazon rose and did as told, this time laying his big, manly feet on the mattress. Antoninus lay at a very close distance.

"Tell me something, General. Do you think a man like Gannys still enjoys the company of women?"

"I cannot speak for him, Excellency."

"I couldn't believe he would… a man who had his balls chopped off cannot possibly still like women."

Antoninus laughed and Comazon joined him, making an effort to relax for the first time during the meeting.

"Alright, alright, let's go back to what you're here for. Tell me how you defeated Macrinus's army."

Comazon began to speak, and Antoninus leaned back against the headboard, gently caressing the general's arm with his long, delicate fingers. Comazon's skin was several shades darker. He had a few moon marks, and hair ran down his forearms to the base of his thick-skinned big hands. Antoninus looked at the face of the man who had saved his life and for a moment lost track of what he was saying.

"…and, of course, you must know that Macrinus was captured and executed, am I right, *Imperator*?"

"Of course, I know," Antoninus said with a serious face. "I ordered it."

Both men burst out laughing again.

Antoninus's touch went further down toward Comazon's hand and then he moved his body toward the general's feet and caressed them. Comazon became distracted by the unusual actions of the emperor.

"Keep talking," Antoninus said, "I didn't tell you to stop."

"Well, I have not told you yet what happened when they broke through our lines… your lines, *Auguste*."

Antoninus had continued to massage Comazon's formidable thighs and was now untying his *subligaculum*. Comazon became nervous. He would not be able to hide his massive hard on. Antoninus removed his loincloth, and Comazon's manhood sprang like a hare in a bushy grassland, spraying some precum on the emperor's face.

Antoninus touched the dickhole with the tip of his tongue and licked it, making a strand with his saliva and Comazon's leak. He slid the skin down to expose the wet cockhead, which he carefully put inside his mouth.

Comazon could feel, but not see, what the emperor was doing down below. Breathless, he leaned back, trying to focus. "Then… your grandmother…"

"Don't you dare mention my grandmother now," Antoninus said, lifting his face above Comazon's tunic, and wiping his moist lips with the back of his hand. He bent down again and continued his task, going lower this time, vigorously sucking the whole length of the fat cock. He moved down to his hairy balls, licking them, sucking them lightly.

"Afterward," Comazon said, panting and lifting his face. "Afterward…" He laid his hands on the emperor's shoulders. "…our cavalry returned, and…" he said amid moaning and groaning, "then we destroyed them, Excellency," he finished, huffing, clasping the sheets.

Antoninus continued the *fellatio* relentlessly up and down Comazon's shaft.

"I'm cumming, I'm cumming!"

Antoninus stopped sucking and jerked him off rapidly until Comazon's hot seed erupted all over his face. After his last moan, the boy leapt up and, without wiping his face, sat down next to the delirious general, who had rested his head again on the headboard and whose breathing caused his chest to heave violently.

"Now I want you to do the same thing to me."

Comazon could not believe what was happening to him. Maybe he had really died and gone to the heroes' afterlife.

The general stood up and the emperor pushed himself to the front of the bed, resting his feet on the carpet. The emperor removed his robe, under which he wore no *subligaculum*. He exposed his long, white, circumcised cock before the mesmerized eyes of the general. Obviously, Comazon had seen many penises before, but this one was particular. In any case, their cocks complemented each other; if Antoninus's was long and sharp as a needle, Comazon's had the girth of an elephant.

He kneeled down and moved his face toward the emperor's crotch. He wanted to do something special. He wanted to really take his time and please his boy. He opened his mouth and inserted half of Antoninus's member inside. Antoninus closed his legs, feeling the abrasion of the general's stubble on his thighs. He raised his head and closed his eyes. Without giving the officer time to get creative, he pushed his face down, forcing him to deepthroat. The general gagged, struggling and gasping for air. The Boy Emperor held his face tight for a few moments longer. When he finally let go, Comazon was red in the face, and coughed hard. Antoninus laughed. He forced him once more onto his cock, this time guiding him up and down. He kept him doing that until he finally blew up. His cum filled Comazon's throat, and as the white liquid began to slide down onto his tongue, the general held it there for a few moments to savor its sweetness.

"Swallow it."

The general complied. The aftertaste was fresh like mint. "My Emperor," Comazon said breathlessly, "my Emperor…"

"I hope you feel rewarded for your service, General," Antoninus said, rising. "Now, leave. I must bathe and get ready for my beautification routine."

Comazon wiped his mouth with the back of his hand, rose, saluted, took his *subligaculum* and sandals and, still with a heavy breath, left the room. An unthinkable sensation of pleasure filled his body; after drinking from the fountain of life, he felt like a twenty-year-old again. But the most surreal feeling was the thrill of love that intoxicated his brain like the morning fog of the frontiers.

Antoninus retreated to the baths. He still had the taste of Comazon's cock in his mouth, and it was fantastic. He had never sucked one before, but he could think of no better reward for a man who had fought a battle to save his life. He was sure it would leave him pleased and satisfied, and ready to defend him again, if necessary. This action, however, had also given him the opportunity to act for the first time on his sexual desires, which he promised himself never to repress again. Before he had been just a boy, sure, the chief priest of Elagabal, but nevertheless a youth, subject to the authority of his mother and—above all—of his forbidding grandmother, but now he was emperor of Rome. The whole world—and its pleasures—were at his disposal.

Δ

News of the battle reached Rome weeks later, prompting a meeting in the Senate House.

"It looks like the boy got his way in the end," Senator Fulvius said.

"I can't say I'm not impressed," another said. "It's true that we hadn't sent Macrinus all the forces he needed, but the Praetorians are not to be underestimated—they're Rome's elite force."

"Well, that has changed now," a third said. "The prime youth of the empire is now commanded by Gannys."

"I would say, by Comazon," Sacerdos said. "According to the news of the battle it was he and his men who provided the greatest impetus for winning the battle."

"Now," Fulvius said, "what do we know about this boy? Is he a complete stranger?"

"Of course not," a senator said. "He is indeed related to the Severan dynasty. At least we know for certain that he came out of Soaemias's womb, what is not entirely clear is whether his lineage indeed came out of Caracalla's cock!"

Laughter erupted in the ranks.

"Fathers, let's not descend into vulgarity," Sacerdos said. "The question of his lineage is the least of our concerns now. He won his war of ascension, and we have no resources to stop him. Not that we necessarily want to, anyway. The question is: what do we know about the boy, about his personality?"

"Not much," a senator by the name of Julius Paulus Prudentissimus said. "All we know is that he holds the highest priesthood of his religion, the cult of Elagabal."

"It's one of those strange Eastern cults, in case you were wondering," another said. "I'm aware of it, because some of the members of Caracalla's family practiced it. It's a queer religion. They dance in front of a rock, which they claim was carved by the god himself."

There were murmurs among the senators.

"I'm actually acquainted with his grandmother," Paulus said. "She kept a low profile during her time in Rome while her nephew was emperor, but she's an impressive woman, nonetheless. I wouldn't be surprised at all if she was the mastermind behind all this."

"The last thing we need is another Agrippina," Sacerdos said. "I do have another surprise for you, dear Fathers."

He gestured to his back. A pair of slave boys entered the hall carrying a large papyrus, about half a man's height and slightly less in width.

"Turn it around," he ordered.

A portrait featuring a young man, richly attired in a purple silk tunic and shawl, was revealed. Ostentatious gold and precious stone jewelry complemented his garments. An enigmatic look came from his hazel eyes.

"Behold, Emperor Antoninus!" Sacerdos declared. "That's the name he adopted at his proclamation."

The senators were flabbergasted. For minutes no one found words to speak.

"But this is outrageous!" one of them shouted. "Those barbaric robes, by Castor and Pollux. How undignified! Is this the man who will rule Rome?"

"He is the man who holds the high office, indeed," Sacerdos said. "He sent this picture expressly to acquaint us with his presence as he makes his way to Rome."

"How long will it take him to arrive?" a senator asked.

"He has announced that he intends to spend the winter in Anatolia. So, we have about a whole year to prepare for his coming."

"May Jupiter help us!" a senator shouted.

"Is there a way we could... prevent that from happening?" Fulvius asked.

"Now, that's seditious talk," Sacerdos said.

"Hold on, honorable Consul," Fulvius said. "I do not wish to encourage disobedience, but I would like to know if... we at least have the option."

"I know that not everyone is happy with Comazon's leadership," a senator said. "I have sources telling me there is potential dissension among his ranks; soldiers who question his role in the rebellion, among other things."

"We should exploit this fact. A strike from within may be the way to prevent the boy from even making it to Rome in the first place."

"That's definitely interesting," Sacerdos said. "But we know what the price for that kind of soldier is. Usually, they want the office for themselves."

"Which we can grant... temporarily," Fulvius said. "At least until we test the waters and find out if he has a manipulable personality."

"But the boy may be suitable in that sense," another interjected. "Can't you see that anyone in that attire will be the laughingstock of Rome? In no way does he project manliness or authority."

"Well, he already won a war, and people know it," Sacerdos said. "Besides, we won't show this picture to anyone, at least for the time being." He considered for a moment. "I would advise going ahead and promoting dissention among the ranks of Comazon. If we can prevent the House of Antoninus from returning to Rome, so much the better. It's always easier to deal with inexperienced upstarts than with pedigree and scheming ladies... and by this, I mean the boy's grandmother. The fact that a woman could be behind all this does not please me at all."

Having come to an agreement on the matter, the meeting ended. One year is what they had. One year and the vague possibility of an "incident" occurring along the way.

CHAPTER 2

PARTY TIME

After an unemotional farewell to Mamaea and Alexianus in Emesa, the imperial family and their entourage travelled slowly for weeks across the arid Anatolian steppe to the winding roads of the Bithynian countryside, where a forest of fir, beech and oak trees surrounded the winding cobblestone roads, providing a deep, fresh aroma that invigorated the mind. It had been Nicomedia, some forty-five miles east of Byzantium, the place chosen by the emperor to spend the winter that year. The court was followed by Comazon and Gannys on horseback, and by the soldiers of the legions *III Gallica* and *II Parthica* on foot, joined by the rebels who had also fought valiantly for Antoninus's cause in the battle that seated him on the throne. A large group of slaves and donkeys carried the vast luggage of the family, and a long line of mules pulled the heavy vaults of the imperial treasure, and especially, the great *baetyl* of Elagabal.

The sun, setting over the dark blue gulf waters, offered a striking spectacle as it illuminated the harbor with its faint reddish rays. The carriage finally crossed the city gates, which were ceremonially opened by guards.

"Look, Grandma, the circus! It's almost as big as the one in Rome," Antoninus said, holding her hand. "Don't worry, we'll be well entertained here."

Unimpressed, Maesa dropped his hand and looked away. It had not been without a fight that Antoninus had imposed his will of making a long stay in that place.

Soaemias looked out the opposite window. "Look at the houses on the hills, Mother. They look as if they were built on top of each other. The gardens are so gorgeous," Seeing that her mother did not answer, she added, "and those rivulets, carrying fresh water from the mountains."

The carriage slowed down as it ventured into the crowded streets, where people were making the last purchases of the day from horse-drawn cart shops. A few homeless people reached out to distracted passersby; boisterous children interrupted their play briefly to drink water from a fountain. On each side of the road more important buildings appeared: the temples of Zeus and Cybele, inherited from Greek times; a Temple of Isis, built by Egyptian immigrants; the great baths of Caracalla; a *nymphaeum*, a theatre, a gymnasium, and, finally, the forum. In front of it was a long colonnaded street that stretched all the way to Hadrian's gulf-side mansion, built during the emperor's visit to the city, about a hundred years earlier.

"I get out here!" Antoninus shouted, banging on the wooden frame to make the driver stop. He jumped out of the carriage and ran down the street, skipping, twirling, leaping, filling his lungs with the fresh maritime air.

Onlookers muttered among themselves that the boy must be a lunatic, wondering if his face was really that of the effigy they had seen on the newly issued coins. Maesa was about to reprimand him, but Soaemias stopped her.

"Let him be, Mother. He's young and needs a little time to enjoy himself before he gets used to the life of responsibilities that awaits him."

"That life of responsibilities has already begun. The people of this city know who he is. They were awaiting us. What will they say about their emperor?"

Antoninus climbed the marble steps leading to the entrance of the mansion that would be his winter home. The guards bowed to him and opened the old cypress doors. The interiors were brightly lit by candlelight. He spent some time admiring the statues and frescoes, especially a life-size marble sculpture on a pedestal of a beautiful young man, who, it was explained to him, was the god Antinous, favorite of Hadrian. Although there were hundreds of statues of him throughout the empire, this one had been carved with special skill—the reason it was featured inside the emperor's home.

The young emperor circled around it, resting his hand on his cheek and chin as he scrutinized it, pausing from time to time to appreciate a particular angle. Comazon and Gannys, who had been outside admiring the facade of the building and discussing its architectural style, entered and joined the emperor.

"Look at this, Comazon. Do you think that such a beautiful young man ever existed, or did Hadrian hire sculptors to represent his own ideal of beauty?"

"I can assure you that he did exist, Excellency. There are more than enough references of his graceful features among writers and poets."

"So, do you think that the features of his body, those slender, toned arms, the firm butt and thighs, the full lips, were all faithfully reproduced?"

"Yes, Highness. We have no reason to think otherwise."

"And… this too?" he asked, pointing to the tiny phallus.

Comazon stifled a laugh as Maesa and Soaemias entered the room, followed by the slaves carrying their luggage.

"Don't you find this boy's statue adorable?" Antoninus said to his grandmother, pointing to the marble. "My ancestor Hadrian definitely had great taste."

Maesa ignored her grandson and shouted orders to the slaves about where to take the various chests. The emperor took his mother by the hand and led her upstairs. "Come, Mother! Let's go find our rooms. I've been told there's a big one for me, and you and Grandma will have one each. That way you won't have to put up with her snoring anymore."

Soaemias smiled.

Once in his quarters, Antoninus jumped on his emperor-size bed and rolled on the shiny sheets. "The best silk in Asia. I can feel it! The people of Nicomedia sure know their emperor's taste. They'll be rewarded."

"Your Excellency is most generous," Soaemias said. "But you must also take care of finances. Too much largess can be dangerous."

"Not if it gets me the loyalty of my people. I know that law and order are what Rome needs. But she also needs a little happiness." He rose from the bed. "No more stupid wars against Parthians, Germans, Moors; it's all over, Mother. I'm going to build an empire of love and peace."

"My child will be the new Augustus," Soaemias said, hugging her pride and joy.

"Just what I promised the troops, Mother… just what I promised," he said, pulling away from her and throwing himself again face up on the bed.

"Keep dreaming of the future, my boy," Soaemias said with a yawn, "your mother is tired and needs to sleep." She came up to him and kissed him on the cheek. "Good night."

As she left the room, she was startled by a man waiting outside.

"Gannys! What are you doing here?"

"Your mother has already retired to her quarters, so it's just you and me here now, sweetheart."

"You surely don't think we can meet here! Someone could be watching!"

"There's no one around. I made sure of it. Comazon left, I dismissed the slaves and told them to continue unpacking things tomorrow. The soldiers retreated to their barracks. Only a few guards remained outside."

Gannys stopped her objections with a kiss. She let out a screech as he took her in his arms, and they entered the *cubiculum* like a newlywed couple. He undressed hastily after laying her on the bed.

"Oh, Gannys!" she said, biting her finger. "My mother won't approve of us meeting here."

"We have to meet somewhere, darling. I don't have a house in this city. It's only natural I stay with you. At least tonight…"

Gannys had been Soaemias's lover for decades. After her husband's death, Maesa had agreed—at her daughter's insistence—that Gannys should continue to live near the family, with the excuse of providing protection, although she did not approve of the man. He had not hesitated to demand extravagant opulence.

The price he had paid for their love affair had been a hefty one: nothing less than being castrated by orders of Soaemias's husband. But the shame hadn't stop their passion. It didn't matter to her that he was now a eunuch; he was still a hell of a man, especially in bed, where he lasted twice as long as her husband in his prime.

She kissed him and caressed his hairy chest with passion, and went down to his member—still only semihard.

"You're so good, my love, keep working on it."

It usually took him a while to warm up, but once he was hard, he could ride her for as long as she wanted.

He moved on top of her, kissing her neck, and sliding his hands on her motherly breasts, making her squeal. "Oh Gannys, Gannys!"

Δ

The next morning, Comazon was summoned to meet the emperor at the opulent throne hall. He arrived in full *legatus* attire, made the military salute, and awaited to be spoken to.

His blue eyes sparkled at the greeting of the emperor, whose ethereal voice brought back memories of that last private meeting. Attired in a purple silk tunic, draped in Caracalla's cloak and with an olive wreath on his head, there he was, the priest of the sun god, the mightiest and most beautiful young man in the world, seated in a posture as if awaiting to be worshipped.

"Comazon, I requested your presence today because I want to communicate important news to you."

Comazon stood at attention.

"It is my wish to appoint you praetorian prefect."

"You honor me with your favor, Excellency," he said, hand on heart. He had already received a more than generous reward for his courage and did not expect to be promoted so quickly. "But we have no Praetorians in this city, they will have to be summoned from Rome if you intend to stay here through the winter."

"There's no time for that. Besides, those of them who survived the battle may still be loyal to Macrinus, even after his death. I prefer that you organize a new guard."

"I will select the best men of our legions, Highness."

"That pleases me. By the way, have they found suitable accommodation at the local camp?"

"Yes, *Auguste*. If there is one good thing your father did, it was to establish housing for the soldiers. The camp is outstanding." Comazon still felt strange referring to Caracalla as *his father*. In the back of his mind, he still wasn't sure if the boy was indeed Caracalla's son. But that lacked importance now, since he was the ruler of his heart.

"Very well. Then go to your men and start the recruiting."

Comazon saluted and turned around. He stopped after a few steps and looked back at the emperor.

"By the way, Excellency. The men of the legions will be going home soon. Of course, those who are not selected for the Praetorian Guard. I am planning a little farewell party… for the boys, you know. It will take place at the camp this Friday night."

"I have no problem with that. Have fun."

"However…" Comazon had thought of inviting His Majesty to attend, but at the conclusive sound of those words he decided it would be an impertinence. "Never mind, *Auguste*."

Δ

Friday arrived and the farewell party with it. Comazon had made sure that everything was provided—game meat, music, and the best wine in the region; still, there was something missing, something that would have been present at any other legion's party: women. Comazon had not decided things to be this way; it had just happened. Since he had been assigned as commander, a few years before, he had indulged in the occasional nighttime amusement with a boy or two; word soon got around the camp, and he made no attempt to hide it. What happens in the camp, stays in the camp. It turned out that many of the legionaries enjoyed that kind of activity, and Comazon made full use of it. They were a Sacred Band of Thebes of sorts. The new men from the *Legio II Parthica* understood it too and got along with the *Gallica* boys quite well. Most of them, at least. It would be a sad farewell.

Winter was approaching and the nights of Nicomedia were colder than those of Emesa. The legionaries sat around huge campfires and shared personal battle stories with their peers as they roasted meat. The wine acted quickly, but it was served without limit, as it was the last time those men would be together in their lifetime.

Before the night was over, Comazon invited his newly appointed Praetorian guards to the headquarters, where it was cozier than outside. The camp at Nicomedia was much larger than the one at Raphanea, had better facilities, and in the headquarters, the walls were covered with bear skins to maintain the heat. Animal skins were also scattered on the floor and served as rugs.

"Well, it's getting a little hot in here, I might as well take my clothes off," one of the soldiers said while the others laughed.

"Yeah, I will do that too," another said.

Soon, everyone had removed their armor and tunics and were left only in their loincloths. Comazon looked at the muscular men in front of him. These were some of Rome's finest males, young in age, but mature in experience. Outstanding in both bravery and beauty.

"I would like to propose a toast," the general said. "To the brave and invincible young men of the *Legio III Gallica* and the *Legio II Parthica*! *Roma invicta*! *Roma eterna*!"

"*Roma invicta*! *Roma eterna*!" the boys repeated.

"I would also like to propose a toast," one of the soldiers said. "To our commander, the bravest and fucking greatest general in Rome, Publius Valerius Comazon!"

"To the general! Long live General Comazon! Comazon! Comazon!" the men shouted amid cheers and downed their wine skins.

One of the soldiers brought a lyre and played a song. The men embraced, sang, danced in circles and with one another, hugged, kissed… and finally took off what was left of their garments. The room vibrated with the rhythm of their bodies as they lay on the floor, trembling and shivering amid caresses, rolling over the animal skins, rubbing their soft skin against each other's.

Each man chose a partner to please, and at some point they lost awareness of their surroundings. The night was young and the passion high. A boy approached Comazon, who had not yet removed his uniform. He knelt down in front of the general and was untying his belt when suddenly the door opened from outside. The legionaries froze. They covered their eyes to protect themselves from the intrusive light of the campfires. Some distinguished a cloaked shadow and thought it to be a ghost or spirit. Comazon unsheathed his sword, and then the door was closed with a thud.

The apparition took one of the candles and held it up to its face. The boys screamed in terror, getting up, reaching for their clothes, fearing for their lives. Comazon was confused. He recognized the visitor immediately. What was the emperor doing there at that moment? Why hadn't he announced his visit? *We're fucked,* he thought. And not in the way he had intended.

Antoninus, wearing the purple cloak of Caracalla, walked gracefully among the men, signaling them to keep calm and sit down. They formed a circle around him, heads low, expecting a rebuke for their behavior. Antoninus waited until a stony silence filled the room. He placed the candle on the floor in front of him and, with a quick movement of his hands, tossed the cloak behind him; he stood there, fully naked, wearing only a pair of high-heeled sandals inlaid with precious stones, a golden diadem of olive leaves, and ruby earrings, in front of the men who made him emperor. For long minutes he remained motionless, in a graceful posture, indistinguishable from a Greek statue.

"Adonis!" one of the soldiers shouted.

"Eros!" another shouted.

"Venus!" a third shouted, to the cachinnation and oohs of his companions. The excitement in the room manifested itself in woo-hoos, lewd whistling and rowdy exclamations.

Antoninus called for music. Immediately, soldiers took up lyres and tambourines, and played a soft melody with sensual undertones.

The Boy Maximus swirled his hands slowly to the rhythm, first to the left, then to the right, moved one foot forward, then backward, repeating with the other foot, and turned around, showing his firm, marble-white buttocks, toned thighs and slender torso to the soldiers, who could not believe their eyes. Some slapped their faces in an attempt to wake up from a dream. The men lay on their sides, embracing each other, rubbing each other's hard cocks, mesmerized by the finest dance show in the universe, causing the temperature in the room to rise to the level of the underworld. Drops of sweat from Antoninus's body sprinkled on the soldiers with every twist, anointing them, blessing them, cursing them, making them victims of a wicked spell of lust.

Comazon, who had not even yet undressed, gazed enthralled at the dancing figure. He wanted to possess all that beauty, squeeze it with his arms, never let go. He was burning with an unquenchable desire to touch and feel every inch of that impossibly smooth body and rub it against his rough hairy skin until it bled. With trembling hands, he removed his tunic and *subligaculum*; his shaft was hard as steel, precum already dripping from its head.

Antoninus abruptly stopped the dance and threw himself face down on Caracalla's cloak, using his hands as support. He looked at his soldiers like a tigress in heat. Then he rose slightly, changed his position to rest his back on the floor, and arched his legs, spreading them with his hands, exposing his pink asshole to the frenzied men. The soldiers stood in disbelief, not knowing what to do, until one of the less shy of the band stood up, knelt in front of him and, surrounding the emperor's thighs with his, grabbed his own hard cock, spat on it, and placed its head in the hairless hole, among cries of: "Go! Go! Go! Fuck him! Take his ass!" He pushed his body forward, clutching Antoninus legs, bending slightly until all of his hard wood went inside. He remained there for a few moments amid the increasing banter and hollering of the soldiers; then he pulled back and pushed back in, sliding with increasing speed. When he finished cumming, he pulled his dripping cock out and another soldier took his place. The second man slid more easily into the already lubricated asshole.

The legionaries lined up to wait their turn to fuck the emperor, while a stunned Comazon stood on the side. That was not the way he had envisioned taking his boy's ass. Not like this. The idea of sharing it with his men did not please him. Was this how the emperor wanted to reward his troops? Was what he had done with him then just a reward, and not the beginning of a special relationship? With these bleak thoughts he walked to a part of the room where he could not witness the lewd action, and two boys followed him. They stood on all fours in front of him, offering their tight, pursed holes, ready and willing to take his pleading cock. The hardness of the shaft was torturing him; he was going to explode. He had to get off.

At the same time, Soaemias wandered restlessly around the palace. The door to her son's room was ajar; she looked inside and found his bed empty. She ran to her mother's quarters and knocked frantically on the door.

"Mother! Mother!"

A sleepy Maesa opened the door. "What's the matter? Are you having bad dreams?"

"Antoninus is not in his room! He's been kidnapped! We must alert the guards!"

With an exasperated look, Maesa gestured for her to come inside. She lit a candle and placed it on a small table. The two women sat on the edge of the bed.

"No, he hasn't been kidnapped. Who do you think would dare to break into this palace?"

"Then? I don't understand…"

"He went to a party."

"A party? But he didn't tell me anything about a party."

"Maybe if you didn't spend all your time with that eunuch, you'd pay a little attention to your son."

Soaemias lowered her head.

"I know he's been sleeping here with you. Do you really think you can keep a secret from me?"

Soaemias looked at her pleadingly.

"I don't care, if that's what you want to know," Maesa continued. "I just wish you had better taste in men… the one you have definitely didn't come from me."

"But he loves me! He really does!"

"Caracalla loved you too."

"But I didn't love him back. Besides, I was just a whim for him. One more married lady to take to his bed." She stood up and looked at her mother. "Really, mother? Are we going to have this conversation all over again?"

"No, we're not. But getting back to your son, it seems like neither you nor Gannys can keep an eye on him. I always have to be the one responsible."

"You're wrong, Mother. Gannys loves him too!"

"Being his father doesn't mean he loves him."

"He won the battle for him."

"We won that day because I rode to the battlefield. All those cowards, including your lover, were ready to abandon us all and let us die. So, you see, Gannys thought of himself first, as he always does."

Soaemias flashed a faint smile. "There was one man who didn't attempt to flee: Comazon." She paused a little. "What do you think is the reason for his loyalty?"

"Some men," Maesa said with a malicious smile, "have certain weaknesses, which with proper care can be turned into strengths."

"I don't understand what you mean."

"It doesn't matter. But, rest assured, my dear. Comazon will be loyal to the end. I can guarantee you that."

"Well, I feel safer knowing that my son is with his soldiers... he couldn't be more protected anywhere... Tell me, Mother, do you think his men really love him?"

In the headquarters, not all the soldiers had yet fucked Antoninus when those who had, began to fuck each other. They formed pairs and groups of three or four, in which a submissive one would take a cock up his ass while sucking another; others would get fucked lying on their sides, others, lying on their backs. The soldiers of the *Gallica* took turns penetrating their comrades of the *Parthica*, and vice versa. The sound of moans, grunts, and groans only differed from that of the wounded on the battlefield in coming from a diametrically opposite state of being. Supreme pleasure and supreme pain don't sound very different, after all.

One soldier fucked another while both were standing, when yet another soldier penetrated the top from behind. A fourth joined the line. The men in the middle took turns moving, fucking, and being fucked at the same time. In another corner, two soldiers were on all fours, taking respective cocks from two other men, kissing each other, rubbing their tongues, while their fuckers also shared kisses.

Comazon, who was done banging his boys, but had not cummed, walked in the middle of the room, astonished, watching his legions in the hardest battle they had ever fought. Antoninus was nowhere to be found. The soldiers who had not taken part in the bacchanal were conversing around a fire. It was useless to ask them if they knew where the emperor had gone. Evidently, he had only come and gone like a shadow in the night—like an apparition, the torturer of his dreams. His men would leave happy and satisfied the next day, but he? He had to stay. Stay so close, but so far away from the embodiment of the cruelest yearning of his heart: the boy whose body any soldier could have, but whose heart was still a virgin. Comazon wanted that heart. He wanted all of it. He could not go on without it.

Δ

The next morning, the soldiers lined up under the weak, warm rays of the sun, ready to walk to the harbor from which they would sail back to Rome, where they would likely be assigned to other legions. In spite of the debauchery of the previous night, they had packed their provisions tidily and were dressed immaculately in their uniforms. An emotional Comazon greeted each one of his men with a kiss and a hug and addressed them with words of gratitude and encouragement, smiling and patting their cheeks. Some had tears in their eyes, some just stoically did the military salute, but all left with a heavy heart and a mind filled with sweet memories of love and war.

When most of the soldiers had left, it was the turn of the second in command of the *Legio III Gallica* to salute his commander. Comazon took his face in his hands, as if he were a child, and was about to kiss him, when the man turned his face away.

"We're not going anywhere, Commander."

Comazon frowned. "What do you mean, Verus? The legion has been formally dismissed. The camp will be vacated, and I will be joining the emperor's entourage as praetorian prefect, as you well know."

"You are not going anywhere either, *domine*. As for the boy, he is emperor no more!"

Comazon took a step back and unsheathed his sword. Two soldiers quickly grabbed him from behind and disarmed him.

"We've had enough of your games and your little boy, Comazon. We are men! Men of honor!" Verus belted, spitting on Comazon's face. "And we refuse to be accomplices in the degeneration you have promoted in these legions."

"Maybe you should try being in the general's bed and you would change your mind!" a boy from behind shouted, who was quickly subdued by the rebels.

"Nobody was forced to take part. It was all voluntary," Comazon replied.

"You are a sick fuck. Ever since you joined the legions, you haven't stopped corrupting the best of Rome's youth."

"They are all grown men, otherwise they would not be in the army."

"Either way, my friend. This little tale is over. We'll get rid of you and your boy, and I'll be the new emperor of Rome!"

"Verus! Verus! Verus!" the soldiers exclaimed.

Comazon couldn't believe that he had not seen that coming. He knew that some of his men did not like to participate in the legion's parties, but he had always respected their preferences. He demanded total obedience on the battlefield, but everyone had freedom to do as they wished in bed. So busy had he been planning to seat Antoninus on the throne that he had not noticed that a conspiracy was cooking in his own ranks. But now he was about to meet his fate. His only regret was not being able to warn the emperor of the impending danger.

Verus stopped talking and put a hand to his heart. He fell to the ground, struck by an arrow. Comazon took advantage of the surprise and broke free from the soldiers' grip. He grabbed his sword and ran toward the gates, where dozens of soldiers rushed inside the camp, engaging in combat with the traitors.

"Gannys!" Comazon shouted, as the general arrived on horseback. "Mars be praised that you are here!"

Gannys barely acknowledged him and charged the rebels with his horse. Then he dismounted and joined the scramble on foot. Comazon joined in and, after a brief combat, the two generals and their loyal men stood in a field of corpses. Comazon approached Gannys and embraced him.

"This did not have to happen," Comazon said, sobbing like a little boy. "We were all comrades, brothers in arms."

"That was obviously not the case, my friend," Gannys said, patting him on the back. "We had only come to say goodbye to your men, but I'm glad we arrived right on time."

Δ

Later that night, Maesa stormed into Antoninus's bedroom.

"Do you know what you have caused? Do you see the consequences of your actions?"

Antoninus looked at her, expressionless, and continued filing his nails. "No, Grandma. I don't know what you're talking about."

"I know you got drunk with the soldiers until the wee hours of the morning at the so-called 'party'. What a way to relax the discipline of the troops. You should be ashamed of yourself."

"Who told you?" Antoninus said, wondering what else she knew.

"Gannys."

Gannys, who had been listening outside, knocked on the door to announce his presence. "Can you give me a little time to talk to the emperor, my Lady?"

Maesa grimaced disapprovingly but disappeared behind the door.

"You shouldn't talk to your grandmother like that," the general said as soon as he was alone with the boy.

"There you go again, Gannys, talking to me as if you were my father. I should ask you to start referring to me by my title. And why were you snitching on me?"

Gannys gave a condescending bow. "You seem to have very quickly forgotten that I was the man who saved your life in battle… Excellency."

"Liar! You ran away like a coward, and it was my grandmother who shamed you into returning to fight. But that's nothing to be surprised about; what can one expect from a man with no balls?"

"A man with no balls, but with an intact ass," Gannys said with a grin. "At least I haven't been fucked by all my troopers, like you, silly boy."

Antoninus's mouth curved into a sinister grimace as he stood up and grabbed a dagger from a side table. He leaped toward Gannys and threatened to stab him. The general pushed him back, sending the wimpy boy tumbling to the floor.

Maesa had been listening on the other side of the door. "Guards! Help! Help! The emperor is in danger! Gannys has gone mad and is in his room with a sword! Run to save his life! Do whatever it takes!"

When the guards arrived, the boy was huddled in a corner with Gannys shouting loudly at him. Without hesitation, one of the guards rushed into the room and thrust his sword into the general's back, while the other slashed his throat. The eunuch's blood gushed out onto the camel-skin rugs, soaking them. His body fell to the floor. Maesa entered the room accompanied by Soaemias, who ran toward the dying man, while Antoninus screamed hysterically, as the knife dropped from his trembling hands.

"Gannys! Gannys, no!" Soaemias wailed.

Gannys took one last look at his lover, and signaled Antoninus to approach him, but as he tried to speak, his breathing ceased and his eyes closed. Antoninus looked at the dead man with wild eyes, as Maesa yelled at the guards to leave the room. Soaemias rested her head on her lover's chest, dyeing her hair scarlet red. She cried aloud, begging Elagabal to bring him back to life, but her prayers were not answered.

Meanwhile, her mother smiled, satisfied. With two guards, she accomplished what she couldn't by sending Gannys to war. Now that the eunuch was out of the way, only she and Soaemias knew the secret of Antoninus's ancestry. Now it was only a matter of keeping her daughter's mouth shut.

CHAPTER 3

"HERE I COME…"

Wintertime was over in the mountains of Bithynia, and the roads, after a lingering snowbreak, were finally fit for the emperor and his family to make their way to the ctcrnal city. After endless weeks of travel by land and sea, the walls of Rome finally appeared in the distance during a brightly lit Sunday morning in the Italian countryside.

The carriage moved slowly forward, lifting clouds of dust along the way. It had been a grueling journey for everyone, not only physically, but also emotionally. Maesa was too old for the trip, and Soaemias, too sad and melancholic. For most of the journey she had merely looked away from the window, letting her mind wander to the afterlife, wondering where her beloved Gannys might be. Her mother had convinced her of the overzealousness of the guards, who, finding their emperor in a precarious situation, did no more than their soldierly instincts told them to do. The men had been conveniently dismissed by Maesa, who bought their silence with a large sum, reminding them that "the safety of their families" should from now on be their only concern.

Antoninus was mostly silent and reserved in the brief breaks his grandmother gave him during her "coaching sessions." Maesa did not hesitate to spend the countless hours at their disposal doing everything possible to prepare him for his encounter with the senators. They practiced rhetoric and showmanship, anticipated retorts and objections, and above all, she made it clear to him that he was to show absolutely no sign of weakness, no remorse or regret of any kind.

"Remember," Maesa said to him, "you must always act with dignity, offended by any insignificance, arrogant, petulant: you must make the senators hate you, but most of all, fear you."

"And how exactly am I going to instill fear in those old men, being as young as I am."

"Acting irrational and whimsical is the best way. They must never know where you're coming from, nor where you're going. You must never let them figure you out. Caligula was not much older than you, and believe me, he was feared."

"He was also assassinated."

"He didn't have Comazon to protect him."

Antoninus was silent for a minute. "I'm not sure I will be able to do this, Grandma... I just don't have it in me to be cruel."

Maesa smiled. "You will get used to it. Cruelty, my dear, is the sweetest of pleasures."

Finally, the carriage came to a stop, as an emissary from Rome, driving a larger and more comfortable couch, met them on the way. The chauffeur of the imperial family descended and spoke to them from the window.

"Excellencies, the delegates from Rome have arrived to take you to the city."

Antoninus, his mother and grandmother got out of the carriage and were helped into the other vehicle, where after a while they resumed their conversation.

"I have a strange feeling coming back to Rome. The city is the same, but at the same time, so different," Soaemias said.

"Everything has changed for the better, dear child, now that we're in a much better position. Besides, here we still have many acquaintances, and many people who love us…"

"And many people who hate us too."

"That's what we have the army for. We can always count on the allegiance of Comazon and his men."

"Let's not forget that it was your money that bought them, Grandma," Antoninus said, at his grandmother's insistence to bring up the general.

Maesa smiled and stroked her grandson's hand. "It is money that has bought allegiances since Rome was founded, dear child. But if that worries you, there are other ways to assure the loyalty of men."

"Yes… and I think I might have contributed a little in that regard," he said with a smirk.

"If only my Gannys could have seen this moment, he would have been so proud…" Soaemias said with a sigh, looking out the window.

When the gates were opened, the carriage struggled to make its way through the crowds that had come from all over

Rome to see their new ruler. The city was not the same as the one Antoninus, still as Bassianus, remembered from some years before. It was not just the garlands of flowers and laurel branches that decorated the streets, nor the heat of the torches or the smell of incense, nor even the radiant faces and white robes of his subjects, no, there was something else in the air, something that perhaps emanated from himself. He had not cared for his fellow Romans when they were only his equals, but now, being their emperor, he felt a strange affection for them, as if they were younger siblings, someone to look after.

The carriage stopped before a grand marble staircase, atop of which the senators awaited. A slave stepped forward to help the emperor, his mother and grandmother, descend from it, and the senators welcomed them as they ascended the stairs. Some of the men exchanged disapproving glances at the boy's notoriously colorful—and barbaric—attire. Comazon, who had been following the imperial carriage with his troops, followed closely behind.

"Senate and people of Rome," Consul Quintus Sacerdos said, who as usual, functioned as the Senate's speaker, "we are pleased to welcome, after his long journey from the East, *Imperator* Caesar Marcus Aurelius Antoninus Augustus, the rightful ruler of Rome, to this, his city, which long awaited his coming."

Cheers emerged from the crowd. Some senators clapped lightly, and others waved the flap of their togas, disguising their disdain for the ridiculous oriental boy. Maesa watched the display with delight; she could see right through them and their thoughts and enjoyed profoundly having imposed her will and left them no choice but to accept her grandson as ruler. Soaemias, a little uncomfortable with the attention, focused her gaze on the speaker.

"The gods showed their good will, freeing us from the tyranny of that most evil man, Macrinus, who by brute force wished to secure the throne for himself; our young emperor, showing great courage under the guidance of Mars, crushed that lion and regained the seat of the Caesars for the honorable Severan dynasty."

Under the guidance of Elagabal, Antoninus thought. He didn't judge it prudent to interrupt the speech. There would be time for such corrections later.

"And what a blessing and a truly enormous gift from the gods it is to have such a chaste, pious, and godlike prince. All anyone who doubted of the lineage of our emperor had to do was look at his effigy to be convinced of his noble origin as the son of Marcus Aurelius Antoninus…"

In this, he's not wrong. This man knows how to speak, the emperor thought.

"…which is indeed what happened to the troops who had foolishly stormed the headquarters of the brave and patriotic *Legio III Gallica* at Raphanea."

Comazon smiled, pleased by the reference to his men. He took a deep breath of Rome's fresh morning air. The feathers of his helmet fluttered in the wind as he enjoyed the dazzling view of the Colosseum, the Pantheon, and the Temple of Rome. He was finally back in his city, which he missed so much. One part of him was happy, but the other… What he had missed during the last night in the camp was now right beside him; the boy he had known on such intimate terms, now stood like a true Caesar in front of Rome's political elite.

"And although he may be young in age, we know for a fact that the gods have instilled in the mind of our prince the wisdom of the ages, and in his heart, care and compassion for his fellow men, the citizens of the empire, who will look to him as a father, to guide and lead them, in all the endeavors that the future holds for our fatherland."

The speech went on with oodles of stanzas of praise and eulogies of the virtues and noble heritage of the prince, his courage in battle and adversity and even his beauty, which did not go unnoticed by the elderly members of the Senate.

When the consul finished speaking, Antoninus looked out at the crowd, smiling, rejoicing in the audience's ovation. This was his moment. This was what he had come to Rome for. At least, in part.

Δ

Minutes later, senators, Praetorians, and the emperor and his family had passed through the posh marble walls of the *curia Iulia*. Antoninus paced speedily in circles over the *pietra dura* floor, forcing his mind to recall the details of the previously rehearsed rhetoric, and at the same time, taming his nerves, which threatened to betray him. He dared not look as the senators took their seats. The Praetorians stood soldierly at the entrance, and Maesa and Soaemias, next to Comazon.

Finally, when a sepulchral silence was made, Antoninus stopped his walk and gave his audience a defiant look.

"Well," he said, resting his chin on the knuckles of his right hand. "It's time for me to give my instructions."

The senators looked at each other uneasily. They had expected a speech, not to receive "instructions" from a boy of barely military age.

"I have been informed," he began, "that my noble birth was not acknowledged by all the members of this honorable house at the time that it was announced." He took delight in glancing at their concerned faces. "It is unfortunate. To err is a human flaw that plagues even men of high office, but I, generous as I am, happily declare that I am willing to forgive, provided that my three following conditions are met."

The senators looked at each other in bewilderment.

"But, Excellency, public thanksgivings were decreed for the restoration of your noble house, as well as the complete erasure of Macrinus from public memory," a senator said, only to be shushed loudly by his nervous peers.

"To begin with, I would like to introduce General Publius Valerius Comazon," he said, looking to his right, "as the new praetorian prefect." The sight of the general gave an immediate boost to his confidence.

Comazon smiled and nodded lightly. A senator immediately rose from his seat.

"*Auguste*, we had thought of proposing for the position Flavius Antochianus, who has a perfect record as—"

Antoninus stopped him with the palm of his right hand. "I haven't finished speaking… Senator."

The man returned to his seat with face flushed with anger.

"As I was saying," Antoninus continued with his peculiar intonation, amid sinuous and swaying hand movements, "I trust no one in Rome more than General Comazon for my personal safety. And I shouldn't have to justify these kinds of decisions, which correspond solely to me, the *princeps* of Rome."

"Such an arbitrary imposition is not constitutional!" another shouted.

"You had better grow accustomed to the idea that I am the sole source of the constitution," he said, approaching the senatorial ranks menacingly. "I have come as the second Augustus; as Augustus, I am eighteen years of age; as with Augustus, my reign began with a war to avenge the murder of my father; and as Augustus, I have received numerous auspicious omens from the oracles. I combine in my being not only his divine wisdom, but that of Marcus Aurelius, plus the impetus of my father, Caracalla, and the unique sensitivity of an artist, surpassing that of Nero and Hadrian."

The hubristic words, and especially the sassy tone his voice had taken, churned up the senators' guts. All their fears were confirmed: this was definitely not a person the divine Augustus would have ever wished to inherit his sacred throne. True, the *pater patriae* had never intended to be equal to other citizens, not even when he had proclaimed himself "*princeps*"—which was supposed to mean "first among equals"—but he had at least kept up appearances. This boy's behavior was already intolerable. They knew he was not much more than a youth, too young to know even the rudiments of politics, but he turned out to be far more cynical and spoiled than they expected.

"Second, I also decree that my grandmother, Julia Maesa, must occupy a senatorial seat." He paused. "With the full rights of her male peers."

An uproar broke out in the Senate ranks. Soaemias gazed, confused, at Maesa's face, in which a beam-smile appeared. The boy was really doing a good job. She had no idea he could be such a fine actor.

"This has never been seen in Rome. This is a disgrace!" one of the senators shouted.

"Who said that?"

Silence reigned.

"Who said that?" the emperor repeated.

"I did," a senator sitting in one of the back rows said.

With head held high, Antoninus approached the senator slowly, almost touching his nose with his. "Take him to the dungeons," he said in a calm voice.

The emperor felt at the peak of his performance. He could not believe the words he had just uttered. But now he had to get on with it. He was playing a dangerous game in which no jokes were allowed.

Comazon and a few other guards approached swiftly. Other senators tried to interpose themselves, but the *gladii* of the Praetorians dissuaded them.

"To the dungeons!" Antoninus shrieked to the astonished faces of the senators. "I want to see him at the next gladiatorial show. Let's see if he's just as brave when he fights there."

As the man was led away shouting words of damnation, Antoninus returned to the center of the *curia* and with steely calm resumed his demands. Inwardly, he had to fight not to burst out laughing. His grandmother was right, being cruel—or, pretending to—was extremely pleasurable.

"Third. I want the image I sent you to be installed right there," he said, pointing to an area above the statue of the goddess Victoria, which presided over the house.

A senator dared to speak amid the prevailing terror and uncertainty that dominated the hall, and said with a trembling voice: "Just for clarification, Excellency, is the image to remain during the hours of ritual and worship of the goddess?"

"It shall remain the whole time," Antoninus said with a murderous glare, which made a drop of sweat run down the senator's temple. "Any more questions?"

"Good," Antoninus said with a smile, to the stunned silence of the senators.

He turned to leave the building but stopped abruptly and turned around. "By the way, there will be a change in the priorities of the religious cult of this city. From now on, the main cult of Rome will be directed to Elagabal, the supreme sun god of which I am high priest. And his cult will be performed in the Temple of Jupiter, which will be rededicated on a date to be indicated by me. All senators are required to attend, regardless of the circumstances."

After those words, he stormed theatrically out of the building, leaving behind not an assembly of senators, but a group of men pale with fear and filled with disgust and an unquenchable anger.

Δ

Inside Maesa's chamber, Soaemias and Maesa were conversing, reclining on their respective divans.

"How I missed living in the palace, darling. This is our true home," Maesa said.

"If you say so," Soaemias said, absentmindedly. She looked around the room, which had already been furnished to Maesa's taste, according to the instructions she had sent from Emesa. "Didn't this room belong to—"

She stopped her daughter with her hand. "It's mine now, and will be until the day I die."

"That's if your swindle is not discovered first."

"Why should it be discovered? Only you and I know the truth. And it will stay that way."

"But, Mother, there will have to come a time when my son... Bassianus... will have to know the truth about his father."

"Antoninus! Antoninus is his name! And he is not only your son, but also the emperor of Rome!" Maesa looked at her daughter with an enraged face. "Never again dare to speak those words, you fool!" she hissed. "Antoninus is the rightful son of Caracalla, and that is the only truth."

Soaemias's eyes filled with tears.

"Dear Daughter," Maesa said, approaching Soaemias and lifting her chin, "we're already here; there is no going back..." She paused and gazed at her sternly. "No going back. No one must ever know who Antoninus's real father is. Not even the boy himself."

Soaemias escaped her mother's grip and stood up briskly. She shook her head in disbelief as she gazed at the woman who had given her life: a woman now completely unrecognizable, a lioness at war. She couldn't stand the sight of her any longer and stormed out of the room.

Maesa was left pacing nervously. Yes, it had hurt to be so harsh with her daughter—the only person she really cared about in this world, other than herself—but it had been necessary. She could not tolerate any weakness on her part that might jeopardize their position. She stopped to consider for a minute. If only her grandson was as manipulable as his mother... things would be much easier. But for now, she was pleased. She had obtained a senatorial seat, something no Roman woman had ever obtained before. She smiled. It was a good first step toward her true goal: total control. If, due to the rules of the patriarchy, she could not be empress of Rome, and therefore could not emulate in her land the likes of Semiramis or Nitocris, then she was determined to be the power behind the throne. Antoninus was totally incapable of ruling. She knew that. She counted on it. His only function was to stand in front of the senators, which he had done very well this day, behaving like a little bully, but she knew that soon, pressure would mount for him to actually rule with some sense. And when that happened, she would be there to offer "advice."

Δ

A selected group of senators had agreed to convene after hours in the back room of the *curia Iulia*. The agenda was simple: the open discussion, in an atmosphere of trust, of the first encounter with the boy. Among those present were Consul Quintus Tineius Sacerdos, leading the reunion; Senator Fulvius Diogenianus, representing the radical faction; Senator Julius Paulus Prudentissimus, representing the moderates; and Flavius Antochianus, the unsuccessful candidate for the praetorian prefecture. Sacerdos opened the informal meeting.

"Friends, I'm grateful for your willingness to assemble at this late hour to discuss this grave matter. Normally I try not to call smaller assemblies, but in this case I wanted to tread on firm ground before holding a full-fledged discussion in the Senate. I'm interested in your impressions of the boy."

"As you can imagine, I think he's a total disaster," Fulvius said. "He's nothing more than a petulant, spoiled little brat, who has no idea how to behave among adults."

"I agree with Senator Fulvius," Flavius said. "We knew he was young and inexperienced, but his attitude adds a level of complexity we had not foreseen. It looks like we are dealing with a barbarian and not a member of the imperial family."

"And the garments didn't help," Fulvius said.

"We are dealing with something extraordinary indeed," Sacerdos said. "A far cry even from Caracalla, who could also behave like a lunatic at times." He turned to look at Senator Julius Paulus. "Any comment, Senator?"

Paulus took a few moments to respond. "I have to agree that he's worse than I expected. However, I think there is a way to talk some sense into him."

"And that is?" Sacerdos asked.

"Through his grandmother. As I had shared with the Fathers before their arrival, I know Julia Maesa quite well. Surely she is the only one who can help us curb his behavior. I wouldn't count on his mother. She is a kind-hearted but weak woman, and undoubtedly the reason for his intolerable behavior."

"Maesa is a '*senatrix*' now," Fulvius said, mockingly. "We will see her in the *curia* quite often."

"And that's not a bad thing," Paulus said. "I know you think it's disgraceful for a woman to take part in Senate meetings, but in these extraordinary circumstances, it's not as bad as you think. I'd rather deal with a woman of reason than with a lunatic boy."

"So, for now you propose to go with the flow and not try anything against him?" Flavius asked.

"Exactly. I think he was trying to make an impression today, no doubt, trying to scare us. And you bet he succeeded, at least with some of us. Let's give him a few days and see how things develop. Besides…"

"Besides?" Sacerdos asked.

"…it's quite obvious that he counts with the wholehearted allegiance of the new Praetorian Guard, and especially, its prefect."

"That's true," Sacerdos said. "Comazon already enjoyed impressive popularity among the plebs, and winning this war so easily has only added to his fame. This is not a good time to try anything that might displease the general."

"We already tried and failed," Fulvius said. "That Verus ended up being quite useless."

"So," Sacerdos said, "do we agree with Senator Paulus's plan to wait and see?"

The men nodded reluctantly. It was already late at night, and they decided to return home before the city became dangerous even for their armed escorts.

Δ

Comazon had given the emperor a few days to settle into his quarters before paying him a visit. He knocked on the tall oak doors and waited for approval. The bedroom featured an extensive bed within a canopy, a *triclinium*, a dressing table with a large silver mirror, two nightstands, all on a brand-new plush wool carpet.

"What do you think," a jovial Antoninus said, turning around with his hands in the air. "I have so much room that I can even practice my dance moves here."

"It is truly outstanding, but no less what you deserve, Majesty."

"Whoever was in charge of furnishing and decorating the room did a good job, but not as good as the people in Nicomedia. Now, that was special." He looked around, slightly displeased. "I don't like the color of the walls, and they didn't put silk sheets on my bed. I've already ordered new ones made."

Comazon smiled. "Are you glad to be in Rome?"

"Yes, of course," Antoninus said, sitting with one arm reclined on the bed. "It is my destiny. Now I can truly feel that I am the master of the world."

"You had an excellent arrival session at the Senate. I did not expect you to be so fierce."

"My Grandma has been coaching me. I thought she was exaggerating when she said I must look firm and ruthless, but now I see her point. Those senators are a force to be reckoned with. But with your help," Antoninus said, caressing Comazon's arm, "I am sure we can keep them at bay."

Comazon sat down on the bed beside him. Stimulated, he reciprocated Antoninus's caresses, moved closer, and tried to bring his lips to the emperor's.

"Not now," Antoninus said, pushing the general back slightly. "We'll have time for fun later. Come here, I want to show you something."

He stood up taking Comazon's hand, pulling him toward the back of the room.

"See this?" he said, pointing to a door.

"Where does it lead to?"

"Open it."

Another wooden door blocked the passage.

Antoninus stepped back into the room. "Push it," he said, as he noisily looked for something.

With some exertion, the door yielded. Both men stooped into the cold and musty passageway, which widened as they walked. Complete darkness surrounded them, yet there was only one direction to proceed: onward. Eventually, they arrived at a shut door with a few crevices through which light seeped.

"I found the key to this door yesterday; it was in a little box, hidden inside Caracalla's treasure chest." He entered the key in the lock and turned it. "Do you recognize this place?"

"It is the imperial passage to the circus."

"Isn't it awesome? Then I can use this little shortcut to show up at the circus, and no one will know where I came from."

"I agree, but I am pretty sure it was built with a more practical approach in mind. Caracalla was obsessed with the idea that someone would try to kill him. He must have built it as a way to escape if things went wrong."

"I see. Unfortunately things went wrong with him far away from home," Antoninus said, shrugging.

Antoninus closed the door and locked it. They returned to the imperial chamber, but before entering, and after some hesitation, Comazon couldn't restrain himself and embraced the boy, seeking his lips again.

"Comazon, seriously, let's leave it for later."

"Why later, when we can do it now? No one is going to find us here."

Antoninus acquiesced and allowed the general to kiss him wet. Afterward, Comazon went down and started kissing his neck and caressing his back and buttocks.

"I have desired you so much, ever since the day I first saw you in the temple," the general said in a whisper. "And I cannot think of anything else but you since we sucked each other's dicks in your house in Emesa."

"It was fun for me too," Antoninus said, pushing him away. "Don't be so anxious, Comazon. We've just arrived in Rome, and we need to get settled before we start doing things. There will be time."

Antoninus smiled at him and tapped the general's cheek. Comazon touched his own groin. His tunic had gotten wet with precum.

"Now, let's go back inside," Antoninus said. "There is much to talk about. I want to tell you my immediate plans."

Δ

A week after the arrival, Maesa attended her first session in the *curia* as a *senatrix*, wearing a white *stola*, featuring the purple ribbon exclusive of senatorial rank. She sat in a preferential seat, given to her out of deference from the senators.

"Honorable Fathers," Consul Sacerdos said. "Let us begin today's session with a prayer to Victoria."

The senators rose and recited a prayer, the words of which Maesa didn't know. She stood in silence, contemplating the portrait of her grandson, which sacrilegiously had been installed above the statue of Victoria; a simple action that symbolized how far she had come in such a short time.

The order of the day began with simple matters, from tax collection to the maintenance of various buildings. The crucial issue of the day came after a few hours.

"Very well," Sacerdos said, "having reached an agreement on all these important issues, there is still one matter to be resolved, and that is the proposed consecration of the Temple of Jupiter to the new god, Ela… Elabagal—"

"Elagabal," Maesa corrected. "And he is not a new god, but the one and eternal god of the universe." She rose. "With all due respect, Fathers," she said, to the stunned silence of the senators, who had never before seen a woman speak in the *curia*, "I do not see why this should be a matter of discussion. It is the will of the emperor, and as such, it must be obeyed."

"But *senatrix*," a senator said, "such a radical action will not be taken well by the people, and requires further justification—"

"You seem to have misunderstood my words, senator. As I have said, the will of the emperor is not up for debate. And neither does it need justification. This is what the divine Augustus established. A one-man government to provide Rome with peace and stability."

"But the divine Augustus never attacked the cult of the gods. Quite the contrary."

"Didn't he deify Caesar?" Maesa said.

"That's hardly an attack on the gods!"

"In this case it is the same thing, only that the emperor is not deifying his father, but merely establishing in Rome the already existing worship of the sun." She paced the room. "Just as Augustus maintained the cult of the gods, so will Antoninus. Jupiter, Apollo, Venus, all will be worshipped in their respective temples. All he asks is that the main temple be dedicated to the one true god. Jupiter has many other places of worship."

"Surely this will bring disgrace upon us all. Jupiter must not offended in such a way!" another senator shouted.

"That's not for you to decide," Maesa said. "And I would like to take this opportunity to make this very clear, honorable Fathers. I am here to defend the will of the emperor. But I also want you to understand that this is a never-before-seen opportunity of collaboration between the Senate and His Majesty, for which I volunteer as liaison. I have unrestricted access to the emperor: all you have to do is ask, and I will be sure to communicate your needs to him. I can assure you that there are only a few things on which the emperor will not compromise his wishes, but many on which he will rely on us to get things done." She paused. "Do not be obstinate, and understand the benefit of sacrificing just a little, if much is to be gained for the welfare of the empire."

With these words, the senators were appeased and Elagabal would make his entrance into the eternal city.

Δ

Not long afterward came the day when Rome would witness the—according to Antoninus—only proper worship service for the sun god. Although other sun deities had been previously worshipped in the eternal city, nothing would compare to the grandeur and pageantry that Antoninus had prepared for the dedication of the former Temple of Jupiter to Elagabal. He intended to put on a performance that the people of Rome would never forget.

The streets were thickly strewn with white sand sprinkled with gold dust, and crowds thronged them, carrying torches and bouquets of flowers in a frenzy of heat and madness, while street vendors rejoiced at their increased sales, and the senators—who had been compelled to attend—waited in silence for the arrival of Rome's latest flame. Their expressions varied between confusion, pain, and gloom—anything but festivity.

After a long wait, the emperor appeared wearing the notorious barbarian clothes of his previous public appearances: robes so intensely hated by his grandmother, who had warned him several times to throw them away and dress accordingly to his new position as head of the empire. None of that diatribe mattered in the least to Antoninus, who in the end—and especially at this moment—was first and foremost the chief priest of Elagabal. His white tunic, embroidered with gold at the seams, was made of the most precious silk of the Orient, since his delicate skin could not tolerate the feel of linen, much less of ordinary cotton cloth.

A chariot adorned with gold and jewels, with great parasols at each of its corners, had been prepared for the conveyance of the *baetyl*; the rock was tied with leather reins to six immaculate white horses lined up in a single row, featuring on their legs gold trimmings encrusted with gems. The horses had no saddles, and the chariot had no driver. Antoninus stood in front of the chariot, bowed to Elagabal, and took the bridles, stretching them away from the vehicle as he walked backwards, never taking his gaze off the icon; he pulled them until the horses moved forward, giving with all this the impression that it was Elagabal himself who guided the horses from its seat.

Musicians playing drums, flutes and tambourines accompanied the march, producing a joyous in tone, distinctly foreign-sounding music, and young male dancers dressed in light white robes cavorted in a sultry, coordinated fashion in front of the chariot. All the dancers, including the emperor, wore green olive wreaths. The women carried vessels of incense, whose tall plumes of smoke reached well into the crowd. The praetorian guard, led by Comazon, walked alongside the emperor carrying Roman imperial standards, and the cavalry walked slowly behind the unmanned chariot. In this fashion they continued the way to the temple, where Elagabal would now take his rightful place as the supreme deity in the Roman pantheon.

Arriving at the ancient abode of Jupiter, four soldiers carried the *baetyl* up the marble staircase with the help of a wooden structure. At that moment, all movement stopped in the parade, and it was only when the soldiers placed the stone facing the emperor that the music resumed. The people of

Rome were about to witness the famous dance of the chief priest of Elagabal.

The crowd went wild with the first movements of his hands; with every twist and contortion he brought the people to ecstasy. Even if he would make an atrocious emperor, nobody could deny that he was a hell of a dancer. His dancers also whirled about, performing a hopping, leaping, spinning dance. To make things wilder, Antoninus climbed a stone column—which had been built next to the temple—through its inner staircase, emerged through an opening at the top and, after basking in the adoration of his people, distributed among them valuable objects such as silver goblets and gold coins with his effigy—which flashed and glittered as they rained on the excited crowd—as well as expensive clothes, and all kinds of luxury items. Many citizens were injured during the scramble by crushing one another; some fell on their hands and knees, struggling tenaciously to pick up a prize. The frenzy was so intense that the Praetorians had to intervene to restore order.

The emperor descended from the tower and ordered some bared-chested men, bulging with muscles, to carry the sacred stone into the temple, where only he, his family, the senators, and designated aids could follow. The Praetorian Guard remained outside for security. Hundreds of white doves were released to signal the beginning of the ceremony to the people and mark the blessings of Elagabal, which were now bestowed upon the city of Rome and its citizens across the world.

Once the god was placed on the altar, an immaculate white bull was introduced into the torch-lit temple. It smelled of the oils and spices that had been used to wash and purify it, was decorated with white wool fillets, and wore a crown of white jasmine on its horns. The beast was brought to the altar before Antoninus, who, after a few prayers, was handed a hunting spear and, without hesitation, stunned the animal with its straight, pointed head and finished it off with its curved side. More assistants quickly approached to collect the animal's blood, which was then poured on the altar for purification: thus began the dedication of the temple to the new deity. Antoninus himself collected a portion of the blood with his hands and poured it over his head, staining his hitherto immaculate garment. A servant approached with a basin of water for the emperor to wash himself.

To everyone's surprise, Antoninus took off his tunic and stood naked before the audience. Some senators covered their faces. He poured water on his head several times, and when he had completely cleaned himself of the blood, a servant approached with a sheepskin and carefully dried him. Then, without asking for fresh clothes, he exclaimed: "Where is my select group of young men of military age?" whereupon the doors of the temple opened to usher in a coterie of young legionaries, who had been chosen by him from among the Praetorians, and who that day had performed as dancers. Judging by their manners, they came from the lowest ranks of society, but they were young, handsome, and athletic, and that was all that was required for the task at hand.

The boys lined up in three rows of three in front of the altar. Antoninus raised his hands in the air and clapped once. Instantly, the dancers stripped off their tunics. A huge gasp emerged among the senators. He clapped a second time, and several slaves lit incense sticks made from the resin of psychotropic plants. It was time to present the ultimate cult of Elagabal: sacred sex. Antoninus had conceived it since his nocturnal visit to the garrison in Nicomedia; he had decided that, if he really wanted to honor his god, he had to offer him for the dedication of his new temple the best possible performance in this world. A god who made men happy, and who had given his special protection to his minister Antoninus, deserved in return no less than the highest bliss of human ecstasy. Dancing for him had sufficed during his youth; now it was time to present the offerings befitting a man. It was time to assert his title of *Sacerdos Amplissimus Dei Invicti Solis Elagabali.*

Antoninus approached the young man in the center of the front row and stroked his chin with his hand. He slid his hand down the soldier's chiseled chest, hard and smooth as a marble statue, gently caressing each of his nipples with his fingers. Next, he moved to the young man on the left, this time softly caressing his penis with the back of his hand, moving it up toward the abdomen, feeling his hairs bristle at the contact. After doing the same with the boy on the right, he returned to the center position and knelt in front of the three of them. After a signal, they approached, cock in hand, ready to serve their emperor and his god. Antoninus opened his mouth, slowly inserting the still soft and uncircumcised member of the young man in the center. He sucked it like a calf attached to its mother.

The scene was too much for Maesa to resist, and she fainted in the arms of a senator. Two other legislators had to help him and Soaemias carry her out of the building. The rest of the men followed behind them, uttering curses and exclamations of indignation. Some vomited outside on the staircase of the temple. Neither the Praetorians nor the people had the slightest idea of what was happening inside.

"Take care of the distribution of meat," one of the senators requested from Comazon. "The bull has already been sacrificed; the butchers should be coming soon to cut it up."

Confused, Comazon saw Soaemias and the men carrying Maesa approaching. "What happened to Maesa? What is going on inside the temple, *domina*?"

"There's no time for explanations," Soaemias replied, shoving Comazon aside. "We must take Mother to a doctor immediately!"

The soldiers watched in confusion how the senators left the building in droves, but did not dare to go inside without an explicit order.

Inside, still kneeling, Antoninus had two fully erect cocks pressing against his mouth. He sucked alternatively one and the other, spitting on them, mixing his saliva with their precum. A tiger skin, brought by a slave, was placed on the floor. Antoninus used it to lie on his back, his head resting on the tiger's head. He arched his legs and spread his buttocks. Two of the other young men drew near him, one filling his mouth with his cock and the other kneeling, getting ready to fill the emperor from behind. The soldier spread Antoninus's legs and poured a little oil on his own cock and on the emperor's asshole to prepare it for penetration. He thrusted the head slowly, but with the large amount of oil used to lubricate, his dick went right inside with hardly any effort. Antoninus gripped the other soldier's cock while he shoved his balls on his face, caressing the scrotum with his tongue. He inserted again the precum-dripping cock into his mouth and continued to suck it.

The soldiers in the rear performed similar actions among themselves, some kissed, others sucked each other, and others had penetrative sex in honor of the mighty Elagabal, who presided silently over the revelry from his throne on the altar, glowing a reddish hue in the light of the torches, absorbing the energy given off by the sexual rite.

While one of the soldiers was still penetrating him, Antoninus gazed at the effigy of his god. He smiled, pleased. If no one—including the senators and his grandmother—had tried to stop him performing his sacred sexual ritual, that meant only one thing. He was really in charge. He was really the supreme power in Rome. He now believed it and would exercise it to the ultimate consequences.

Outside, Comazon pushed the door ajar, and an otherworldly sound of pleasure deluged his ears. He immediately understood the reason why the emperor's grandmother had fainted. Antoninus was truly a nymphomaniac; the farewell party was not going to remain a one-time occasion. He had no idea that, without his knowledge, the emperor had selected a few legionaries to form a covenant with his god. How would he, Comazon, deal with that? When would the sun boy have his fill? And, above all, how could he win his heart? Was the emperor's heart even available? Or were orgies all he cared for? A tumult of questions tormented his brain, and his heart trembled with uncertainty, but for now, he only regretted being left out of the action once again.

CHAPTER 4

MARITAL DUTIES

A year had already passed since the infamous dedication of the temple, and while during that time Maesa had done a fine job handling affairs of state as smoothly as it was done in the times of Severus and Caracalla, things were still not quite as she wanted them to be. Although she had tried with all her might to bury the lubricious performance away from the public mind—going so far as to forbid the subject from being mentioned in the palace and in the city—her actions did little to keep the emperor and his lewdness from being on the lips of every Roman, citizen or slave; his liberal lifestyle—with frequent, flamboyant late-night parties—was the cause not only of astonishment, but also of disapproval and disgust for many of the city's inhabitants, especially the noble and wealthy families that feared for their sons, and who she feared were secretly plotting his demise.

Her power was in jeopardy as long as her grandson's position as emperor was not fully consolidated. There one essential action that could contribute to gaining him a little respect from the community, and that could also probably put an end to the life of excess that the stripling had set out to live. Maesa had convinced Julius Paulus

Prudentissimus—who remained one of her true supporters in the Senate—to grant his daughter Julia Cornelia Paula in marriage to the young ruler. After all, the matriarch argued, the boy's extravagant behavior could be explained as a juvenile response to the tremendous authority and responsibility vested in him at such a young age; she vehemently assured the senator that his demeanor "was just a phase" and made it clear that "the ways of the Greek" were more common in Asia than in Italy among the youth.

After months of negotiations and formalities, the matrimony took place in autumn, in the *atrium* of the *domus* of Julius Paulus, as the tradition dictated. The vows were read and then the newlywed couple and guests proceeded to the ballroom, where food and wine were served in abundant quantities and the evening was enlivened with music and entertainment.

The young couple occupied the main divan. On the bride's side lay her father and mother, her brother, and other relatives. The emperor's side was less populated: Maesa lay next to Antoninus, then came Soaemias, and next to her was an empty space, since no one else had been judged worthy of such proximity with the emperor.

The bride looked pale and tense, as if convicted of a crime, but for the people around her this was completely normal, since it was precisely what the Roman tradition dictated for any woman of virtue: that she should dread leaving her parents' home to go live with a man. And it this case, it was completely true.

Antoninus hardly noticed her, busy chatting with Soaemias. "Who is that guard, mother?" he said, chewing a grape.

"Who are you talking about, Son?"

"That boy over there," Antoninus said, pointing to a handsome young man in impeccable Praetorian uniform. "I hadn't seen him before. Do you think he's old enough to be in the guard?"

"He must be," Maesa intruded. "Why do you worry about such things? Besides, you're ignoring your bride. Why don't you talk to her instead?"

Antoninus rolled his eyes and continued gobbling grapes. Soaemias smiled and wiggled her fingers at invitees she met eyes with. Deep down, her nerves were eating her up and she was trying hard not to show it.

Hours passed and, as the invitees feasted, the mood in the main *triclinium* continued to deteriorate. Paula looked stiff as a stick and pale as a ghost. She had laid her forearms on the divan and was constantly fiddling with her fingers. Careful to avoid the gazes of others, she feared crying at any moment. Antoninus made no attempt to hide a huge yawn and rested his head on his palm.

Maesa, not wanting to expose the couple to further humiliation, rushed things a little. "It is time for you to take your bride to the master chamber of the palace," she whispered in her grandson's ear.

"Am I supposed to carry her…" he replied in a whiny voice audible to the rest of the table. "…all the way to the palace?"

"Of course, that's a Roman tradition!" she hissed, "And it's really not that far!"

Antoninus stood up before the murderous look of his grandmother. "Let's go," he said to his wife. "We must retire to our chamber."

Julia looked at her mother in terror.

The older woman nodded and held her forearm. "It will be alright, my dear."

Antoninus awkwardly took her by the hand, heading for the exit. As they approached the door, he placed one of his arms under her thighs and the other on her back. He tried to lift her, but, although she was a small and delicate woman, her weight was still too heavy for his feeble arms.

He quickly gave up after the second attempt. "Comazon!" he shouted, to the gasps of the guests. A heavy silence followed. "Comazon! Pick up this lady and carry her to my chamber."

With a swift movement, he lifted the girl as if she were made of straw. Julia felt comforted for the first time that night and wished that her husband would also ask this man to be his substitute for marital affairs. Unfortunately for her, Antoninus dismissed him as soon as he carefully deposited the "parcel" on the imperial bed. A long night awaited them.

Comazon left the palace and headed out into the cold, empty streets of Rome. For a regular citizen it would have been terribly dangerous to walk alone in the middle of the night, but his uniform commanded respect. He headed toward the usual tavern and ordered a goblet of his favorite dry wine. He gulped half the cup in one swallow and wiped his mouth with his forearm. Alcohol could not make him forget what was happening that night. Antoninus, his dear Antoninus, that boy he loved, would be deflowering a woman… for the first time? That woman was now his wife. Surely he couldn't love her. That marriage couldn't have been for love. He took another sip. Tears began to well up in his eyes. How silly, how foolish to think that the pale emperor would one day be for him. Now the obstacle was not only the debauchery of his social life, but a solid institution, sacred to the Roman people: marriage! Now there would never be even the remote possibility of demonstrating him his love, to ask him if perhaps there would be a little place, a dark corner in his heart, for him to occupy… Maybe there had never been one; maybe he had been a fool all this time to indulge such thoughts. Such a display of emotion was unworthy of a Roman, especially a soldier. He finished the cup and asked the taverner to top it off again. He knew that the emperor would not require him until late the next morning, so that night he was planning to get besotted with wine.

After several hours, he stumbled out of the bar. He proceeded down a dark road he knew well, even in his semiconscious state. With luck, he would find the usual youth still looking to make a little more money that night. Many effeminate youngsters were loitering leaning against the walls. A few approached him, but Comazon waved them away. At last, he found what he was looking for. It was not the boy with whom he had visited in the past, but one with smooth, ivory-white skin, deep, wide hazel eyes, and, above all, a feathery mustache. That sold him.

He took the young man into a dark alley and turned him to face the wall while he lifted his tunic and caressed his silky buttocks. Comazon pulled his cock out of the tunic and rubbed it against the boy's creamy, pale, hairless ass. He kissed him on the back of his ear, breathing heavily as he lightly bit his lobe. He heard the boy retch as the stench of his alcoholic breath seeped through his nostrils and he covered his nose and mouth almost completely with his thick hand. The abrasiveness of his stubble reddened the delicate skin of the young man's neck.

After spitting on his hard cock, he inserted it into the tight, lustful asshole. He moved fast, frantically, anxiously, as if a quick satisfaction might succeed in undoing the insidious thoughts that tortured his mind. In his fantasies, it was Antoninus's hole he was fucking. The boy moaned, trying to breathe under the heavy muffling, placing his hands on Comazon's thighs, begging him to slow down. But he would not do it. He would fuck him hard until his cum showered his man pussy.

After some time, he felt the sweet sensation of jism spurting out. In the midst of heavenly relief, Comazon closed his eyes with bated breath and loosened the grip on the boy's mouth. He tucked his dripping cock swiftly back into his loincloth and tightened his belt. Before leaving, he placed a coin in the boy's hand. He took a deep breath, a little sobered up. Now he would go home. And sleep.

Having dismissed Comazon, Antoninus returned to the bedroom. Deeply distressed and on the verge of tears, Paula pulled back the thick silk sheet and covered herself up to the neck. The emperor stared at his beautiful trophy wife with an inquisitive look, his index finger under his chin. He pulled the other side of the sheet and, without changing clothes, slipped under it, an inch away from his lady. Minutes went by in a dreadful silence.

"How do you make a man fall in love?" Antoninus asked out of the blue.

Paula stared at him in bewilderment. "Excuse me, my Lord?"

"I asked how a man falls in love."

"I… I don't know what you mean…" Paula said in a trembling voice. Did the emperor think she was not a virgin? Why would he ask such a thing?

"Of course you do. You are a woman; your mother must have taught you something before…" Antoninus caressed her cheek with the back of his index finger, "…allowing you to marry."

"Oh no, my Lord, she didn't say anything, she said that everything I needed to know… I'd learn tonight…"

Antoninus got up and yanked the sheet from her hands.

"So, you come here, to my bed, and tell me you know nothing about love? Nothing!" He drew near her wagging his index finger. "This is the only reason why I accepted to bring you to the palace, so you could tell me what a woman should do to make the man she wants love her."

This time Paula couldn't hold back her tears. "Well, maybe your Highness could have asked your mother about that."

"So now I have a wife, a pretty wife, but utterly useless. What is the purpose of a woman, if not to catch her man?"

"That's something that can be learned, I'm sure that if we try…" Paula said, sitting on the bed.

"I am already experienced in those matters," the emperor said with a smirk. "I know what I like in bed, and I know what men like, I just thought… there must be something special that women do to bewitch and enrapture men and keep them."

Paula stood up, embracing him from behind and caressing his torso. Antoninus squeezed his eyes shut and breathed heavily.

"It's useless. I am unresponsive to a woman's touch," he said, pulling away from her abruptly. "I made a mistake in bringing you here. I should never have listened to my grandmother. This is all a big blunder!" He looked at her with piercing eyes. "Get out of here. Get out of here, now! You are dismissed from my presence! You will not stay in my room another minute!", he said pointing to the door.

"But my Lord, you will disgrace me, think of my family, they have been loyal subjects of the empire—"

"Your family is the least of my concerns right now. I'm done with you. You're nothing but a pathetic little creature, and I want you out of my sight!"

He opened the door and continued pointing to the exit. She wiped her tears with the back of her hand and exited the bedroom, with no time to fix her clothes and disheveled hair.

"I will divorce you tomorrow!" Antoninus shouted, slamming the door behind her.

Δ

Comazon was summoned to the emperor's chamber the next day around noon. The door was ajar when he knocked.

"Come in," the emperor said with his distinctive feminine voice.

He was reclining on his divan, enjoying a bunch of juicy red grapes. There was no trace of his wife.

"You look terrible, Comazon," he said, looking the general up and down. "What the hell happened to you?"

"Excuse me, Excellency. I am not feeling very well today."

"Well, that's obvious. Where were you last night? I needed you to take the former empress back to the motherland."

Comazon frowned. "*Domine*, I am afraid I do not know what you mean."

"I sent her back to her mother's," he said with his mouth full.

Comazon's mouth gaped open. "You did… what?"

"It was a big mistake to bring her here. I should have never listened to Grandma. And I had to send her in a litter with two of the lower ranked guards, as if it wasn't enough humiliation for her… I'm sure her father is furious. But I truly don't give a dormouse's ass." Staring at Comazon, he continued, "but don't just stand there like an idiot. Say something! Where were you last night and what were you doing?"

"I… I went to the tavern, Excellency."

"I see. And you got yourself wasted. Too bad, Comazon. I can't let the praetorian prefect behave like a damn smith. You have to be here for me at all times. Do you understand?"

Comazon liked the sound of those words. *To be there for him at all times*. He smiled. His headache had disappeared and now he felt like fresh out of the bath. "Yes, *domine*."

Maesa entered the *cubiculum* unannounced, with a distraught face that foreshadowed a nasty conversation.

"*Imperator*, I need to speak to you right now."

"Comazon, leave us alone."

The prefect hurried out of the room, looking at Maesa with eyes gleaming with joy and a wide smile on his face—his teeth unusually white for a Roman soldier. His stubble had grown since the night before, but it still did not hide the cute dimple in his cheek.

"Well, he sure looks happy." Maesa guessed what was going through Comazon's mind. "But I'm not."

Antoninus flipped his hand upward and rolled his eyes. He invited his grandmother to join him on the divan, offering her a bunch of grapes, which she refused.

"I already know of your actions last night. Julius Paulus demanded to see me early this morning. As you can imagine he was—"

"Yeah, I know. Don't bore me with the details. What does he want, money?"

"He wants you to restore his daughter's status as *Augusta* immediately."

"That's not going to happen."

Maesa stood up abruptly and paced the bedroom. "You can't do this," she said stopping in front of her grandson, wagging her index finger. "You just can't do this! You had agreed, you had understood the benefits of marriage." She resumed her nervous pace and turned around to Antoninus. "You know the reputation you have earned, right, my Son? That you are a whore! That the emperor is nothing but a sex toy!"

Antoninus was taken a bit by surprise by his grandmother's harsh words, but he pulled himself together quickly. "Rome doesn't have to understand me nor approve of me, Grandma. I am her Lord, and she has only to obey my commands."

"You've really taken to heart everything I've been telling you but it's not as easy as you think. There are traditions here. There are values like honor, virtue, family… Rome cannot suffer her emperor to fornicate with her youth inside the temple."

"So that is the problem."

"Yes, that is the problem. That, and your clothes, your parties, your debauchery, your effeminacy, the way you talk and walk, the things you say!" She paused for a minute. "I didn't make you emperor for this, my dear child, but to be a man!"

"What if I don't want to be a man?" He stood up. "Have you thought about that? Maybe I want to be a woman," he said with glacial calmness, facing her raging gaze. "Yes! Woman! Queen! Empress!—"

Maesa's hand fell down hard on his cheek, which reddened quickly. He gaped and touched his face in disbelief. He turned away, looking for the bed. He wanted to cry, but his fury was greater than his pain. He turned around to face her, spitting as he spoke.

"Alright, alright! I'll marry again! Not that dull woman, though, but a vestal."

Maesa's eyes widened in disbelief. "You can't do that…" she hissed. "Those women are sacred, they are like goddesses, holy to Rome and her people. The Senate will not allow it!"

"You should know by now that I don't abide by what the Senate says, Grandma. You saw them in the dedication. Meek and docile sheep following me around. Did they try to stop me from performing the sacred sexual religious acts in the temple?"

"You are insane… out of your mind! There's no way you're going to get away with that, Antoninus. No way at all!"

"You'll see," he said with a smile. "I have a great idea of how to get it done."

Maesa left the room indignantly. Antoninus stayed inside, his mind occupied not with his grandmother's harsh words, but with his own: *to be a woman…* did he really say that? Or, more importantly, did he really mean it? The thought of it seemed so liberating. It all began to make sense in his mind. The next step to truly be a woman was to find his man.

Δ

Julius Paulus received in the peristyle garden of his *domus* fellow senator Quintus Aquilius Sabinus, an aged nobleman, and member of one of the most prominent families of Rome. Aquilius walked slowly, admiring the peculiar features of the residence, unrivaled even among the elite. Its garden had a pool cornered by four cupids, merrily serving as fountains by peeing into it. Between the columns were numerous shrubs of medicinal and ornamental plants. Statues of *lares* in niches, and frescos of ancestors adorned the walls. As they crossed the *portico*, Aquilius saw fit to start the conversation with topics such as trivial legislative matters, and the weather.

"I don't mean to interrupt you," Paulus said after a few minutes of small talk, inviting his peer to sit on one of the benches. "But I'm sure you've come to visit on a more important matter than senatorial disputes."

"Indeed." Aquilius's face darkened at the question.

"So, what is it?"

"First I would like to express my regret and sympathy regarding—"

"I know. You don't have to say it. It must be on everyone's lips in the city. The disgrace the emperor brought upon my family is more than what decent people can bear." He paused. "However, we have no need of your compassion. My daughter is not dead."

"But it's almost as if she was. It may now be hard to find a suitable husband for her, after all that has happened."

"That won't be difficult, believe me. That little prick did not touch her. Her virtue is intact. But that shouldn't surprise me from a deviant whose birth name is Varius. Do you know why he was given that name? Because not even his mother knows who the father is, of the *various* men she slept with."

Aquilius did not laugh. He was taken aback by the candid words of his interlocutor, especially coming from the mouth of a man who just a few days ago had been one of the few supporters of the emperor in the Senate.

Paulus looked at him straight in the eyes. "Listen, Aquilius. I don't care if you go around saying what I now think of the emperor. He's nothing but a beast: a depraved, pathetic weakling, not even a man. In fact, never a man!"

"You should be careful, Paulus. Sometimes it's better to keep your mouth shut and not to air your thoughts. He who cannot be a man can very well serve himself of men to crush his enemies."

"Are you talking about Comazon?"

"Not only him, but the former legionaries, the new Praetorians. They are unconditional addicts of the emperor. You have seen what they do with senators who oppose His Majesty's will."

Paulus reflected for a moment. "They are addicts to Maesa's money; there is no better way to open the hearts of men. But listen, Aquilius: a man that can be bought, can also be bought by his enemy."

"Unfortunately, money is not the only problem here. We have the issue of the deep... ehm... sexual alliance between the emperor and his young elite troops. You saw that happening in the temple."

"Do you think Comazon approves of that?"

"I doubt there's anything he can do about it. The supreme commander of the armed troops is the emperor himself."

A moment of silence ensued.

"There's one more thing you probably don't know, Paulus. Next week he will marry his god to Vesta."

Paulus stood up and walked in circles, making furious gestures with his hands, snorting like a spurred bull. Turning around, he hissed, "How do you know?"

"My daughter told me."

Julia Aquilia Severa was the *vestalis maxima* of the Temple of Vesta, patron goddess of Rome since the foundation of the city.

"Everything has a limit," Paulus said. "He can insult Jupiter and Victoria, but his attack on the House of Vesta cannot be tolerated."

"I understand your rage," Aquilius said, getting up and trying to calm his friend. "But we must be reasonable and think of what can be done. My daughter is every bit as horrified as we are… She has prayed day and night, lighting the sacred fire with more wood than usual, but it seems that even the goddess is helpless before the determination of this evil man. He has ordered the fire to be taken to the temple of his god, where he says it will reside from now on."

"This is an outright desecration! What do the people of Rome think? And more importantly, what does Maesa think?" Paulus said with wide eyes.

"Maesa. It is interesting you mention her. We can't deny that without her leading the empire *de facto*, Rome would have collapsed by now. But she has only one flaw: she is a woman and can only do so much. Jupiter knows that if she were a man, she would surely be a new Augustus."

"I agree. She's our only hope amid the chaos, though her power is not as strong as I once thought. She was unable to make Antoninus recant his decision to abandon my daughter." He paused. "Surely, she cannot approve of this new marriage…"

"I'm sure she doesn't."

"What do the other senators think?"

"They're in shock, as you can imagine. There seems to be nothing sacred or untouchable to this boy. And about the people, there is gossip, yes, but as long as the emperor's largesse keeps coming, they don't really care. They're nothing but a mass of atheist, ignorant donkeys. Besides, the emperor has ordered games to start right after the ceremony. That's why he's not worried about what people think."

Paulus struck a porcelain vase, causing it to shatter on the mosaic floor. He grabbed Aquilius by the shoulders. "There must be some way to stop him. By Jupiter, there must be a way!"

"Maybe in time, dear friend. For now, we have nothing to do but play his game."

"I'll be watching." Paulus let go of his peer, "I'll be watching and at the first mistake… by Castor and Pollux, I'll make that provincial nobody pay. He'll be sorry he ever left that dusty Syrian village."

Aquilius smiled faintly. He excused himself to leave. Paulus called a slave and ordered him to escort his guest to the door. He sat on a *solium* alone in the garden and sank his face on his hands. He wept, not only for his family, but for Rome and her dwindling future. His breathing was agitated and his face, flushed with uncontainable fury. As he fixed his piercing eyes on an indeterminate point, an idea came to his mind.

Δ

The Temple of Elagabal had been carefully decorated for the great occasion. The sacred fire of Vesta had been carried in procession during the night and stood to the right of the *baetyl*, trembling and quivering like the terrified heart of an abducted maiden. In front of the altar stood the emperor, attired in a purple silk tunic specially made for the occasion, and behind him, the six vestal virgins wearing their sober *stolas*, their heads covered by the *suffibulum* and their hair combed in the traditional manner of seven braids entwined with strips of colored cloth. Among the women was the *vestalis maxima*, Julia Aquilia Severa, a woman already far from the dawn of youth, whose dour face, whittled by strong lines of age, certainly lived up to her cognomen. She had been selected to join the cult when she was six years old and had been in the temple for over twenty-five years, and in all this time had never witnessed an event even remotely similar. Behind them, on either side of the *cella* stood the emperor's family, plus senators, patricians and, above all, the Praetorian Guard, without which this ceremony would have never taken place.

An old man, acting as *auspex*, led a meek white lamb to the altar for sacrifice. With a knife, he slashed the throat of the animal, which collapsed on the floor quietly after uttering a weak bleat. After pouring its blood on the altar, he removed its entrails with his bony hands and laid them on the marble. Carefully, he scrutinized them amid a tomb-like silence. After a while, he turned his attention to the emperor and shared the news: the auspices were favorable for the union, since the viscera of the animal contained nothing abnormal. Antoninus, who had been a bit tense during the procedure, sighed in relief.

After kneeling for the opening prayers and rising again, Antoninus turned his back and asked the *vestalis maxima* to accompany him in front of the altar. She looked around, confused. She was the ultimate authority in matters of morality, so it was only natural that the emperor asked her to join him at the front. As Severa stood next to the emperor, he held her hand at shoulder level and asked her to recite the matrimonial vows on behalf of Vesta, as he would do on behalf of Elagabal. At a signal from his other hand, two slaves approached. After bowing, they knelt on one knee and, with their eyes directed to the floor, held papyri in front of them. Antoninus looked to the side and nudged Severa slightly with his elbow to prompt her to read.

"I, Severa, high priestess of Vesta and woman of virtue, declare: *Ubi tu Gaius, ego Gaia.*"

"I, Antoninus, high priest of Elagabal and man of virtue, declare: *Ubi tu Gaia, ego Gaius.*"

He turned to her, and, to the shock of everyone present, especially Severa herself, pressed his lips to hers. Without releasing her hand, he made her turn with him to face the audience.

"Just as our supreme deities, the almighty Elagabal and the most honorable Vesta have become forever one, as husband and wife, so have we, Antoninus and Severa, joined our lives in the sacred vow of matrimony."

A series of gasps resounded in the temple. Two of the vestals fainted. Paulus made fists and snorted, while Aquilius looked around in bewilderment. He had not expected the emperor to marry again. Not in the former Temple of Jupiter. Not a vestal. Not his daughter.

"This is unheard of!" Aquilius yelled. "Not only unheard of, illegal! You can't do this; you can't take my daughter! She has sworn to remain in the sacred service of Vesta. You are desecrating Rome and our ancestors! You, you, filth—"

Antoninus nodded and before Aquilius could finish the sentence, Comazon advanced, muzzling the senator with one hand and tying one of his hands behind his back with the other. Severa put her hands to her head and shrieked. Aquilius and Paulus were dragged out of the temple by several guards and the rest of the Praetorians drew their swords menacingly to maintain order. Some vestals fell at the emperor's feet and begged him not to take their sister. He ordered the rest of the soldiers to carry them back to the House of Vesta, cold and deprived of the sacred fire as it was. Amid the mayhem, Antoninus led his new wife out of the temple, toward the carriage that would take them to the Palatine Hill.

Δ

In Antoninus's chamber, Severa stood rigid, like a cornered cat; and just like a cat, she was ready to claw and bite if the emperor tried to remove her *stola*, lay a hand on her, or steal another kiss. Antoninus tried to approach her with a firm stride, like a tamer.

"Come on, woman, I'm not going to hurt you. I just want to… talk to you."

She crossed her hands over her chest and looked at him with sharp murderous eyes.

"Get out of there," he said, taking her by the hand when he was sure she wouldn't scratch, and led her to the bed. "Just sit here, and we'll have a peaceful conversation."

She kept her hands together, never taking her eyes off the floor. She didn't utter a word.

"You may be wondering why I married you and brought you here."

She gazed at him frowning and nodded.

"So we can make holy babies!" he exclaimed, laughing hysterically.

She shrieked and covered her ears.

"Why not? Just as Elagabal and Vesta are now husband and wife, so are we, for the good and unity of the empire." He stood up. "This marriage was only the first step. One day, all the Roman cults will be absorbed by a single monotheistic cult: that of Elagabal."

"Vesta did not wish to marry your god any more than I wished to marry you," Severa cried. She ran to the door and pulled hard on it several times but couldn't open it.

"Don't be silly! Why don't you be a good girl and talk to me?"

"And what do you want to talk about? I won't talk to you unless you release my father."

"You father, your father…" Antoninus said, walking around her. "You father needs to learn to keep his mouth shut." He drew near her face, piercing her with his eyes. "Very soon you and he will learn that there's only one way to serve Rome, and that is to serve me."

"I don't understand what the purpose of all this is," she said with tears in her eyes. "His Majesty had already married Julia Paula—"

"It was my grandmother who wanted me to marry. She wouldn't stop pestering about it. Julia Paula was a mistake, so I thought I'd marry you, a woman who obviously wouldn't be interested in any kind of bed transaction with me. Do you get it? I'm brilliant, am I not?"

Severa looked at him in horror, her breathing quickening.

"Don't worry," Antoninus continued, "I'll give you time to adjust to your new life as a married woman… you know, living here in the palace and pretending to be my wife. I can always blame you for the lack of children."

"But my Lord, I will be released from my religious duties in just a few more years, then you can marry me without disturbing the traditions of Rome," she said, desperate for any solution that would help her return to the temple immediately.

"There's one more thing, perhaps even more important."

"What is it?"

"Gold is always needed in the treasury to keep people happy. Therefore, the House of Vesta must pay for your dowry."

"What? A dowry? How can you expect the House of Vesta to pay for a dowry, especially for a marriage without consent."

"You consented to the marriage; you recited the vows."

"I did not suspect the trap you had set for me."

"Trap or not, you said the sacred words. Then it is done; we are husband and wife. You must arrange for the dowry to be paid at once."

Severa considered for a few moments. "I'll do it… only if you release my father."

"Is a vestal trying to impose conditions on the emperor?"

"If you don't release my father, I'll never do it. You can throw me to the lions and have them tear off my flesh, but I won't do it!"

Antoninus sighed. "Alright, have it your way. I'll order Comazon to release him tomorrow."

"Tonight!" Severa shrieked. "He can't spend a night in that stinking jail. And you must free Paulus too!" she exclaimed, throwing herself on him, beating his chest. He tied her arms and tried to calm her down.

"Alright, alright," he said, dragging her to the door. "Guards!" he shouted as he opened it with a key. "Come inside and take this lunatic to her quarters! She's indisposed to fulfill her marital duties tonight."

The guards stepped inside and dragged her out of the room.

Δ

A little later that evening, Comazon visited the cell occupied by Paulus. Given the status of the senator and the fact that he had been Antoninus's father-in-law for a day, he was given one of the "preferential" accommodations. Still, it stank in there.

"You may leave, Senator. Aquilius has been released as well."

Paulus rose from the minuscule bed, dusted off his toga in a dignified manner and gazed at Comazon. "Nice to meet you, Prefect. I don't think we had been introduced before," he said, holding out his hand.

Comazon reciprocated the gesture. "It's a shame it had to be under these circumstances."

"A shame indeed," Paulus said, straightening his clothes. "If possible, I would like to have a conversation with you one of these days, General."

Comazon thought about it for a moment. "Where? In a tavern?"

Paulus cringed at the thought of those nasty joints. "No, I would like to invite you to my *domus*." Then, after a pause he added, "To dinner, maybe?"

"Sure, Senator. It will be an honor for me—"

"…and your wife?"

"I do not have a wife, *domine*."

"I see. Well, it'll be just you then, Prefect," he said as he left the cell.

Comazon wasn't very sure of the man's intentions. He remained a few minutes inside the cell before leaving and locking it back up. The emperor would not be amused to learn that the praetorian prefect accepted invitations behind his back… Well… maybe he didn't have to know. A tinkling sensation crept through his stomach. For some reason, he was interested in what this man had to say. Mostly because he wasn't happy with the actions he had to take. Orders are orders, and peace has to be kept, but the senators had a point. That marriage had been forced. But why?

Δ

The following night, Comazon had been standing outside the palace after visiting with his men, when the sound of footsteps made him turn around.

"Majesty, are you leaving the Palace… unaccompanied?"

"Does the emperor require your permission to visit his own city?"

"Would you at least allow me to join you?"

"No. There are a few things I'd like to do on my own. I feel like a prisoner followed by Praetorians wherever I go."

"But I need to talk to you."

"Right now? About what? Please hurry, Comazon. It's getting late and I need to get to my destination."

"I want to talk about us."

Antoninus froze. He saw the expression on the general's face, like a dog pleading for attention. Comazon had been waiting for the right time to finally express his true feelings to the emperor. He wanted him to know that he had more than just passion for him. However, until now there had been no "right time" and he suspected there never would be.

"There's nothing to talk about. I'm married now. Have you forgotten?"

"No, but that marriage is about everything except love." He pulled the emperor closer. "You can't love that woman. If you did not love Julia Paula, who at least was young and beautiful, how can you love this lady who seemed destined to be an old maid?"

"You're right. It's not about love. I married a woman to appease my grandmother." He broke away from Comazon's arms. "I can't love anyone; my heart is not ready. I just want to live, Comazon, to experience life, and do all the things I want to do before I die."

"We can do it together."

"How? Tell me how, please. You're the praetorian prefect. I'm the emperor of Rome. How would it look if we paraded hand in hand in the street? Is that what you want?"

"No, of course not. But I thought that we… Well, no one has to know."

"So that's what you want: a romance in the shadows. Surreptitious encounters in a dark alley, while we lie to the world? No, Comazon. That doesn't appeal to me. I do everything in the open. Even my sacred sex performances are public. I'm not interested in living a double life."

"But…"

"No buts. Now, do me a favor, will you? Go find me a litter to take me to town."

Comazon remained silent for a minute. "I could conceal two guards in the seats. Nobody will notice them."

"Praetorians traveling inside my litter? That's beyond ridiculous. I said, no, Comazon. I'm going on my own, I just need carriers."

Comazon procured one of the luxurious palace litters and four carriers—whom he armed without the emperor's knowledge.

"Are you sure this is where you want us to take you, Excellency?" one of the carriers asked, upon hearing Antoninus's instructions. "This part of the city is not safe at all, especially—"

"Yes, this is where I'm going. Don't you fear and do as you're told. I have given notice of my visit, and trustworthy people await me."

After some time, they reached a conspicuous part of the city, famous for its "nightlife." The carriers stopped in front of an old guesthouse, painted in once bright colors.

Antoninus ordered them to wait outside as long as necessary. They helped the emperor down from the litter and he entered the building quite naturally, although it was his first time in that place. The walls inside were painted with obscene acts, not unlike those commonly found in the houses of the long-gone Pompeii. Two young ladies in bright make-up greeted him.

"I'm looking for Plautina. Tell her the emperor is here."

The two girls rushed inside. A few minutes later an obese, gaudily dressed woman appeared.

"Highness," she said, bowing. "So, you did come to visit us tonight."

"I always keep my word, Plautina. Can you show me my room?"

The woman waved her hand to lead the way through an entrance covered with strings of colored beads. They arrived at the room—the finest in the property—that Plautina had prepared in advance for the momentous visit. A large bronze-framed couch, intricately gilded and decorated with exotic wood and mother-of-pearl inlays, and ornately carved and turned legs, occupied most of the space. Its plush mattress, stuffed with feathers—and aromatic herbs to ward off bugs— invited one to jump on it on sight. Equally cozy were the luxurious red wine silk beddings and pillows, and the golden comforter, furnished exclusively for the emperor. Frescoes depicting explicit erotic scenes covered the walls, and the floor was of quaint marble mosaics partially covered by a carpet with a stitched image of a tiger on the attack. Two candles in penis-shaped holders provided illumination to an otherwise dark, windowless room.

Plautina's brothel was the best in Rome, not only for its lavish amenities, but for the privacy it offered its patrons, who were usually wealthy and reputable functionaries; her ladies knew that the punishment for indiscretion was expulsion, which meant homelessness or worse. However, Plautina knew that her house wasn't suitable for an emperor… especially one with such exquisite taste. Therefore, she busied herself rearranging the decor of at least that particular room, thinking he would appreciate a slight touch of the east.

"Not bad, not bad at all…" Antoninus said, throwing himself on the bed. "This is something like what I would have conceived myself."

"Thank you, Majesty, your words are deeply appreciated," she said amid a sigh of relief.

"Now, don't be shy and get yourself over here," he said, tapping the bed.

The mattress yielded over the excessive weight of the woman, who carefully pushed herself closer to the emperor. She was a little disconcerted. Whenever emperors procured women for their entertainment, they always did so in the palace. At least that's what the mighty Caracalla had done— she had sent him many girls there. So, she wasn't sure why Antoninus had asked to meet there… besides… she didn't recruit boys in her house, and she knew, like all of Rome, the emperor's preferences… so… what could be the reason for him to be there at that moment?

"Now, Plautina, I just have one question." The emperor paused for a moment. "How do you make a man fall in love with you?"

After a few seconds of confusion, the woman burst out laughing uproariously. She laughed with such impertinence that Antoninus became furious.

"What are you laughing at, bitch? I asked you a very simple question."

"With all due respect, Lord, I suppose you already know that."

"No, I don't. I may be very experienced in matters of sex, but… mere sex seems to be far removed from true love and devotion."

"True love, Excellency, doesn't exist. At least, not forever. You can see signs of it in a person, but that doesn't mean their feelings won't change later on."

"What signs?"

"They're subtle. A look. A smile. A caress. Some things can't be faked."

"If it's that simple, my first wife should have known it already."

"She's a virgin and surely her parents hadn't allowed any men to court her, so there's no way she could have known."

"I know that, but isn't there some kind of feminine instinct to attract a man, something that comes naturally without having to seek it out?"

"Not really, Highness. Everything a woman needs to know about how to please a man, that is, her man, she will learn from him and no one else." She lay on her side to look at him. "You see, every man is different, every man has his own needs, and what a man may like, another may not care for."

"So, it's just a matter of letting go and doing the things that give him the most pleasure?"

"Exactly, Excellency."

"But there must be some trick, some peculiarity that all men fall for."

"Food. They say the way to a man's heart is his stomach. But I bet you can't cook," she said, laughing.

"You're right about that."

"Well, there's another one, and that is his penis. If only women were less prudish, they would discover a world of pleasure for their husbands and themselves. And I would be out of business!" she shrieked.

Antoninus laughed. "You're funny. So you're telling me I should just keep sleeping around until I catch the right fish?"

"I'd say yes. Give everyone you like a chance, but one-on-one. You won't find him at an orgy. And look for the signs of true love. I'm sure you'll recognize them."

The signs of true love. He thought of Comazon, and what he had just confessed to him. He felt foolish for trying to find out how a man falls in love. It was obvious, and right in front of him. And what had he, Antoninus, done to provoke it? Nothing. There was only one problem. Plautina had addressed it too when she said: "Give everyone *you like* a chance." Comazon was just not his type. He was too old and hairy; he wanted someone younger, not someone to be his dad. Sure, he was nice and sweet, but he just couldn't see himself with him in a real relationship. Besides, everything he had told him was true: his very office prevented Comazon from being close to him as a life partner. They would become the laughingstock of Rome.

"I will," Antoninus said, coming back from his thoughts, and giving the fat woman a big kiss on the cheek. "By the way, how much do your girls make in a night?"

"On a good night, they can make about twenty sesterces each."

"I'm sure I can double that. You want to bet?"

A high-pitched laugh erupted from the woman's mouth. "You got it!"

The emperor got up and asked her to take him to the place where the girls usually waited for their clients. Some waited inside the brothel, even in one of the rooms, but the younger ones, who didn't yet have a clientele of their own, usually waited in the *atrium*.

"I'll stand here, and you'll see what happens."

The emperor stood next to the confused-looking girls, when the first men began to arrive. "Hey, which one of you wants to lie down with the emperor tonight?" Antoninus yelled.

"I do!" one of them hollered.

Antoninus led him to his room. Without thinking, he went down on his knees, untied the man's *subligaculum,* and sucked his cock and balls with a mastery the stranger had never experienced. The man threw his head back and moaned.

Plautina watched from the door, which had been left ajar. "He surely wastes no time," she whispered to one of her girls.

The word quickly got around that the emperor was servicing Rome's men for a fee. As more patrons arrived, a glut of sesterces and even *aurei* coins produced a sharp ching as they poured like rain inside the copper pot placed at the entrance to Antoninus's room.

The emperor lay on his back, taking a man up his ass while sucking another. Antoninus's sloppy hole was becoming increasingly lubricated with the white slime deposited inside by the young and old studs of Rome. He kissed none of them; this was exclusively a "fucking" business. Dozens of men penetrated the lusty young man that night: on his back, on all fours, riding their cocks while as they carried him in their arms, with entry facilitated by the distension of the anus and the slick lubrication.

In the early hours of the morning, Antoninus stumbled out of the room, carrying with difficulty the overflowing copper pot before the astonished faces of the ladies, especially Plautina.

"See, ladies? This is how it's done. Now, keep this money and be sure to make more next time."

The strumpets burst in cries of joy as the boy danced his way out of the brothel, looking for his ride back to the palace. Some of the girls threw coins in the air. Nobody could say that the emperor was not a man of his people, in every possible way.

Δ

Two nights later, it was time for Comazon to visit Senator Julius Paulus. Unsure of what to wear, he wore his Praetorian Guard uniform with full regalia, except for the feathered helmet. He was going to dinner, not to war. Although at that moment, the two things did not seem very different.

A slave ushered him into the *atrium*, where Paulus greeted him and introduced him to his wife and, especially, to his daughter Julia. Comazon kissed the girl's hand. She looked beautiful—his sexual preferences did not make him blind to feminine beauty—even more so than when she had been in his arms on the night of her wedding. He had no idea how much Julia had longed to be in them ever since that moment.

"Please lie down with us," Paulus said, leading Comazon to a divan in the *triclinium*.

Slaves brought a plethora of Rome's finest delicacies: oysters from the Adriatic sea, seasoned with *silphium* and rue; exotic dried fruits from Asia; cheeses from the mountainous regions of Gaul and Helvetia; and to top it all off, the finest wine from Tuscany. Paulus had an amphora preserved for more than three decades opened for the occasion.

"I am overwhelmed by your hospitality, *domine*," Comazon said, after gulping down one of the seasoned oysters.

"We are honored that you have accepted our invitation," Paulus replied. "We want to show you how much we appreciate your service in defense of the fatherland."

Comazon nodded with a smile, and the small talk turned into a conversation about life in Rome those days, war stories, senatorial reforms, and, as the goblets of wine went on, even personal and family matters. In his drunkenness, Comazon confirmed that Paula was indeed a very beautiful lady. That dark hair, curling at the sides, was a perfect frame for her ivory white skin and her delicate features. He regretted for a moment that he was not the type of man who enjoyed intimacy with a woman. He had had intercourse with females in his youth but had quickly lost interest as soon as he gave in to his true desires and felt the sweet warmth of a male's tight inside. And there was no return from that.

"My dear officer," Paulus said after a few hours, "I think it's time to let the women retire to their quarters while we discuss serious business in my office."

Comazon agreed. He rose and followed the senator, not without his goblet. They entered the *tablinum*, whose walls were lined with shelves of ancient papyri. A cluttered desk and a pair of leather chairs were the other few pieces of furniture. Paulus sat on his side of the desk and asked Comazon to take a seat.

"You're probably wondering the real reason I asked you to visit my house."

Comazon nodded and took another sip of wine.

"I know all about your service under the great Caracalla, and your work commanding the *Legio III Gallica* in the east. I have to say that I truly admire your work and leadership; not many men have achieved the fantastic pacification results you and your legion accomplished in the harsh lands of Syria."

Comazon gazed at him unperturbed. "Is that all you wanted to tell me?"

Paulus stopped him with his hand. "However, I am also aware of…" He paused to make sure he chose his next words carefully. "…the manner in which our current emperor was proclaimed."

"What do you mean, *domine*?" Comazon said with suspicion in his voice.

"I do know that there were some… irregularities in the way the proclamation was made. You and your legion were loyal to Macrinus and suddenly… you changed your allegiance to the new Antoninus."

"Macrinus was a usurper and a traitor," Comazon said dryly. "Antoninus is the legitimate heir to the throne, being the son of Caracalla."

"And what proof do we have of that? Maesa's word?" Paulus smiled and got up. "All we have is the word of an old woman? A woman who had much to gain from the proclamation?"

"The resemblance is extraordinary," Comazon said. "Looking into the eyes of the emperor is like looking into the eyes of the mighty Caracalla."

"They are related, there's no doubt about that," Paulus said, as he paced the room. "And that kind of eyes is common in Syria. But I'm still not sure about the emperor's paternity… besides, there is the fact—"

"What fact?"

Paulus stood behind Comazon's chair and massaged his shoulders. The general immediately felt relaxed by the touch of the strong hands. Paulus was still a very good-looking man for his age. Undoubtedly, his daughter got her beauty from her father.

"The fact that you and your men received gold from Maesa in exchange for the proclamation."

Comazon rose violently and glared at the senator. "Who told you that?" he snarled.

Paulus turned away and resumed his pacing.

"That kind of secret never stays hidden for long. Your soldiers bragged about it for weeks as soon as they made it to Rome," he said, returning his gaze to the general.

"Why did you not do anything about it then?"

"It was too late. Antoninus had won the battle against Macrinus's forces; there was nothing to do."

"So, if there was not anything to do back then, why is there something to do now?"

"Now things are different, General. The emperor—your emperor—is losing support as days go by. He has insulted the Senate, harassed its members and, as you well know, even had one of them thrown to the dungeons!" Paulus's eyes bulged out of their sockets. "He disgraced my daughter and the Temple of Vesta, installed a foreign god in the Temple of Jupiter, ordered his ridiculous painting to be hung over the image of Victoria in the Senate…" He made an oratorial pause. "There's nothing of Rome and her glorious past that he will not sully. He will destroy this city and our civilization if he's not stopped!"

"And what do you want me to do?"

"At the moment, the Praetorians are all he has. The Praetorians and the people. I am not worried about the latter;

as soon as the games and the largesse are over, they too will see his vices and turn against him. They admire his bottomless vanity and eccentric behavior, however crass and inappropriate, but admiration also has a limit. It's the Praetorians who matter." He put his hands on Comazon's arms. "You're a man of reason, General Comazon... we all know that if Antoninus loses the support of the Guard, well, if you help make that happen, we will be free to remove him from office and banish him back to Syria where he belongs!"

"What makes you think I will do that?"

"I'm aware of your love for your country... it is to that patriotism that I appeal."

"Do not try to entangle me with your words, Senator. Antoninus's rise was legal. Macrinus was a murderer and a usurper. Sure, some things have changed in Rome, but no emperor is without eccentricities... take Tiberius, Caligula, Nero, even Trajan and Hadrian, for Jupiter's sake. Besides, Rome has been doing fine lately. There are no serious crises to speak of. What you senators have a is a personal grudge against the emperor, a grudge I want nothing to do with!"

Paulus paced around a little more. "Very well. I regret to see that my arguments were unable to convince you."

Comazon turned to leave.

"Wait."

Comazon stopped.

"Answer with the truth, General. Regardless of the legal status of the boy... you wouldn't have done what you did to put him on the throne if money hadn't been involved, would you?"

Comazon turned to the old man, glaring at him with iron eyes.

"I'll ask you plainly," the old man continued. "How much do you want this time to turn things around, and… leave the legal matters to us?"

Comazon clenched his hand into a fist. He walked up to Paulus and punched him in the face. "There is my answer," he roared and stormed out.

Paulus stood there in silence, leaning on the desk with one hand and touching his bloody mouth with the other. So, it wouldn't be that easy. After all, Comazon wouldn't be bought off just like that a second time. Fine. That would have been the easy path. Fortunately, he had another plan in mind. A plan that would provide him with a trap to force him into his camp. But he would have to be patient and wait for the right moment to set the bait.

CHAPTER 5

A DAY AT THE RACES

The celebration of the marriage of Antoninus and Severa lasted several days. Among the events, a crowd favorite was the chariot racing at the *Circus Maximus*. On the opening day, the emperor, his wife, and their entourage arrived at the circus amid a storm of cheers, which erupted as soon as their figures were visible to the people. Millions of saffron crocus flowers were thrown into the air from the upper tiers, filling it with their grassy scent as they fell. An ominous silence reigned in the ranks of the senate, consciously ignored by the Boy Maximus, who allowed himself to get lost in the spellbinding adoration of the crowd. He waved his hand gracefully as his wife walked stiffly beside him. She still wore the same somber *stola* she had worn in her temple days and did not yet seem at ease with her life as the first lady of Rome.

The emperor took his seat in the *pulvinar*, his wife on the right and his mother on the left. Maesa sat next to Soaemias on the far left. Comazon—always on the lookout for possible aggressors or even gestures of disapproval—and two more Praetorians sat behind the imperial family. The remaining five vestals were also in attendance. They had refused to appoint a replacement for their superior, although they knew that the emperor would soon force them to do so. They still had hopes that Severa would return to the temple; every day they visited the sacred fire in the Temple of Elagabal to pray to that end, under the excuse of praying for the imperial family.

The initial procession began. The *editor* of the games and his companions paraded figurines of the different gods; priests chanted arcane hymns and waved censers.

Soaemias looked behind her, smiled to Comazon, and then drew near her son. "You must be very happy to have Comazon to protect you, right? Especially on these occasions."

"I certainly am, Mother," Antoninus said, without taking his attention from the procession.

There was one more person paying attention to Comazon. Next to her father, in the senatorial stands, sat Julia Paula, who, without being indiscreet, turned her gaze to the handsome prefect whenever she had the chance. She sighed as the wind ruffled the feathers of his helmet. The cruel Cupid had shot a second arrow aimed at her heart during the general's visit to her home, and now she could hardly eat, drink, or sleep, without thinking about him.

Antoninus looked toward the *carceres*, where the twelve chariots belonging to four teams, white, blue, red, and green were ready to start. In addition to wearing ribbons in their team colors, the tall and muscular horses were decorated with gold and silver amulets on their breastplates, which gleamed in the sunlight. The neck and tail hair was braided with semiprecious stones, and the—less elegant but more important—reins were tightly wrapped around the charioteers' chests to allow for better control. The charioteers also wore outfits with their team color, as well as breastplates and sturdy steel helmets.

Trumpets announced the end of the procession, and the *editor* looked up to the emperor, waiting for a signal. Antoninus nodded, and the man dropped a handkerchief to mark the start of the race. A stunning silence inundated the arena. The slaves who leveled the sand ran out of the field and joined the assistants and doctors who were ready to jump in if necessary. The judges gave a signal and the doors of the *carceres* burst open. The chariots darted like arrows whistling in the wind under the deafening cheers of three hundred thousand souls. A chariot of the blues took the first position.

"Who's that driver?" Soaemias asked.

"No idea, Mother. I wish we would have consulted their names before the race started."

A chariot of the whites pulled in front of the blue and gained a slight advantage. Another white car threatened to take over; the blue driver spurred his horses to prevent it. The space between the two chariots narrowed. A crash was imminent. Suddenly, a loud crunching of wheels and a huge gasp emerged from the audience. The blue charioteer did not have time to cut the reins and was dragged about one hundred feet by his out-of-control horses. Soaemias covered her eyes. Severa kept watching the scene with no emotion whatsoever. Several doctors and assistants rushed onto the field to pull the unfortunate driver out, before the other chariots would complete the turn and trample him to death.

"Mother, don't be silly. This is what we came to see."

Julia watched over a delighted Comazon, who snacked on raw oysters and sipped mulled wine, while commenting on the action with his peers. On the *spina*, the first of the seven dolphins indicating the number of leaps was flipped down. The three red cars hurriedly chased the white chariot that had escaped. Their drivers whipped their horses' backs with fury and shouted incomprehensible words: many of the charioteers were of foreign origin. Soon the white driver got trapped on the inside of the track and was forced to slow down to avoid a collision with the *spina*. A driver of the greens took advantage and sped his chariot from the outside. One of the reds realized the maneuver and took off in pursuit. He soon managed to run alongside. The eight horses, four green and four red, ran as if in rehearsed synchrony. Then the red chariot began to ram the green one and forced him close to the walls near the brick and marble steps. The crowds went wild with excitement. Both cars were quick to go around the remains of the blue chariot that had crashed on that spot. The red took advantage of the distraction and began to drill the right wheel of the green car with the axis of his left wheel. The second dolphin was flipped down. The red chariot continued to drill the green chariot's wheel until it shattered into pieces and the green chariot fell apart, tipping to one side, dragged by the gone-wild horses. The charioteer was quick to cut the reins and save himself from certain death. His body came to a halt amid a cloud of dust, right in front of the emperor's balcony.

Antoninus put a hand on his chest and rushed down the stairs, to the gasps of the audience. Comazon sprang out of his seat, grabbed his sword, and tried to follow, but Maesa indicated him to stop and wait. On the track, the charioteer got up, dusting off his torn green tunic with his face burning with anger and indignation. He tightened his belt after reaching for his helmet, and seemed less worried about the scratches on his knees and elbows than about his hurt pride.

Feeling the urge to look up to the stands, he found the emperor staring at him like a hawk at its prey, with the sun at his back. He shielded his eyes and positioned himself so that the emperor's head obscured the sun, and saw his face clearly.

"What is your name?"

The charioteer eagerly fixed his sleeveless tunic, trying to remove the lingering dust as quickly as possible. "Hierocles, Excellency," he replied, turning the gaze of his emerald eyes back to the emperor. His voice was firm and masculine, and had a pleasant, youthful, bell-like timbre.

Antoninus gazed admiringly at the man beneath him. He relished in the charioteer's toned arms and tanned skin from many hours under the sun. His curly golden hair and scruffy beard belonged in a Greek god statue. Some chest hair protruded from the torn collar of his tunic. However, the smile on Hierocles's face was what sealed the deal.

"Meet me at the palace. Immediately."

Δ

It took Hierocles a little longer than "immediately" to arrive at the palace. He had to reach the front door after climbing the steep steps of the Palatine Hill, only to be met by guards who had not yet been notified of his visit and found him impertinent; while Antoninus had returned to his room directly from the circus, using his secret passage.

For a moment, Hierocles thought of going home and changing his clothes, but he understood the command well and did not want to displease the emperor by being late. Once allowed inside, Hierocles was met by a tall man in uniform. The man looked him up and down with a surly expression.

"You must proceed to the baths," Comazon said, pointing the way. "It is an order from the emperor."

Hierocles walked down the hall, contemplating the stucco walls adorned with intricate carvings, the polished marble floor gleaming under his feet, and the fired clay ceiling soaring above him with sophisticated patterns. Never in his wildest dreams had he imagined being surrounded by such grandeur even for a moment.

"What are you looking at? Walk!"

Hierocles looked at the man with contempt. Whoever that fellow was, he was not someone to mess with. However, being used to dealing with tough men, he was able to keep calm and walked down the corridor as directed.

A cool breeze from the windows greeted him as soon as he entered the *thermae*. The baths consisted primarily of a huge pool of pristine water from a spring, surrounded by Greek-style columns and several marble statues of nude ancient heroes on pedestals, among which was one of Antoninus, in a provocative position, bending over and sticking out his ass, wearing only a cape over his shoulders. Hierocles took off his sandals and enjoyed the comfort of the heated floor, made of elaborate colorful mosaics. The guard did not leave when he took off his clothes.

"Are you going to stand there watching?"

"Yes."

"Why don't you join me then?"

Comazon responded with a smirk. As the charioteer descended into the water, Comazon couldn't help but admire his sturdy physique: the strong, muscular arms and legs, the heavy built torso with some perfectly located chest hair and, in particular, that thick phallus hanging from his crotch; phallus that looked massive even through the dense forest of golden pubes. His low-hanging balls looked proportionally big, like those of a mature bull ready for sacrifice.

"How old are you?" Comazon squatted.

Hierocles submerged for a few seconds and emerged with his wavy hair smoothed over his head. He wiped the water from his face and looked at Comazon with his deep green eyes. The beauty of his bearded face was undeniable.

"Twenty-seven."

Only twenty-seven. Nine years of advantage. Comazon remained still, piercing his rival with his gaze as if with his sword. The whole thing unfolded before his eyes in the circus. The emperor had become completely smitten by this man, this low-class thrash, this beast, this barbarian. Yes, barbarian, since he definitely did not look Roman to him.

"Where are you from?"

"I'm from Caria, it's in Anatolia—"

"I know where that is."

Hierocles did not feel intimidated by Comazon's interrogation. If anything, he was amused. He dipped back into the deliciously warm water. "May I know your name?" he asked, emerging for the second time.

"You may not." Comazon rose abruptly and walked toward the exit. Before leaving, he turned around. "Here are some towels and fresh clothes. You may leave the rags you were wearing right where they are." The sounds of his footsteps echoed off the walls. *So, a Carian. Not surprising.*

Hierocles remained seated for a few more minutes on the submerged steps in one corner of the pool, with eyes closed and arms resting on the edges, enjoying the rhythmic lapping of the water on his brawny chest.

Brought back to life by the delightful bath and feeling refreshed in the white light-fabric tunic with which he was provided, Hierocles followed Comazon, who had been waiting outside, through the corridors of the palace to the imperial chamber. The door was already ajar and Comazon opened it wide for the guest. After stepping inside, Hierocles waited an instant to see if the prefect dared to enter as well. He did not. He had closed the door behind him.

In front of him was a bed larger than anything he had ever seen before. A green lace canopy wrapped it like a cocoon. He opened the curtains, and there was the Boy Maximus, wearing a delicate, simple purple robe, lying in a suggestive pose, biting his index finger. A rock carved in the shape of an erect penis— the precious *fascinus*—hanged on the wall behind him. It was the first object of veneration that Antoninus had demanded from the vestals as a part of the dowry.

"I've been waiting for you."

Hierocles stood still for a minute, unsure of what to do. He tied the curtains to the sides and waited for instructions. The emperor pointed to a jar with oil on an adjacent table as he removed his purple robe and lay on his chest on one side of the bed. Hierocles took the jar and poured some of the warm oil over his rough hands. Instinctively, he spread it lightly over the emperor's back, arms, and legs, taking a little more time to massage the firm, pale buttocks. He took a few moments to remove his own cloths, and there they were: emperor and charioteer, master and slave, transacting with each other wearing nothing but their manliness. Hierocles poured a few more drops on the emperor's lower back, right above the buttocks. The oil ran smoothly down the crack; the rosy hole trembling upon the feel of the sticky substance. Hierocles spread the youthful cheeks apart, rubbed his hands over and between them, exposing and fingering the stretchy hole. He moved closer to the neck and gave Antoninus long strokes from the upper back down to the buttocks, pressing firmly with his manly hands. Antoninus's moans made Hierocles's cock grow hard fast. The massage continued for a few more minutes, Hierocles applying pressure with hands and forearms, sliding gracefully and deftly over the slick skin.

The emperor turned over and lay on his back. Expeditiously, Hierocles covered the long, fully erect, dripping hot rod, and the hairless balls with oil. He massaged his chest, while "incidentally" elbowing the hard penis. He went down to the steel hard cock, grabbed it, and massaged it up and down, slowly at first, then vigorously, pausing only to give the balls a lick. Spitting on the glans and letting the saliva run down the shaft, he inserted the thin rod into his mouth, and masterfully took first the entire length all the way down his throat, then lingered for a while on the head, sucking it, liking it, kissing it, while massaging the balls and pinching the nipples. He continued sucking and jerking the imperial cock as he rubbed his legs, chest and fingered his asshole. He went down to the imperial hole, and gave it a couple of licks, noticing the emperor's reaction to the tickle. The boy had never been pleased that way before and got goosebumps all over his body. Hierocles inserted his tongue in the pink hole, sliding it in an out, and had to grab Antoninus by the ankles when his body began to twist out of control.

The charioteer moved up, grabbed Antoninus's legs and pushed them down, lifting his ass in the process. He climbed onto the bed and placed his thighs on either side of the emperor's buttocks, his hard organ pointing right at the imperial anus, which could wait no longer. He used the remaining oil on his hands to lubricate his own member and, holding Antoninus's legs apart, entered him.

The initial insertion was slow and careful, not because of lack of lubrication, but because of the dimensions of Hierocles's manhood, of which he was perfectly aware.

Antoninus moaned and whimpered, clutching at the shiny silk sheets, while his ass was being stretched as never before. Finally, the whole of Hierocles slid inside and there he remained for a few moments, waiting for His Highness to get used to his sheer size.

Moving slowly, his breath matching every lunge, he reached a certain rhythm, after which he let Antoninus's legs relax. He locked eyes with him and rejoiced at the sight of the boy squirming, moaning in exquisite pleasure. Hierocles's cock grew thicker and harder with each penetration and Antoninus wrapped his lover's back with his legs as he vigorously jerked his own dick. Hierocles leaned down and brought his mouth close to the emperor's; he breathed into it and lightly brushed his thick lips over the emperor's delicate, rosy lips, but did not kiss, leaving him yearning. He lifted his torso and placed his hands on the bed to gain support and fuck harder. As he moved, easier and deeper each time, Antoninus moaned so loudly that his cries could be heard all the way down the hall.

At the door, Comazon's heart was a volcano in eruption, pumping his blood with an impulse so strong that it made his face red hot and caused his pulse to lacerate his wrists. He gripped his sword with twice the force he would have used to slay an enemy on the battlefield. He, Comazon, the legendary commander of the *Legio III Gallica*, hero of a thousand battles against barbarians, used to enduring all kinds of hardships under extreme heat and cold, never before defeated in battle, was now being defeated in bed. And by no more than a brute from the streets. Unable to stand it any longer, he walked away from the door, still restraining himself from making noise.

Inside, Hierocles had put Antoninus on all fours. He kept fucking him steadily, with constant vigor and pace. The young man squealed as a virgin. A virgin he was, but only to a ten-inch monster cock. Hierocles locked hands with his emperor and kept pounding him harder. The fury he had felt at the defeat in the racetrack was slowly leaving his body. He let go of his hands and spanked Antoninus until his ass turned red. He grabbed the emperor's cock and jerked it while he kept on impetuously banging him from behind. And then, when he was about to climax, he laid the boy on his back again, to allow him to marvel at the expression of his masculine face as he impregnated him. He kept pounding as he gripped the boy's wrists, pinning him to the bed. He placed his forehead over the emperor's, noses touching, breaths mixing, until he reached the point of no return. Hierocles's balls spasmed and his cock released a copious amount of cum inside Antoninus's hole. While feeling the heat of the syrupy liquid inside his guts, the emperor admired in rapture the bearded chin of his man, as Hierocles lifted his face toward the ceiling, in a bestial scream of infinite pleasure at the moment of release.

Hierocles slid his cock inside a few more times after he was done, letting it soak in his own cum. Moments later, still with heavy breathing, he threw himself on the bed, closed his eyes and almost immediately began to snore. Antoninus lay down on him, letting his chest hair tickle his nose, inhaling the manly scent of the charioteer. He hadn't cummed, but all that mattered was that his man had, and inside of him.

He had finally found love: he had seen it in his smile, that first moment at the circus; he had felt it in his hands, sliding with long strokes all over his body; he had seen it in his eyes, as he made him squirm with the most exquisite pleasure. He had found love in a real, tough, rough, but nevertheless beautiful man. He felt happy and satisfied. Not long afterward he joined Hierocles in his sleep.

"Oh Mother." Soaemias sobbed in Maesa's lap. "How can he do this to us? How can he do this to himself?"

Maesa did not say a word. Her gaze was lost in the walls of her chamber as she stroked her daughter's back.

Soaemias rose and wiped her tears. "I feel so sorry for Severa. She must be—"

"She's alright. I don't think she cares about any of this."

"Should we invite her to come?"

"No. I don't like strangers in my room. And that woman is still very much a stranger to me. I can't understand why my grandson chose to marry her, since he could have had any woman he wanted."

"I'm surprised you still don't understand, Mother." She stood up and looked at her. "He doesn't want a woman."

Maesa looked away.

"I noticed a strange behavior in him since he was little," Soaemias continued. "He was not a normal boy. He played with dolls, befriended girls, spied on the maids and asked them to teach him how to cook… He was never interested in swords or bows and arrows…"

"I honestly thought it was just a phase. I didn't lie to Julius Paulus when I asked him to give him his daughter… And now…"

"Now there's nothing we can do."

"I'm not so sure about that," Maesa said, trying to regain her composure.

"Really, Mother? What do you think can be done? Whatever we did wrong was a long time ago. It's too late to change his ways."

"It's not his ways what really bothers me," Maesa said, looking at her daughter. "If only he would be more discreet with his private life, things wouldn't be so bad. What the senators think, that's the real problem. You know very well that those old weasels are conspiring behind his back and are just waiting for the right moment to strike a blow. And if he falls, we fall with him, dear."

"That's all that matters to you, right, Mother? Status and power?"

Maesa cracked a smile. "Someone must wield power while your son is not mature enough to rule on his own. But I can't be of help if the senators don't respect him."

Soaemias gave her a nasty look. "You can rest assured. As long as he has Comazon and the Praetorians' allegiance, all will be well."

"Yes, as long as he has Comazon…" She paused meditatively. There lay the real danger. How would he take this?

In the imperial chamber, Hierocles had just awakened when Antoninus, dressed in the light white tunic that the charioteer had worn in the baths, returned to the room with a plate of green grapes. Antoninus sat down beside him, with his back against the headboard and his feet on the bed, and teased him with a bunch until Hierocles plucked one of the grapes with his teeth. Antoninus put the plate aside and gave his mouth to his lover, engaging with him in a battle of tongues fighting for the elusive fruit. The emperor let him win, and rested his head on the pillow. They both looked up at the ceiling, their bare arms touching.

"Where have you been all my life?" Antoninus said.

Hierocles moved quickly and tickled the young emperor until he begged for mercy. They embraced, letting their skin slide over each other, and kissed until their tongues were dry. They lay on their sides, facing each other, Hierocles lightly squeezing Antoninus's nipples. They didn't speak, they just smiled, like two people who had just stumbled upon the fact that there was someone in the world just for them. Hierocles lay again on his back and put his left hand behind his head. Antoninus lay on his chest and Hierocles laid his right arm around him.

"Here. I've been here," Hierocles said, running his fingers through Antoninus's hair. "Rome is my home."

"But it hasn't been your home all your life."

Hierocles was going to ask him how he knew but realized that it was surely because of his accent. "That is true. I am from Anatolia."

"I was born in the East as well."

"I didn't know that."

"And there's many more things you don't know about me."

"And you about me."

"But yours is easy to find out. I'm the emperor of Rome; nothing is hidden from me. Have you forgotten?"

Hierocles chuckled. "No, I haven't forgotten."

Antoninus gently punched him on the abdomen. "I never dreamed there could be someone as perfect as you in this world," he said, playing with his lover's chest hair.

"Is that right?"

"Yes, I mean… there are many handsome men, but you… you are something else."

"May I ask what it is about this humble charioteer that has driven the emperor of Rome so crazy about him?"

"I wish I knew. I just know… that I never want you to leave," he said, playing with his beard.

Hierocles turned his face toward him. Then he leaned back on the pillow. "I will be where my emperor wants me to be." He paused. "Just keep me away from that grumpy Praetorian."

Antoninus frowned. "Oh, Comazon? Don't worry about him. Not at all."

"Then what will you have me do here? I can be your chauffer, of course, taking you all over Rome. I bet you don't know the city as well as I do."

Antoninus thought about it for a moment and then exclaimed, jumping on the bed: "No, we'll do something better."

Hierocles frowned and leaned on his side.

"We will marry!" the emperor shouted, clapping his hands.

Hierocles shook his head as he squeezed his eyes shut. "Marry? The emperor wants to marry me?"

"Yes! Two people who love each other belong together."

"But what will you do with your wife?"

"Forget about her. She will be gone tomorrow before the cock sings."

"It's funny you should say that," Hierocles said with a chuckle.

"Why funny?"

"Because another cock will be singing all night too!"

He jumped on Antoninus, making him roll with him and fall to the floor, pulling the sheets. Antoninus squeaked like a piglet, while Hierocles, grunting and snorting, rubbed his rough face across the boy's smooth chest, licking, sucking, and biting the delicate skin, out of control like a ravenous bull.

Δ

The next day, Antoninus summoned Maesa, Soaemias, Severa, and Comazon to the throne hall of the palace before dawn. They stood in silence under the skylight, in the middle of the immense room, surrounded by marble columns and colorful walls covered with rectangular tiles of dark green, terracotta and ochre. The emperor appeared, strutting arm in arm with his brand-new lover, who walked with extra care trying not to slip on the polished marble floors. After ascending the stairs, Antoninus took a seat on his throne and crossed his legs femininely, while Hierocles stood beside him, hands clasped in front.

"Dear Mother, dear Grandmother and faithful Praetorian Prefect," Antoninus said with his usual, if somewhat exacerbated mannerisms, "I would like to introduce you to my fiancé, Hierocles."

Comazon's eyes exuded fury. Hierocles looked at him with a condescending smile. Soaemias stared in confusion at the appalled, somewhat stoic expression of her mother.

"But, Excellency, how can you speak like that in front of your wife, don't you see that she's here?" Maesa said.

"She will be dismissed at once. I will grant her the divorce she has so insistently requested."

Severa ran out the palace without even waiting to be formally asked to leave. For the first time, a smile appeared on her face.

"Yes, you may leave!" Antoninus shouted behind her back. "But forget about the dowry and the *fascinus*, those will stay!"

"This is impossible!" Maesa shouted, unable to maintain her composure anymore. "How can a man marry another man? How can the emperor marry a barbarian, who is not even a Roman citizen? How can you have such contempt for Roman law and customs?"

"He's a citizen now. I have granted him his freedom as well as full citizenship and have ordered the tailors to cut him a toga. They are working on it as we speak."

Comazon's hands clenched into fists.

"As for the law," Antoninus continued. "I am the law. We will marry in three days in the Temple of Elagabal."

"Do you expect the senators to attend? This cannot be arranged on such short notice," his grandmother replied.

"Yes, it can. And they will attend. They will do what I say, just like everyone else."

"Is that all, Excellency?" Comazon said.

"Yes," Antoninus said, glacially.

Comazon gave a martial salute, turned around and stormed out of the room, his cape billowing in the air. Maesa followed. Soaemias shrugged her shoulders. Antoninus smiled at her and caressed his lover's hand.

Δ

Maesa reached Comazon and asked him to follow her to the studio. Both were distraught and furious, but Maesa was able to control herself faster.

"Comazon, please calm down, we must think, and anger doesn't help the brain."

"How could he do this?" he asked as he paced the room. "Does he not see the kind of man he is bringing to the palace?"

"I won't lie to you. I'm as shocked as you are. I knew he'd taken him to bed after the races, but I had no idea that their affair would last more than one night."

"There must be a way to stop this."

"Not without removing him from power. He's the emperor, after all, and not obeying his orders would significantly defile his office in the eyes of the people."

"He just cannot do this!" Comazon said, leaning against the desk.

"I know how much this must hurt you," Maesa said, putting her hands on his shoulders. "I'm aware of how much you love him."

He turned to look at her, his eyes wide open.

"Let's talk heart-to-heart, Comazon. Like we have never spoken before."

Comazon's eyes watered.

"I knew it from day one," she said, embracing him, "just by the way you looked at him and your body reactions. I confirmed it by your valor in battle and the zeal you have always shown to defend him. And I know that you have remained behind your line, out of respect for the empire and your position as praetorian prefect; your sacrifice is exemplary, dear General: you wanted to be near him, to protect him, but at the same time, you understood the importance of his office for all Romans, and the stability of the empire."

"But now, everything will go to hell anyway!"

"There's nothing we can do for now. We had better wait. After all, the people did not approve of his marriage to a vestal, anyway. They know his ways; I doubt they will be shocked by his decision. If anything, they'll be amused."

"And the Senate?"

"Leave it to me."

Δ

Maesa convoked an extraordinary session of the Senate. She stood in the center of the *curia*, waiting for the Fathers to take their seats.

"Honorable Fathers, I have called this session today to communicate you important news from the emperor."

The senators waited in silence.

"His Majesty has decided to repudiate his current wife and remarry."

Quintus Aquilius rose from his seat. "Praised be Vesta! Thank you for answering my prayers, dear goddess! My daughter will watch with her life that your fire be well tended!"

"And who will be the next spouse?" a senator asked.

Maesa took a little time to compose herself and contain her displeasure.

"A man by the name of Hierocles."

Jeers and shouts erupted from the seats.

"Order. Order!" Sacerdos shouted. "*Senatrix*, please continue."

"I will not deny that I'm as shocked as you are. But, honorable Fathers, let me ask you this: Weren't Rome's laws and traditions defiled more when the emperor married a *vestal*, a woman dedicated to praying for the welfare of the fatherland?"

"I have to agree with that," Aquilius said, who, even as disgusted as he was with the present solution, would do anything to free his daughter. "Besides, there's a precedent. Nero had already married men in several occasions."

"But Nero was a tyrant, whose memory has been damned!" a senator shouted.

"A tyrant indeed," another shouted, "just like your grandson!"

Maesa looked at him with piercing eyes. "I must remind you, honorable Father, that you must never refer to the emperor by any other name than one of his titles."

Silence ensued in the audience.

"Moreover," Maesa continued, "as you know, the will of the emperor is the law, and the sole function of the Senate is to administer it." She paced around the room. "However, all is not darkness in this hour. I'm convinced that if you show no opposition to the emperor's desires, he'll also show his gratitude by allowing this House the freedom it needs to legislate. After all, the good of the emperor is the good of Rome."

What she really meant was that if the emperor got enough dick in his bedroom, he would not care much about ruling Rome, and the senators promptly understood it.

Δ

In a few days, everything was ready for the unusual wedding. In the temple—from which the fire of Vesta had notoriously already been removed—stood the newly formed couple, dressed in white silk tunics and laurel wreaths; behind them Soaemias, arm in arm with her distraught mother, and lastly, the senators. Comazon had remained outside; he had the excuse of watching for signs of unrest, but in reality he had neither heart nor stomach to be present at yet another abominable wedding ceremony.

After the sacrifice of the bull and the inspection of the entrails, in which—conveniently—nothing strange was found, the religious minister held in front of the bride and groom the same papyri that had been used in the previous wedding.

"Excuse me, Highness, who…" he hesitated as he tried to find the politest words, "will recite the words that correspond to the female?"

"I will. I'm the woman," the emperor said promptly, to the gasps and murmurs of the attendants. He turned to the left and took Hierocles's hands, looking into his eyes. "*Ubi tu Gaius, ego Gaia.*"

"*Ubi tu Gaia, ego Gaius,*" Hierocles replied. Antoninus pressed his lips against those of his now husband.

Δ

The emperor's new wedding festivities were for the dumbfounded people of Rome like a continuation of those of his two previous marriages. This regime was nothing but a never-ending circus. Since, in his largesse, the emperor had ordered the distribution of cattle and game, incense, spices, and even gold to the masses, most people didn't care whether he married a vestal, a slave, a man, or a dog, for that matter. That, however, did not prevent malicious gossip in the streets.

One evening, two women enjoyed a friendly chatter while sweeping the porches of their homes, paying little attention to their children's games.

"We need to hurry up and talk less, Matilda," one of them said, named Martia. "You know it's bad luck to sweep after dusk."

"Look, mama!" one of the ragged infants shouted, pointing to the street.

The two women turned their heads toward an approaching cloud of dust and the trepidant sound of galloping horses. As the cloud dissipated, the offending vehicle appeared; it was none other than the flaming, highly adorned chariot of the young emperor's husband, racing with Apollo's celestial speed.

"Did you see that?" Martia said.

"How could I not see it?" Matilda replied, mocking Martia with her gestures. "He almost ran us over."

"That indecent man. He will bring ruin to all of Rome!"

"He's the emperor's favorite. Who are we to question Augustus's preferences?"

"Not just his favorite, fool. His husband!" Martia said, her eyes about to burst out of their sockets. "Yes, his husband! As horrid as it sounds." Her sharp voice trembled slightly. "That deviant, shameless Asian youth has disgraced the house of the divine Augustus."

"Shh! Don't let anyone hear you," Matilda hissed, looking around them. "You know what happens to those who oppose him. Besides, didn't you and your family enjoy the lamb that the palace men brought to the neighborhood last week?"

Martia looked down and continued sweeping.

"You did, didn't you?" Matilda continued. "So, who cares? I for one find this man extremely attractive. He's so muscular, so handsome, and has such beautiful eyes. It's exciting to see him walking the streets all dressed in fancy clothes and wearing all that jewelry; I don't care who he takes by the arm, it will never be me, anyway."

"You wish it were you, don't you? It's precisely that vulgar display of wealth what bothers me. He's a nobody, a slave from the province who just had the good fortune to fill the emperor's eye. That doesn't give him the right to parade before us and shove his success up our face."

"Don't be such a hypocrite, Martia. What would you do if you were rich and powerful and ruled the world? I'm telling you; you'd have thousands of dresses and earrings and jewels, you'd eat turbot and caviar every day, and decorate your palace with millions of roses, daffodils, and violets. I am glad that one of us has made it that far. I rejoice in witnessing what he's doing with his luck. Instead of being so bitter, you should join us, his group of admirers."

Martia looked at her, frowning.

"There's one more thing that might change your mind," Matilda said, giggling. "They say that he's got a club so big it touches the ground."

After a while, Hierocles and his slick white chariot arrived at one of the many breweries in the eternal city, run—like most—by immigrants, since beer drinking was decidedly an un-Roman tradition. He may have upgraded his ride, but neither his taste in beer nor his friendships had undergone the slightest change. He stepped out of the car, making sure not to stain his toga, and was greeted by Gordius, a large man in his fifties with black, wavy, tousled hair, hairy like a boar, who wore an oversized brown tunic. He approached Hierocles with a smile from ear to ear and gave him a bear hug and a kiss on the cheek. Hierocles could smell the alcoholic stench on the man's breath.

"So, you've already been drinking. Without waiting for me."

"Come on man, it was just to get in the mood while you arrived. Your new home is farther from here than the junkyard where you used to live. By the way, what did you do with all your stuff?"

"It can burn, for all I care. I have no need for any of that."

"Not even your old chariot, from what I can see."

Hierocles had certainly improved in that regard. The first thing he asked for as a wedding gift from his wealthy husband was a new chariot. It was a splendid machine, unlike anything he had ever owned before; the guard was of the most expensive pine wood, painted white and trimmed with real gold, not just cheap steel with gold paint; it also had detailed carvings of protector gods and fauns on rims and wheels. Even the reins had been skillfully cut from the most expensive bull hide. But the finest detail consisted in the never-before-seen folding bronze steps, a true touch of innovation.

"By Castor and Pollux!" Gordius exclaimed, walking around the chariot. "Look at this. It's got room for two, so you'll have to take me for a ride."

"Not enough space for you, fat man," Hierocles said laughing, as he tied his horses to a pole and fed them grapes.

Gordius looked at him reproachfully. "And the horses! By Apollo, I've never seen such beautiful animals. Pure immaculate white. Why only two and not four?"

"Why would I want four? This car isn't for circus racing. Besides, it has more of a sporty look with just two, don't you think?"

The man nodded. He put his arm around Hierocles's shoulders and led him inside the brewery. They found two empty stools by the bar and ordered beer.

"To the health of the emperor's consort!" Gordius exclaimed raising his cup, inviting the other patrons to the toast.

"To his health!" the patrons replied, raising their respective cups.

Hierocles took a sip of the beer that had been his favorite since his arrival in Rome. It was as good as ever, and not unlike what could be found in faraway Caria, but now that he didn't have to risk his life in the arena to afford it, it tasted different somehow.

"It's amazing how things can change in a moment," Gordius said.

Hierocles nodded with a smile and drank. Platitudes—the only kind of conversation he could have with his old mentor.

"Indeed, but not everything is perfect yet."

"What do you mean? You got gold, jewels, servants; anything you want is at your disposal."

"Yes, but I don't have any authority."

"What, you want to be the emperor of the Romans?"

"Why not? I don't want to be a consort all my life."

"Cheers to that!" Gordius raised his cup again.

"There's one more thing that worries me," Hierocles said, lowering his voice. "That bitter praetorian, Comazon… He still makes me nervous. He doesn't like me and I don't trust him at all."

"He's at your husband's command. Why should you fear? He won't do anything against you."

"Are you a fool? Don't you know how many times Praetorians have assassinated an emperor to replace him?"

"He doesn't seem that kind. He has quite an honorable reputation."

"That remains to be seen. I'm going to have him investigated. There must be something in his past that I can use against him."

"Why don't we talk about more pleasant things," Gordius said, patting Hierocles's shoulder. "Like old memories. It doesn't seem like years ago when I bought you in your hometown for just a few sesterces," he continued, taking a huge swallow.

"You still have to remind me of that, don't you?"

"Don't get angry, my friend. We're here to celebrate your success. I want to rejoice in the past as much as I want you to live the moment."

"It's interesting that now you dare to call me friend. Just a few days ago you were still my owner."

"I got good money for you from the emperor."

"That means you'll be paying for our drinks tonight."

"And the next round for everyone!" Gordius shouted, to the cheers of the attendees. He took another sip and set the goblet on the bar. "You know why I bought you?"

"You just couldn't resist it, right?"

"Just like the emperor. You were the most beautiful boy in the universe."

"Were? I still am, you prick."

"Undoubtedly. Now even more beautiful. Now you are a man. Back then your features had not yet fully developed. Your arms, chest, legs did not have the size and hardness they have now. All of which, you have to thank me for, because it's due to the training I provided you with." He gazed coquettishly at the Carian. "And certainly, your…" He slid his hand over Hierocles's thigh toward his crotch.

"Not here. Not now," Hierocles said, gripping the old charioteer's hand tight. "In fact, never again."

Gordius withdrew his hand and jerked it in pain. "You mean you'll never visit me at night like you used to?"

"Now I have something better to stick my dick into."

"That pale little ass? Come on, Hierocles. You couldn't have changed that much. I know what you like. You like a big, hairy, heavy ass to ride you like a horse."

Hierocles considered for a moment whether he should speak his mind. True, he had had some of the hottest sex of his life with that man, but just to get ahead. Fucking Gordius had given him an advantage over the other charioteers of the Greens. He had gotten the best horses, the best whips, even the best clothes. No. It wasn't the right time to tell him. He didn't want to ruin the moment. He smiled and stroked Gordius's hand, guiding it back to his dick, which had grown hard in the process.

Gordius felt of that solid, sturdy shaft with gusto. "By *Fascinus*, how good this feels. You're the best endowed man in all of Rome, there's no doubt about that."

Hierocles allowed himself to enjoy the strong, manly hand rubbing his cock over the expensive fabric that now covered his privates. A little precum arose. Gordius moved his hand discreetly, first under Hierocles's toga and then under the tunic and *subligaculum*. Hierocles held his breath upon the feel of the rough hand sliding the prepuce down from his lubricated cock head and the thick, calloused fingers touching his balls.

"What the fuck is going on here?" a man from behind yelled, who had been watching them since they arrived. "This is not a whorehouse. Get the fuck out of here!"

Hierocles stood up, accidentally slamming his cup. "Make me!" he shouted, standing an inch away from the man's chest.

The man raised his arms to push him, but before he could do so, Hierocles punched him in the face, causing him to stagger and fall onto a chair a few feet behind. The other patrons were speechless amid a stony silence. The man got up, touched his face, and was held by two of his companions as he was about to return the blow.

"Let me go, you idiots! Let me beat this bastard, this disgusting prostitute. Yes!" he said looking Hierocles in the eye. "That's what you are, you vile piece of thrash, nothing but a fucking whore!" He spat on the floor.

Hierocles rushed to give him another blow but was held back by Gordius and the brewer. "I will kill you! I will fucking kill you! You're dead, you son of a bitch!"

"Take him out, come on, let's get out of here!" a distraught Gordius said. He and the other man dragged Hierocles away, who was still cursing and yelling. Once on the street, Gordius instructed the brewer to leave them alone and go inside to control the situation. "Hey, calm down," Gordius said, as he held Hierocles against the wood guard of the chariot. "It was all my fault. I got all horny looking at you dressed like this; I shouldn't have done what I did."

Hierocles pulled Gordius's hands away and freed himself from the grip. "Don't you ever tell me what to do," he yelled, wagging a finger in his face. "Don't do that ever again, did you hear me?"

"Alright, alright," Gordius said with hands up.

Hierocles fixed his toga. "That scumbag. Who the hell does he think he is? I will keep my word. Tomorrow, he'll be fucking underground. There's nowhere in Rome he can hide."

"Yeah, do what you want tomorrow, but let's not ruin the night. Wanna go to my place?"

Hierocles looked at him incredulously. "You're fucking crazy," he said, as he untied his horses. He climbed into his chariot and drove away.

Δ

Hierocles returned home, straight to his bed. Gordius must have been really out of his mind to think he would trade the imperial bedroom, with its carpeted floors and rose-scented oils, for his fetid, filthy den.

There hadn't been a single night in which he and the emperor didn't fornicate like wild rabbits. Hierocles's vigor and Antoninus's lust had unleashed an uncontainable force. That night, though, there was something different. Had Antoninus not been so focused on his own erotic sensations as he rode Hierocles's cock, he would have noticed his lover's vacant stare and apparent lack of interest. When they were done, Antoninus fell asleep in his arms, exhausted, but the charioteer remained awake well into the night.

A slave girl served them breakfast late in the morning, which they ate undressed. After finishing their meal, they put the dishes aside and went back to cuddling.

"I want to ask a favor of you, sweetheart," Hierocles said, running his fingers through his lover's hair.

"Anything you want, love."

"I want you to order the death of a man."

Antoninus rose and stared at him. "What?"

Hierocles licked the residues of fruit juices from Antoninus' fingers. Antoninus licked his fingers wet with Hierocles's saliva.

"What did he do to you?"

"He insulted me publicly. And in doing so, he insulted you too, Majesty."

"Where?"

"In a brewery."

"In that shitty place you went to with your friend? Now I know why you came back so early." He paused for a moment. "Why didn't you tell me last night?"

"I didn't want to ruin our time together." Hierocles gave him the kind of kiss that made him forget the world around him. "But this is important. I want that man dead by tonight."

"Granted. Anything else?"

Hierocles nodded with a smile.

"Yes? What does my husband want?"

"You may not be aware of this, but people say nasty things about me on the street."

"Why do you care? Aren't you with me right now? Isn't that all that matters?"

"Yes, of course, but... it's not pleasant to roam around my city and notice all the chatter around me. It makes me uncomfortable and sad. Even when I ride my chariot, I see people pointing at me and whispering things in each other's ears."

"There's not much I can do about it, honey. Even the emperor's power is not unlimited. I can't order the patrolling of the streets to arrest people for gossiping. I guess that's something you'll have to live with."

"The problem is that they see me as an upstart, a nobody who was just lucky that you noticed him. I want to show them that I am more than that. Is that so bad?"

"And how exactly do you want to do that?"

"See, we're married, right? Legally I'm your husband."

"Yes."

"And I think we both agree also that I am the man in this relationship, right? You said so yourself in our wedding vows."

"Yes."

"I think that it's time for me to do the things that befit the *dominus* of the house. I want to have authority, authority of my own, not to have to depend on my wife for everything."

"Your wife?"

"Yes, my wife, isn't that what you are?"

"Yeah, I guess so... I'm just not used to the way it sounds."

"Well, get used to it. Because that's how it's going to be from now on. I'm your husband, and you're my wife."

"Alright, alright... yes, yes! I like the idea! It's exciting... I will have dresses made and start wearing makeup. How about that?"

"That's very good, but—"

"You know, darling, it's as if you had read my mind; I've been wanting to tell you this, but I hadn't found the right moment…"

"You can tell me now," Hierocles said, slightly annoyed at the interruption.

"I've long since realized that… I want to live as a woman; that I am truly a woman. I just didn't know how you were going to take it. But now I'm sure that's precisely what you want from me, am I right, love?"

"Yes, of course," Hierocles said, a new light in his eyes. "And as you know, it's not proper for a woman to be at the head of the government… in Rome, men are in charge, that's how it's always been."

"Then you want to assume my position as head of government?" Antoninus said with a disappointed look on his face.

"Yes. And that can be done only in one way. Otherwise, nobody will take me seriously."

"And that is?"

"You must officially name me Caesar."

Antoninus got up abruptly and paced nervously around the room.

"Caesar? But I am the only Caesar. How did that idea crawl into your mind?"

"I've been thinking about it since our first night together. But now it has become really necessary. And you have just told me that you want to live as a woman: how can a woman be Caesar?"

"Wait a minute. So, all this time, all you've been thinking about is becoming Caesar." He went up to him and slapped him in the face. "And I thought you loved me!"

Hierocles tied Antoninus's hands with his. "Listen. I do love you. But, you have to understand my position. I am a man. And I can't allow other men to treat me as I am not good enough. I am a man, I have a family, and I must be the head of that family. There's no other way, Antoninus."

Antoninus's jaw dropped. "You called me by my name!" He freed his hands from the grip and walked away.

Hierocles followed him and locked his arms around him from behind. "Listen," he hissed in his ear. "So far, since I've been in your house, I've given you everything you've wanted. You want a good fuck? I give it to you. You want a massage? You got it. You want me to stay in bed all day? I've done it. I gave up my life, my career, just to please you. I love you, I can't live without you, but you can't deny me the honor I deserve as a husband."

"You don't respect me. All you want to do is take advantage of me! It's clear to me now," Antoninus said, trembling, sweat running down his temples.

"I don't have time for this hogwash," Hierocles said, forcing Antoninus to look at him. "I'll tell you just one thing. You will name me Caesar. You will do it tomorrow. And from now on, you will do only what I tell you to do." He threw the helpless boy to the floor, grabbed his clothes, and slammed the door behind him.

Comazon entered the guestroom adjoining the emperor's chamber, since he thought he heard noises. A butt-naked Hierocles was spreading his clothes on the oversized mattress.

Startled, the charioteer looked back. "Oh, it's you."

"What are you doing here?"

"I owe no explanations to the praetorian prefect."

"Yes, you do. I obey only the emperor."

Hierocles smiled. "Since you're here, why don't you help me get dressed? I still haven't got used to properly putting on a toga by myself." He handed the *subligaculum* to the general, who hesitated. "Come on, Comazon, can you do it as a favor?"

Comazon took the *subligaculum*, walked behind the naked man and placed the cloth over Hierocles hairy bottom. He tied the front just above the pelvis, inadvertently pulling some pubes inside the knot.

"Ouch! Be careful!"

Comazon undid the knot and tied it again. He noticed how Hierocles's cock had gone from flaccid to semihard. Not wanting to see any more, he quickly folded the rest of the *subligaculum*, not without carelessly touching his cock as he did so. It was impossible to get around that huge thing.

He stood behind Hierocles and took the tunic from the bed. As he slipped the opening over Hierocles's head, the sweet, sexually charged fragrance of the charioteer intoxicated him. Sliding the robe down the fit body, he rested his chin on Hierocles's neck, scratching it with his stubble, exhaling into his ear, while his own cock grew hard. After placing one end of the toga over Hierocles's left shoulder, he unfolded the cloth all the way to the other end, wrapped the man with it, and tied the other end snugly. He stood in front of him and made the final adjustments.

When the prefect finished, Hierocles looked him straight in the eye. He had to look up, as Comazon towered over him by about six inches.

"You're attracted to me, aren't you?"

A cold silence fell between the two men.

"Not everyone here is a victim of your charms," Comazon said, without breaking eye contact, his heart betraying him with its rapid beating.

"I know that," Hierocles said, lowering his eyes and straightening his clothes a little. "I just thought I sensed something from you. An energy of sorts."

Comazon turned away.

"I haven't told you to leave," Hierocles said, in a glacial tone.

Comazon returned and stood a finger away from Hierocles, his face flushed with fury.

"I have already told you that I only take orders from the emperor," he bellowed, waving a finger.

"That will change soon. His Majesty has named me Caesar and will ratify it tomorrow before the Senate."

Comazon's expression hardened. "That is impossible!"

"It's not, since it has already happened."

Comazon ran in the direction of the emperor's chamber. Hierocles hastily put on his sandals. From the outside, the prefect thought he heard sobbing inside. He palmed the door vigorously.

"Excellency! Excellency!"

Hierocles arrived quickly and put his hand on the door. "I'll handle my matrimonial affairs personally. You're dismissed, Comazon," he said, pointing to the corridor. Since the general refused to move, he said: "As you can hear, my wife is crying, I must attend to her." Hierocles took advantage of the general's surprise at those words and pushed him aside.

Comazon stood in the hall, immobile, unable to process what he had just heard. His... wife?

When Hierocles entered the room, Antoninus was still lying on the floor, naked, helpless like a newborn fawn. "Have you had time to meditate on my request?" he said, coming to his side.

Antoninus rose, and wiping away his tears, stood for a few instants in front of Hierocles, breathing anxiously. He couldn't contain himself and threw his arms around him. "Yes, yes, yes... Please forgive me, my dear husband. You are the man of the house; I must understand that." He kissed him all over his face. "Tomorrow I will do as you wish."

"There's one more thing. I also want you to grant my mother her freedom and a place among the wives of senators and councilmen. If your mother has the honor of being in that circle, then my mother should have it too."

"Yes, my dear," Antoninus said, embracing him, not wanting to let go.

"Very well," Hierocles said, forcing some distance. "I'm glad you've come to your senses. I must leave now. I have many things to do. I'll see you again tonight." He gave Antoninus a quick kiss on the lips and left.

Δ

Antoninus had rehearsed the speech he was about to give in front of the senators, but he was still a little nervous. He had ordered two *solia* to be placed in the center, one for himself and one for his husband. Both were wearing laurel wreaths and pristine togas. The legislators had awaited the arrival of their majesties for six hours and were in the worst mood possible. Hierocles took his seat immediately, while Antoninus paced the room for a few moments before speaking.

"Honorable members of the Senate," he began in a firm, contrived voice, "we are here today to discuss important matters regarding my role in government."

The senators looked at each other. Some even smiled. Was the boy going to announce his abdication? That would make the wait worthwhile.

"As you well know, a few days ago I married the man you see on my right."

Hierocles waved his hand and smiled.

"Therefore, I consider it my duty to announce an important decision for me and for Rome." He paused for a minute, as if trying to recall his words. "I have decided to name Hierocles Caesar and rightful heir to the throne."

"This is outrageous!" one of the senators shouted, rising from his seat, and raising a fist. "This man is not a citizen of Rome and does not possess the rank nor the lineage to occupy the throne."

"And he won't occupy the throne," Antoninus regretted the sound of those words. His husband wouldn't like them. "As least not as long as I live," he rectified. "But if anything should happen to me… He would immediately succeed me as emperor and Augustus."

Jeers erupted in the crowd.

"However… however," Antoninus said, gesturing the senators to maintain order, "I'm still here. I have no intention of going anywhere."

Sighs of disappointment came from the ranks.

"Dear and honorable members of the Senate," he continued, speaking over the legislators, "I have a husband, yes, I have a husband; thus I am a wife. And as you well know, in Rome it is not appropriate for a woman to deal with men's affairs. Therefore, from this moment on you will refer to me as lady, empress, or queen, both in public and private, and my husband will represent me in all matters of government, political and economic, and you will have to listen to him and respect him, as if it was me who stood on this ancestral floor."

A renewed eruption of heckles inundated the rows. Most senators got up from their seats.

Antoninus was ready to leave the *curia*, but she remembered one thing. "I also decree the freedom of my husband's mother, who is to be brought to Rome from

Anatolia, and be given the place in society that rightfully corresponds to her new status as my mother-in-law!"

She had to shout those last words, as the clamor in the room almost made her voice inaudible. She ran out of the room, frightened, followed by a smiling Hierocles, who walked leisurely, mocking the frantic old men with a repertoire of obscene and vulgar gestures.

Antoninus looked for Comazon as she left the Senate. "Comazon, send the Praetorians to put order in the room."

"Will do, Majesty," Comazon said, as he signaled his men to go inside.

"One more thing," she said, as the general was leaving. "From now on, you must protect my husband as if he were me. Promise me, Comazon."

The general's expression hardened.

"I'm sorry we haven't had the time to talk about this. Things have happened so fast."

Comazon took a hard swallow. He was struggling to hold back tears.

"I love him, Comazon. I'm sorry, but I really do. Hierocles means the world to me."

"But you had told me that your heart was not ready to love."

"It wasn't then. It is now."

Antoninus led Comazon to a place where they could talk with a little more privacy. She looked at his face as tears fell along his cheeks. She wiped them dry.

"I'm sorry. I never meant to cause you this pain. But no one can master their heart. Not even the empress of Rome. I'm sure you will find someone to suit your needs."

"But I need you," Comazon said, grabbing her hands. "There is no one else in the world for me but you."

"There are plenty of men in Rome, dear Comazon. I'm sure you'll find one to be with you in secrecy, the way you want it. And you and me will always remain close friends."

Comazon was taken aback by those words. His mind began to understand a little. In a way, it was true. Even if Antoninus loved him, they could never be together publicly, the way Antoninus was with Hierocles now. And not because of the empress, but because of him: he was not willing to pay the price.

"Now, do you promise to protect me and my husband?"

"I do, Excellency."

Δ

Back in the palace, Maesa requested an immediate private audience with Hierocles. She was sitting impatiently at the desk when the newly appointed Caesar arrived, still wearing the toga and laurel wreath on his head.

"You could have changed into simpler clothes," she said with a grim face. "I haven't forgotten where you came from."

He walked a few steps and rested his hands on a chair.

"I understand that you want to have a word with me, *domina*."

She gestured for him to take a seat.

"Until now I had refused to talk to you, but what you've done today has gone too far."

"You mean, what my wife has done today. I just sat there doing nothing."

"Don't you play the fool with me," she said, as she stood up and started pacing around the room. "This was supposed to be nothing more than one night of fun." She looked him up and down. "I'm well aware of the emperor's preferences. But I didn't know he liked to collect waste from the sewers."

"If you just asked me to come to insult me, I can tell you that—"

"There's nothing you can tell *me*, young man. I know all about your kind. You're nothing but the worst filth of Rome: a charioteer, a barbarian, a nobody who just happened to be in the right place at the right time. But I promise you this: it won't last."

"With all due respect, *domina*, that's not for you to decide. It is my wife who makes all the decisions."

"You think you're so smart, don't you? What do you know about how Rome is governed? Do you really think *he* makes all the decisions?"

"All I know is that she just appointed me Caesar in front of the Senate. That's good enough for me for now," he said, looking her in the eye. "And I'm going to play my part, whether you like it or not."

He turned to leave but looked at her one last time before opening the door.

Maesa's eyes seemed to pop out of her face. "We'll see about that!"

CHAPTER 6

THE SMELL OF ROSES

"Stephanus, mirror."

The slave swiftly approached his mistress with an oval mirror, framed in silver and inlaid with precious stones. Antoninus gazed vivaciously at her own image, fixing her elaborate, bouffant hairdo.

"There's still a few left to pluck here." The empress pointed to a spot on her face.

The slave rushed for a pair of pincers and extracted the tiny hairs.

"Ouch," Antoninus exclaimed, startling the young man. "Do it. Don't just stand there, finish it!"

When Stephanus was done, the empress admired the smoothness of her face in the mirror again.

"Now, makeup!"

Stephanus fetched a box of pigments. Antoninus applied white lead on her eyelids. Then alkanet as eyeliner. After a few moments, she continued with the base and foundation, and with a thick brush, put blush on her cheeks. She picked a red ochre lipstick, almost unknown to Roman women, but quite fashionable in the East, and applied it liberally with her little finger. She pursed her lips.

"What do you think?"

"Even Venus would be jealous, mistress."

Antoninus smiled.

"Is your husband attending the gathering?"

Antoninus's expression saddened. "I doubt it. He hates my social circle. He says he has no patience for girl talk." She brushed her face a little more. "And to be honest, I don't care."

Stephanus did not quite believe his mistress's last words. "But my queen spends so much time here lonely, I think the master should be home more often."

"Really, Stephanus?" She stopped her actions and gazed at him.

Stephanus lowered his head.

"Don't be silly and raise that head."

The slave obeyed.

"Now smile."

A faint smile appeared on his face.

"Good. Leave me now," she said, waving her hand.

As Stephanus headed for the door, Antoninus stopped him. "Your service and company are very much appreciated, Stephanus."

The slave bowed.

"And, well… it doesn't hurt that you are a eunuch. Hierocles would never have allowed an intact man to be so close to me."

"Always at your service, Empress."

When she was left alone, Antoninus regretted her last words. Stephanus was well aware of what he was; it had been heartless to remind him of it. Perhaps it had been an unconscious response after the slave's remark about her husband, which had pierced her heart a little.

He had been her closest companion since her wedding to Hierocles, two months earlier; months that, in the midst of longing, anxiety and desire, had seemed like an eternity. The first weeks had been incredibly fun, but, as much as she had tried to hold it, the original high was already gone. Caesar—as he demanded everyone call him now—was away from the palace most of the time, even in important occasions: in fact, she had almost had to force him to attend the opening ceremony of the Saturnalia with her.

Although she was not entirely fond of the lingering worship of the gods of old, Antoninus did not want to do away with the December festivities. She enjoyed the lighting of candles, the hanging of wreaths, the giving of gifts and, of course, the raving parties. A week in which Rome forgot all her rigid formalities and allowed the pressure accumulated over twelve months to dissipate was a tradition worth preserving. Maybe one day, all of this joy would go to the worship of the one god, Elagabal, but for now, the occasion would help her forget the gloom of her marriage and enjoy herself, if only a little.

A splendid sculpture of a *quadrigae* carrying Apollo and Diana, placed on top of an arch, received the numerous guests at the palace that night, the second of the Saturnalia. In the atrium—where a fountain of bright rose color gave off the scent of violets—a medley of high society people coalesced with a rabble of singers, mimes, musicians, dancers, poets, tricksters, miracle-wrights, taletellers, and jesters, all too eager to receive the bucket-loads of sesterces they expected from the invitees that night. All attendees, regardless of their status, had to find their way to their divans on their own, as slaves had the week off and were just performing minimal chores during the festivities. The patriarchs of the patrician families had taken the trouble to put on colorful dinner clothes, while their wives rocked fantastic oriental tunics and wore their hair arranged in the shape of towers or pyramids, with the primary purpose of not going unnoticed before the empress, her mother and grandmother, during the festivities.

Maesa and Soaemias—who wore respective robes of amethyst and daffodil colors, necklaces of immense pearls, and elaborate hairdos—greeted them at the entrance with kisses and holding hands. As the increasingly louder sound of conversation was overtaking the splashing of the fountain, Antoninus—whose head was adorned with a jewel-encrusted golden diadem of olive leaves—made her entrance strutting through a vestibule lit by the glow of multiple candles mounted on penis-shaped candleholders, and was received by a generous ovation.

Inside, a vast number of dishes had been laid out on a large table, from which the attendees procured their own meals and carried them to their *tricliniums*, petting along the way the tame tigers and leopards that lay tied to the marble columns. Among the food selections were stuffed artichokes, fried cod, *gustatio* salad, eggs of different birds, a variety of dried fruits and, naturally, the outlandish dishes that could only be found at Antoninus's court: sow's breasts in Libyan truffles, camel heels in sumac, nightingale and peacock tongues in cinnamon, ostrich brains, yellow pigs cooked in the Trojan fashion, sea wolves from the Baltic, sturgeons from Rhodes, fig-peckers from Samos, African snails, and, of course, the spectacular braised flamingos stuffed with fruit.

Antoninus had greeted the guests and taken her seat in the main *triclinium* when, to her surprise, Hierocles entered the hall. He sported an elaborate updo, consisting of an asymmetric front row braided wig, tied with a medallion over his forehead, and sprinkled with gold dust—with almost a whole corsage of winter blooms weaved into it—in harmonious cohesion with his blond hair and beard. He also wore a jade-colored Greek *synthesis* robe that brought out the shine of his emerald eyes and the honey-gold tone of his skin. His neck was decked with multiple chains of pure gold. All of this made Antoninus think that he might have changed his mind after all and would join the party. She made room for him beside her and tried to meet him with her eyes, but he wouldn't look her way. Hierocles looked around, displeased; he did not feel comfortable among people who considered him unworthy. A thousand knives cut through Antoninus's body when he left the room. She turned her attention back to the table and pretended to be interested in the conversation, and in eating appetizers.

After dinner, a slow but steady fall of rose petals was sprinkled over the room through revolving panels installed as a second ceiling, while the guests were drinking, chatting, and eating desserts. The sweet scent intensified with each wave.

Some tried to catch the petals as they swirled in the air. The women laughed when one fell into their drinks. "Well, we can officially call this wine a rosé," one of them said, to the laughter of her companions. Musicians played soft music in the background as the performers of the night visited each of the tables.

Comazon stood near the food table, taking a sip of his favorite wine, when a lady approached him.

"General, it's so nice to see you again."

Comazon, startled, looked to his side, and found Julia Paula, who looked extraordinarily beautiful in her colorful ball gown. A delicate floral scent emanated from her skin. She wore a long emerald necklace and pearl earrings that seemed too heavy for her small earlobes. He thought all that jewelry was excessive. Her natural features were more than enough adornment for a party.

"My lady, the pleasure is all mine."

"Don't call me Lady, General… why don't you just call me Julia instead?" she said smiling coquettishly.

While his mother and grandmother were dealing with most of the conversation, Antoninus noticed a young man whom he had not seen at the court before; he had olive skin and wore a subtle chin strap beard and a garland of roses on his head. He was gaily sipping drinks in a nearby *triclinium*, next to an elegantly dressed middle-aged lady. The empress rose from her divan, walked over to theirs and was greeted cheerfully by the lady, who offered her her seat with the excuse of fetching another drink and going to converse with Maesa and Soaemias.

"You must be new here," Antoninus said, making herself comfortable on the couch. "I haven't seen you before. What's your name?"

"My name is Aurelius Zoticus, my Lord Emperor."

"Call me not Lord, for I am a Lady," Antoninus said, giving him her hand to kiss.

Zoticus placed his lips gently on it.

"May I ask where you are visiting from?"

"From Smyrna, Empress. The lady I was talking to is my aunt. She has lived in Rome for a long time and is well acquainted with your grandmother. She told me that Maesa thought that since I was in the city, perhaps it would please Her Majesty to meet me."

As Zoticus spoke, she smelled with pleasure the scents of marjoram and mint emanating from his body. She loved that Greek men were so attentive to their personal grooming.

"It surely has," Antoninus replied in Greek. She hadn't spoken in that language in years—since she had had her last tutor—but still felt competent enough to carry a conversation in it. "So, what do you do back in Greece?"

"I'm an athlete. I participated in the Olympic Games this year."

"I can see that," Antoninus said, feeling the muscles of the young man's strong arms, ornamented in the Oriental fashion with two broad golden bands fastened above the elbow. "Are other parts of you as big as these?"

Zoticus blushed. He wasn't sure if he had understood the question correctly.

Antoninus laughed. "Just kidding. So, what else do you do when you're not training or competing?"

"Well, I'm also very good at cooking. My friends call me Cook."

"So we have a cook here! You're talking to Rome's greatest food connoisseur. What's your specialty?"

"I can prepare some heavenly stuffed dormouse."

"That's disgusting!" Antoninus said, sticking a finger in her mouth. "Come on, I'm sure you can do better than that."

"Well, I do prepare some excellent *olivarum conditurae*."

"That's better. But I'm craving something sweet. Something really…" Antoninus said, licking her lips, "sweet."

In the meantime, two athletes, wearing only loincloths, were preparing to offer guests a wrestling spectacle.

"Look!" Antoninus said to his new friend. "You're going to love this."

The men began to wrestle, and their powerful bodies, glistening with olive oil, formed a single mass, as they crunched each other's bones in an iron clinch. Roman eyes followed with delight the movement of the tremendous backs, broad thighs, and brawny arms. Antoninus took the opportunity to slip her hand under Zoticus's tunic and noticed the young man's growing arousal down there.

"See? I told you you'd like it."

Comazon's blood boiled as he witnessed Antoninus's display of affection for the stranger. He had to dissimulate, not wanting Julia Paula to notice his distress.

"So, is your father here too, Julia?"

"Yes, he's sitting over there," she said, pointing to one of the *tricliniums*.

Comazon turned and met Julius Paulus's gaze. Both men nodded. Julia accidentally glanced at Antoninus and Zoticus and couldn't hide her disgust. She looked at Comazon.

"There's the emperor, with what he always wanted… a man. It's obvious that even without his 'husband', he always finds ways to entertain himself."

Comazon was not amused by these comments.

"So," Julia said, holding onto his muscular arm, "you mentioned in our house that you don't have a wife. Why is it so, General?"

Comazon's hand started shaking. He put his goblet on a table, fearful of spilling the wine. He was about to come up with something when Antoninus lay on Zoticus's chest, and a lump formed in his throat. At that moment, one of the guards approached him. Comazon thanked the gods for the intervention.

"General, I'm sorry to interrupt, but I think you should know that Caesar is not in the palace. He did not say where he went, but we fear for his safety."

"Thank you for letting me know, Sergius. I must go find him right away." He carefully disengaged from Julia's grip and excused himself.

Julia, speechless, had no choice but to return to her father's *triclinium*.

After an evening of good food and excellent brews, away from the pedantry and pretensions of the upper class, Hierocles found himself walking aimlessly through the busy streets of Rome. Although many of them were lit with torches and had a festive look about them from the wreaths and gilded ornaments hanging on walls and doors, most of the city remained dark and gloomy, and to wander about was to risk one's life. Regardless, he was taking a walk to let the cold night air clear his thoughts. For the same reason, he hadn't taken any of the Praetorian guards with him; he needed to ruminate on everything that had been happening in his life for the past two months.

His luck at the circus was unbelievable. Since that day, he had gotten everything he ever wanted and more. It couldn't be that easy. It just couldn't be. He had to remind himself that his new life was not a dream, that he was now Caesar, heir to the throne, however chimerical it might be to reach it. His wife was much younger than he was, so it was highly unlikely that he would ever succeed her as emperor of Rome.

That thought took him to Antoninus, his stupid little wife. Did he love her? No, he just couldn't convince himself of that. Had he loved her at least in the beginning? He thought about it for a moment. Sure, the first weeks had been fun: lots of sex, drinking, and entertainment; just what he cherished most in life. But afterward... things had become complicated. She demanded so much of his time that he now felt suffocated. He still wanted to live his own life, do the things he liked, and not just be a companion for the empress. He tried to talk to her about it, but she just wouldn't listen. She always thought she knew what was best for them.

Then came his responsibilities as Caesar. Not that he really cared, but he did want to exercise his power in some way. He had to keep a tight grip on those senators, even if he didn't understand one iota of what they discussed in their sessions. But the empress took no interest in his work or his ambitions; she only wanted him by her side. Making love to her day and night. It made him sick. The issue was that they were spending too much time together; how can passion be maintained that way? He wanted to free himself a bit, but that had only made her bitter. She would claim that he didn't love her as before, and then he had to insist, to swear that nothing had changed. And she would constantly bring back every little offense she had perceived from him.

One time she said something that had really frightened him: "Hierocles, darling, why don't we forget everything and run away to the desert together? Just you and me and a sky full of stars? Make love outdoors in the cool of the night?" The stupid things that someone in love can say.

In the middle of these thoughts, he found himself walking into a dead-end alley, dark as a wolf's mouth. He hurried to get out of it, but before he reached the street, he was pulled by a pair of chunky hands back into the darkness.

"Hello, Hierocles. It's been a long time," a deep, harsh voice said.

Antoninus had not left Zoticus's company for the rest of the evening. In the *triclinium* the two of them remained alone, as the other diners—understanding their desire for privacy—had left with other guests. The music had changed to a lively burst of zithers, lutes, Armenian cymbals, Egyptian sistra, trumpets and horns. Beautiful boys sprinkled the feet of the guests with perfumed oils, while others fanned them with bunches of ostrich feathers attached to golden wires. The rose petals falling from the revolving ceiling had formed a sort of pool that covered the invitees up to the waist.

"The slaves really got it going with the petals," Zoticus said.

"Now, watch this." She took him by the hand and led him up the stairs to a gap between the false ceiling and the real one.

She signaled to Stephanus, who instructed the slaves to pull golden ropes to make the false ceiling collapse, causing a torrent of petals to pour down all at once on the crowd. Men shouted expletives while women shrieked in terror and confusion. Most were gagging and coughing, suffocated by the intense aroma. Soon, the invitees were trying to escape the room, but all but one of the exits had been closed. Antoninus and Zoticus laughed to tears as the guests tried to find their way through the chaos and stepped on each other's feet or bumped into furniture.

After the flowery "slaying," Antoninus led Zoticus down a long corridor, dimly lit by candlelight and aromatized by Indian and Persian incense sticks. They reached her room and, as soon as they stepped through the door, she pinned him to a wall and kissed him. Unsure of what to do, he at first kept his mouth shut, but she bit his lips and forced her tongue into his mouth. She dragged him toward the bed and pushed him onto it. Then she jumped on him, kissing him more ardently, and this time— though somewhat shyly—he reciprocated the kisses. She untied his belt and removed his robe, exposing his smooth, muscular torso. She punched his chiseled abs, but it had no effect on him.

"Punch harder," he said, grinning.

Antoninus moved down his body removing the *subligaculum*, and then a huge uncircumcised, slightly curved cock sprang in her face and sprayed it with precum. She immediately took the meat into her mouth like a hungry bird, letting the head touch the inside of her cheek. She sucked it all the way to the base, having a hard time accommodating the huge Greek member inside her mouth and throat. Zoticus was well aware of the ways of the men of his homeland, but he had not imagined the pleasure of such activities to be so intense.

She asked him to get up as she took off her dress, undid her hairdo, and bent over—face down leaning against the side of the bed—ass up, ready to take him. His manhood was already wet with saliva and precum and it was easy for him to slide it into the sloppy hole. Antoninus moaned in pleasure. Zoticus gave in to his manly instincts and continued to thrust himself into her, enjoying the pressure and warmth of the imperial hole. After a few moments, she lay on her back so he could fuck her while she admired and caressed his athletic body. He had a smile to die for, which made her cock moist.

When he felt his seed was about to burst, he slowed his pace and leaned in to kiss her with a soft, long, passionate kiss, biting their lips, touching the tips of their tongues, breathing into each other's mouths. He moved down her neck, rubbed his incipient beard on her face and caressed her chest, until the moment came when he could control himself no longer. He cummed abundantly, filling Antoninus's hole. Some semen dripped onto the carpeted floor and sheets as he pulled his cock out. He took a shaky breath and closed his eyes, letting his hands rest on the empress's legs as the flaming arrows of ecstasy set his mind on fire.

Three men carrying torches stood behind, while Hierocles was pushed against a wall and lifted a few inches above the ground by the stranger.

"Nice to see you again, my friend," the man said. The stench of his breath pinched Hierocles's nostrils like a dagger and made him close his eyes and jerk his head to the side.

When he could open his eyes, he recognized the face in the torchlight—Celer, a charioteer from the red team, who had been his main rival during his time at the circus.

"What the fuck are you doing? Let me go immediately! You're touching Caesar!"

The men laughed. "Caesar, Caesar!"

"Caesar, my balls!" Celer roared. "It looks like the pretty boy has forgotten very quickly where he came from."

"What's that thing on your head anyway?" another said. "Did your feminine ideas finally 'take root'?"

The other men guffawed.

"What do you want?" Hierocles said with fear in his eyes.

"We want to know why you haven't responded to our messages."

"I don't know what you're talking about."

"Yes, you do. But maybe 'Caesar' no longer has time for his friends."

"We were never friends, idiot."

"It's never too late, don't you think?"

"There's nothing I can do for you. The empress is the one who makes all the decisions regarding the conditions and pay in the circus."

"You mean your little… 'wife'?"

The men fell about laughing.

"Yes, the empress! My wife! Now let me go or you will regret it, motherfucker."

Celer put him down and put his hand on the wall to prevent him from running away. "It looks like he's not willing to cooperate, fellas. What should we do with him?"

"Cut his throat! Slit his guts!" the men exclaimed.

"Wait. Wait! Alright. Let's make a deal. What exactly do you want?"

"We want to be free from slavery. And we want to be citizens."

"There's a big difference between freedmen and citizens. I'm afraid that such a big leap is not possible."

"It was possible for you."

"But you don't have my attributes."

"You mean we couldn't fuck that slut every night? Hell, we can. We can satisfy her better than you do, boy."

"You know why his name is Antoninus? Because he can fit *a ton* in his *anus*!" another said, to the laughter of the thugs.

"It's not about sex, it's about love!" Hierocles replied.

"Did you hear that, guys? Now he talks about love!" Celer said.

The men laughed themselves to tears, clutching their bellies, and stomping the ground. One laughed so hard he began to retch.

"Fucking kill him now," another said. "I would very much like to see his guts drained on the floor tonight."

"What the fuck is going on here?" a strong voice behind them shouted.

Hierocles turned to look and there was Comazon, accompanied by a couple of Praetorians.

"Who the fuck are you?" Celer asked.

Comazon grabbed him by the collar of his tunic. "You know very well who I am. Now, get the fuck out of here, before we slit your throats like goats!"

Celer raised his hands and Comazon released him.

"Alright, alright, *domine*," he said to Comazon. "We will go now. But you," he said, facing Hierocles, "you are not a man if you refuse to race against us in the circus!"

"I ain't a charioteer no more, *stultus*!"

"Once a charioteer, always a charioteer. You're no Caesar if you can't be a man first!" he shouted, pointing at him. He signaled his men to leave.

Comazon ordered his guards to return to the street and leave him alone with Caesar. He grabbed him by the neck with a force that made the veins pop out of his temples and pinned him against the wall.

"What do you think you are doing here?"

"I don't have to answer to no public officer. Besides, why are you here? Were you following me? Who authorized you to do that?"

"Unfortunately," Comazon said with an intimidating grunt, "your life is a matter of state security. Otherwise, rest assured, I would have let you die. I could not care less if your guts get spattered in a sewer."

"Well, my wife sure cares about me. She sent you here to follow me, am I right?"

Comazon's face reddened. He let go of his neck, grabbed him by the balls and squeezed them hard.

"Come on, Comazon, squeeze harder! I don't even feel you!"

Comazon tightened the grip on the ox balls.

"I'm just starting to feel it," Hierocles lied. In reality his balls were about to burst. "Your hands are kind of weak for a soldier."

Comazon let go of the grip. He could have gelded the motherfucker right there, but his soldierly prudence brought him back to his senses.

"Thank you," Hierocles said, straightening his clothes. "Now, are you going to send your men to escort me back home? I'm kind of tired."

The lovers, totally exhausted, had been in bed for a while, Antoninus laying her head on Zoticus's sweaty chest. After a while she rose, sitting with her back against the headboard.

"Sit next to me, please."

Zoticus sat up next to her, their arms touching.

"Is this your first time?"

He nodded.

"How old are you?"

"Twenty-six."

"Twenty-six years old and you've never been with a woman before?"

"That's right, my queen. We don't have much time for love at the gymnasium."

Antoninus was silent for a minute. "You must be asking yourself why I brought you here in such a hurry."

"I'm no one to question my empress," Zoticus said, turning slightly, and caressing the empress's loose hair.

"You're so sweet, Zoticus… so different from my husband."

"Does Caesar not treat you right, my Lady?"

"He used to. He was great in the beginning, I thought he really loved me, but now…"

Zoticus smiled with his eyes.

"Now he's always busy with politics: meetings, dinners, days and nights out; I hardly see him anymore."

"It must not be an easy thing to run the empire. I am sure he does nothing more than what his obligations demand."

"Yes, but still… it feels wrong. I put him there. I made him Caesar. He wanted me to be his wife, and I… well, I did want to live my life as what I've always been at heart, a female… I wanted to run the house, supervise the kitchen, make sure everything is nice and tidy for when he comes home…"

"But it's not enough?"

"No, it's not enough." Antoninus's face saddened. "I just… I need a friend, you know? I need someone who really understands me… Ever since I left Emesa, things have been so… overwhelming… I feel like I have no one to talk to. My mother doesn't understand me, my grandmother is always thinking about power and money, and I… I'm always so lonely. You see, when he makes love to me, I have the feeling that his mind is somewhere else, that it's only his body that I have in the room with me, that I don't have his heart…"

She hugged him. Tears ran from her eyes. They cuddled for a long while. He didn't try to stop her sobbing; he simply let her feelings flow unrestrained. She rose again and wiped away her tears.

"Please don't cry, my lady… It breaks my heart to see you cry…" he said, finally.

"I'm sorry, I'm sorry, I'm just so emotional right now… Thank you for being here… Thank you…"

"You don't have to thank me for loving you," Zoticus said and offered her his mouth. They merged once more in the most heavenly kiss.

On the way home, Hierocles remembered the party at the palace and guessed that it was probably not over yet. It was about to dawn, but he knew his wife's tendency to stay up until the first hours of daylight. He didn't want to go home. He had a better idea.

The Praetorians following at a distance noticed Caesar's change in course. Comazon had long since left the scene, leaving them in charge of his security. They watched him walk toward a house of ill repute and discussed among themselves what to do.

"What do you think he went there to do?" one of them said.

"Don't be a fool. Isn't it obvious?" another said, making obscene gestures with his fingers.

The other men laughed.

When Hierocles entered the house, Lucretia, an overweight woman wearing excessive makeup, stood to greet the leader of the world.

"Caesar! Welcome! We hadn't had the pleasure of seeing you around lately… Not since your wedding. Congratulations, by the way."

Hierocles waved her off. "Is Lucia here?"

"Yes. She's ready in her room. She hasn't had any clients tonight, so she'll be excited to see you."

Hierocles walked into the place. The excess of perfume in the air made him feel nauseated. He opened the curtains of Lucia's room and found her lying on the bed filing her nails, naked to the waist, wearing only copious beaded necklaces, cheap earrings, and a long red wig with a few braids.

"Oh! By all the gods! Hierocles! I thought you forgotten me." She jumped into his arms and showered his face with kisses.

He took her mouth, thrusting his tongue down her throat, choking her words, and grabbing the generous tits with his manly hands. It has been a while since he had kissed a woman, and her lips felt so good. She pulled him down onto the bed and removed his tunic, exposing his masculine torso. She leaned down to his crotch, untying his *subligaculum*.

"Full service, I believe, am I right… Caesar?" she hesitated as she said his new name.

He nodded with a smile. How good to have a woman's lips going down his shaft. Sure, it had been great to fuck Antoninus for a while, but he had grown tired of it. The other half of his manhood clamored to lie down with a woman. He was sick of fucking ass. He wanted pussy this time.

Once she got him all prepped, she made him lie down on the bed, and sat on the huge erect cock, making him shiver from the first instant. She locked hands with him and moved up and down. He grunted and growled with pleasure. Then he took control and fucked her aggressively. He had to get off from all the unpleasant emotions of that night. His balls still ached after Comazon's tight grip. He smiled, though; if anything, that would just make the sensation of cumming more intense.

Near Comazon's house, a litter guarded by four men waited in the dark. After eternal hours, one of the men alerted the person inside that someone was arriving. Julia Paula slipped through a small opening in the curtains. Comazon. But he was not alone.

The tall general stumbled, and the person next to him kept him from falling. The pair approached the door, and Comazon reached for the key as his companion offered their mouth. The general did not refuse. The torchlight that illuminated the porch showed her the truth. The person joining the general was a man. A young man, nevertheless, but undoubtedly a member of the male sex.

Horrified and with tears in her eyes, she slammed the curtains shut. The stunned carriers lifted the litter to take her back home. She had paid a large sum to be taken out in the darkness to give herself to the man of her dreams, only to find out once and for all why he was not the marrying kind.

Δ

The next day, once the sun had fully risen in the sky, Hierocles arrived at the palace and found his wife sleeping peacefully. A sweet scent of sex wafted in the air; he sniffed, confused, but decided that it must be his own smell after the wonderful night he had just spent in the brothel. He was tired but knew there was no time to sleep. Antoninus sensed him and woke up. Hierocles sat beside her.

"Oh, you're finally here. Where have you been all night?" Antoninus said, yawning and stretching her arms.

"Here and there. How was the party?"

"Fun. But I'm sure the details would bore you."

"You're right about that."

They remained silent for a while.

"There's something I want to tell you," Hierocles said.

Antoninus rose. "What is it?"

"I want to race again. You know, in the circus."

"What? Caesar can't take part in the entertainment of the plebs."

"Commodus used to fight gladiators, right? I don't see why I couldn't drive a chariot. I miss it."

"You can drive as much as you want on the streets. In fact, you're the only one allowed to."

"It's not the same. I miss the thrill, the danger, the rush… Things have become a bit boring since I became Caesar."

"Since you became, or since *I made you* Caesar?"

"It's the same thing, isn't it?"

Antoninus stroked his arms. Hierocles looked away.

"And what color do you want to wear? Pink?"

"No! Purple—the color of royalty."

"And my favorite color too! I'll have a special tunic made for you. With golden embroidery and all."

"Thanks, darling."

"Just thanks?"

Hierocles leaned down and kissed her lips.

"I will bathe now. I have an assembly with the senators this afternoon. I don't want them to see me in shaggy clothes."

And you don't want them to smell you, either, thought Antoninus. Hierocles had a funny smell this morning. Not just sweat, at least not just his sweat. Had he been playing last night? *That wouldn't surprise me*, she thought. Especially since she had been doing the same thing. Her mind wandered back to Zoticus. Where would he be right now? Would he think of her?

"Wait," Antoninus said, getting out of bed. "I had this made for you. Isn't it lovely?" She showed him a man-sized, lush dark green *stola*. "Do you like it? Try it on after your bath."

"A dress for me? What's wrong with you?"

"Why not? There are temples in the East where Hercules is worshipped in female dress. You could cause a commotion on the streets, more than you already do."

Hierocles grimaced. "Hell no. I'll never wear a dress. Now, if you'll excuse me…"

A nude Hierocles dipped his toe in the water of the baths. "It's cold, damn it! The water is fucking cold!"

A frightened slave ran to him. "I'm sorry Caesar; we didn't expect you to use the baths this morning and the hypocaust was not lit—"

"Who are you, fucking imbeciles, to decide when or if I take a bath. The bath water must be warm at… all… times!"

"Yes, Caesar, it won't happen again," the slave said, bowing nervously.

"By Jupiter's cock, I will have to go to the Senate like this!" he said looking at himself. "At least go fetch me a fresh toga. Move!"

Later, Hierocles arrived at the Senate in his chariot. His pristine toga did little to mask the filthiness of his body, and he was perfectly self-conscious of his foul body odor. The laurel wreath he had donned in haste could not entirely conceal his untidy, greasy hair either. Though his shagginess made him a little uncomfortable, he thought it would show those slaves in togas how much he despised their institution, and especially, an extraordinary session held during the Saturnalia. He nodded to Comazon and the guards, who were posted outside the building, and climbed the steep staircase with contrived confidence.

The senators—Maesa among them—were chatting when he arrived, but a deep silence ensued as he made his way to the throne. He sat down and looked at them with a stony face.

"Highness," one of the senators said, "we have convened this extraordinary assembly to discuss some of the most burdensome problems facing the empire at the moment, which we must resolve before the new year. We request your approval to start the session."

Hierocles nodded impassibly.

"The first point to be discussed today is the economy—"

"First," Hierocles said, "I would like to ask the honorable *Augusta* to leave this house. These are important matters that concern only men."

Hierocles had been thinking about this move since his initial meeting with Maesa, but finally felt bold enough to carry it out. He knew well that his only leverage against the matriarch was his gender. By appealing to the misogyny of many of the senators, he hoped to get rid of her influence, and perhaps gain some sympathy.

Maesa was so shocked by the request that she didn't even protest. She wasn't going to add to her humiliation by futilely begging to stay. She would settle matters later. She rose and left the room with a dignified tramp.

"As your Highness is aware of," the senator continued, "commerce has not yet recovered from the turmoil that followed the unjust assassination of our emperor Caracalla. Inflation has ruined the welfare of many families throughout the empire. The currency has lost much of its purchasing power since then."

"Why don't they mix gold with copper and issue more currency then. That will give the people more means to pay for things and stimulate the market."

A few chuckles came from the senatorial stands.

"But Excellency," the speaker said in a trembling voice, "that would only bring… more inflation, as you surely know…"

The chuckles turned to laughter.

"If you already knew that, then why did you ask the question?" Hierocles barked.

"Sorry Highness, but I hadn't asked the question yet… The question is… well… what to do about it?"

"Stop being a smartass, Senator. You people think I'm an idiot, but I assure you I'm not. I have already given my answer."

"Highness, but I'm afraid that your answer—"

"My answer is the answer of Caesar, not that of an economist. If you can't do your own job, maybe you should be replaced by more capable people."

"May I bring up the second topic, Caesar?" the speaker said with hesitation.

"You may."

"The Goths have invaded parts of the Dacia, Moesia and Dalmatia, Excellency. We suggest the dispatch of at least ten legions—"

"No! The empress wants peace. She has expressed it clearly. We will send an ambassador to reason with them."

"Reason?" another senator said, springing from his seat. "Does Caesar really think that it is possible to reason with barbarians."

"Perhaps His Excellency thinks so because he is one of them," a senator said from his seat, in a not so quiet voice.

Hierocles sat still for a moment, then placed his right leg on the armrest of the throne. He opened up his toga and lifted his tunic, under which there was no *subligaculum*. Loud gasps filled the *curia*. Some senators stared open-mouthed at the sheer size of his endowment, as he let his bull-sized dick and balls rest on the seat, while others looked away in disgust. He remained in that position for an uncomfortable length of time, then rubbed his balls, stood up and walked toward the young senator who had dared to call out his origin. With a quick movement, Hierocles covered the senator's mouth and nose with his man-smelling hand. He grabbed the back of his neck with the other hand and forced him to take a deep sniff. The senator struggled, and after a while Hierocles eased his grip; the senator sprang and hurried out the room, gasping for air amid violent coughing and retching. Vomiting was heard a few moments later. Hierocles looked fiercely at the assembly.

"These balls rule in my bed," he vociferated, pointing to his crotch, "and these balls rule in Rome too!"

There was a deadly silence for a moment, until a few senators began to shout profanities. The whole assembly soon erupted in clamor against the inexperienced ruler. Hierocles tramped for the exit.

"Comazon! Comazon!" he shouted into the air.

The prefect appeared.

"Put order in the room. The senators are a bit rowdy today."

More Praetorians arrived and subdued the senators who threatened to attack Caesar, who proceeded to a room in the back. Comazon followed him.

"What did you do over there?" Comazon yelled behind him.

Hierocles turned around. "I ordered you to put order in the room."

"And I demand to know what happened."

"That's none of your business, Prefect. Do as you're told."

"I will not act until I receive an explanation."

Hierocles stood in front of the general. He looked up into his turquoise eyes and saw fire in them, but not the kind of fire to make him afraid. He rose up on his toes, leaned toward him, and stole a little kiss.

Comazon's stomach turned and his blood boiled. What had that bastard just done?

Hierocles smiled. "Do your job, General." He walked gaily out of the room.

In the palace, Antoninus paced anxiously in circles in front of the throne. Knocks came from the door.

"Yes?"

The doors opened. A short young man appeared and bowed.

"Excellency, Sura, the man you requested has arrived."

"Let him in."

An old man, wearing a somewhat threadbare tunic, entered the hall and bowed to the empress. He was the main judge of the *Circus Maximus*; the man who had the last word in a race if the outcome it was disputed and, most of all, the one who watched over its legality.

"It is an honor for me to appear before the mighty empress of Rome. To what do I owe the privilege?" the man said in a tone of adulation.

"I want a race organized for next week."

"For next week? May I ask what the occasion is, *Augusta*? I'm not aware of a festival—"

"The occasion is that it is my wish that a chariot race be held. With all formality. Twelve chariots, as is customary. Well, thirteen, actually."

"Thirteen? But *domina*, there are only twelve stalls in the field…"

"Here's the thing, Sura. This race is to celebrate Caesar, my husband. He will compete as an independent charioteer, with colors of his own. Twelve or thirteen chariots, I don't really care. I'll let you solve that part. But I do want drivers representing each team, is that clear?"

The man bowed. "I will do everything within my power to organize the race expeditiously, Highness."

Antoninus dismissed him.

"One more thing," Antoninus said, as Sura was leaving.

The man turned around.

"My husband really wants to win that race."

Sura's eyes widened and a panicked expression appeared on his face. He took a hard swallow. "Understood, *Augusta*," he said in a faint voice.

Δ

A distraught Maesa paced nervously inside her quarters. She put a hand to her chest as she heard a knock on the door.

"*Domina*, General Comazon is here. He said you wanted to talk to him," a slave said.

"Let him in," Maesa said, almost breathlessly.

Comazon nodded, hand on heart, as he entered the room, where he had never been.

"Did you see how that brute expelled me from the Senate meeting?"

"Yes, *domina*, I am aware of what happened."

"And you won't do anything about it?"

"I do not know what I can do, other than restore order."

"I had no idea he would go this far. It's one thing to entertain the emperor in bed, and another to pretend to rule the empire."

"It is the emperor who put him in that place. But I honestly do not see how he can last. The senators are furious. You may not know yet, but his actions in the room after you left… were little short of indescribable."

"What did he do?"

Comazon told her how he had "subdued" one of the senators. Maesa put her hand to her mouth in shock.

"So this is what the government of Rome has come to? By Elagabal, we must do something, Comazon, we have to get rid of that man."

"I have been thinking about it, and perhaps it is best to let things fall under their own weight. The emperor has just told me that he wants to organize a chariot race for Hierocles. I know for a fact that there will be contestants there who hate him to death. I would not be surprised if they have conspired to…"

"Kill him?"

"Yes, *domina*."

A smile peeked over Maesa's lips. "Thank you for the news, dear General. It is always a pleasure to speak with you. I'll take your advice. This race will sure be fun to attend."

Δ

The day of the competition arrived. The people of Rome couldn't have been more delighted with the celebration of another race. The last one had taken place not so long ago, when the emperor was still married to that vestal woman, but this one came as a surprise because it was not customary to hold races after the Saturnalia, when preparations were already underway for the New Year's celebrations in the Temple of Janus. Things had changed radically: not only had the worship of the Roman gods declined due to the new cult of Elagabal, professed by more people with each passing day, but also the emperor—or rather, empress—had gotten married again, and this time to a man; a man who was in charge of all governmental affairs and who—despite the fierce opposition of the Senate—had taken the title of Caesar.

The empress, wearing a brand-new purple silk tunic and a bejeweled gilded tiara, emerged in the imperial box of the *Circus Maximus* followed, as usual, by her mother and grandmother, and took a seat amid wild ovations. This time, however, dressed in white, and wearing gold earrings and eye liner, stood beside her none other than her new acquaintance, the young Greek visitor.

Comazon had also joined the occasion and sat next to Maesa, who was in a spectacular mood. "Who is that young man accompanying the emperor?" he asked her.

"That boy? He's Zoticus, his new… 'friend'…" she said with a chuckle. "Haven't you met him yet?"

Comazon now remembered the boy from the palace party. He didn't like her emphasis on the word "friend."

"No, *domina*," he lied. "Never seen him before. He looks like a sturdy youth."

"He certainly is. He's an athlete from Greece and competed in the Olympics this year. I'm good friends with his aunt."

A Greek. That explained what Comazon had seen that night. Knowing of the ways of those men, he didn't want him anywhere near Antoninus. He turned his attention to the field, where the parade had just begun.

Maesa, meanwhile, took another squint at the spectacular young man. What a brilliant move to ask the young man's aunt to take him to the Saturnalia ball. He was just what she needed to slacken the amorous grip Hierocles exercised over her grandson, especially now that the Carian had had the nerve to throw her out of the Senate. The best way to get rid of Hierocles—in the event that he survived the race—was by providing Antoninus with the attentions of another beautiful young man. And one with some class, this time, by Elagabal!

The richly decorated chariot of Sura, the *editor,* was the first to appear on the field. As it passed in front of the imperial box, he bowed to the empress, who nodded in acknowledgement, while whispering something in Zoticus's ear.

In the stable, the charioteers were supervising the final preparations of their cars, when a slave announced that the drawing of lots to determine the starting positions was about to take place. Celer and the other competitors had already gathered in the center of the open space. It had been agreed that it would be a twelve-chariot race, with the greens giving up a position for Caesar, since he used to belong to their team. Hierocles was the last to arrive, wearing his royal purple and gold tunic and Caracalla's cloak over it, walking carefully so as not to stain his fine sandals too much with mud and manure.

"Caesar is finally honoring us with his presence," Celer said with a sarcastic bow.

"Indeed," Hierocles said, ignoring the gesture. "We may now begin the drawing of lots."

The main judge brought a vessel containing clay tablets. "As Caesar and ruler of Rome, Your Excellency has the honor of drawing first," he said, bowing before Hierocles.

Hierocles looked at his competitors with disdain and drew a tablet. He showed it to the judge without looking at it.

"Four," the judge said and quickly dumped it in another vessel, full of other tablets.

Hierocles smiled. So, Antoninus had done her part. That was the best position, right in the middle of the track.

The next man to draw was Celer. He got the number eight.

"You will die," he grunted as he walked past Hierocles, giving him a hostile look.

Hierocles blanched. He had to be careful. The little wife could have arranged everything, but out in the field anything could happen. This race was no joke.

"He cheated, that's for sure," another competitor whispered to Celer.

"No need to complain," Celer said. "He's a loser. I've beat him before, and today it won't be any different."

Gordius, still the coach of the green team, approached Hierocles. "Good luck, Caesar."

Hierocles looked at him while adjusting his rings. "Thank you," he said, absentmindedly.

Gordius drew near him and tried to kiss him on the cheek.

"Not now," Hierocles said, pushing him away, and looking in all directions. He walked to his chariot.

Once all the tablets had been drawn, the slaves helped the charioteers lead the horses to the brightly painted stall gates. The horses pawed the ground between loud neighing and snorting, their breath forming misty clouds on their noses. In the erroneous belief that it would prevent the horses from trampling over them in the event of a fall, several charioteers had smeared themselves with dung. Hierocles had never done so, and never would, especially on an occasion like this, when he was to shine in all his glory.

In the field, slaves worked assiduously leveling the sand while the judges were taking their positions. The *erectors* set up the traditional seven stone eggs and seven dolphins. Excitement ran through the crowd. The air was sparkling, as if Jupiter had struck the stands with a bolt of lightning. But it was all an illusion; Jupiter ruled no longer in Rome. His place had been taken by Elagabal.

In the imperial box, Antoninus and Zoticus were enjoying a snack of olives, fruit, and roasted pine nuts, which they stuffed gaily in each other's mouth. To eat in the circus was inappropriate for upper-class Romans, so Maesa tried to concentrate on the parade and ignore the tomfoolery around her. Comazon was also doing his best to avert his gaze. His feelings were hurt. The emperor, however, had every right to entertain guests as he wished. Who was this Zoticus, anyway? Just a visitor who would soon leave. No one to worry about. Another thought crept furtively into Comazon's mind. A vicious, piercing, electrifying thought. He licked his lips, remembering the softness of other lips that had dared to touch his… *No!*

Trumpets came to rescue him from his thoughts as they loudly announced the start of the race. All eyes turned to the stalls. The charioteers each climbed into their cars amid the violent neighing of the horses. The slaves took their positions at the side of the track, ready to remove the wreckage of any fallen chariots and drag the injured for medical attention between laps. Sura, the *editor*, waived a white handkerchief in the air, looking for the empress with his eyes. Antoninus nodded and Sura released the handkerchief. The judges gave a signal, and the stall traps were flung open. The vehicles raced down the tracks, fighting for a better position from the start. Hierocles whipped his horses and immediately took the lead. The crowd went wild.

"Caesar is first!" an excited Zoticus exclaimed to Antoninus, who was more concerned with feeding her guest with grapes than with what was happening on the track.

"Yes," Antoninus said, without ceasing to admire the young man's face. She assiduously fixed his hair, which had been messed up by a sudden gust of wind. "He's the best, darling. He will win."

Celer, starting from position eight, had a much more difficult task than his hated opponent. Living up to the meaning of his name, he accelerated aggressively and managed to outrun two other chariots. He was now two positions behind Caesar. He had participated in many races and had been cheated before, so this scenario was not new to him. He knew that Gordius's protégé was nothing more than an apprentice, and that day he would show him what a real charioteer was. He couldn't wait to humiliate him in front of the entire city of Rome. If conditions were right, he would also make sure he didn't make it out alive.

The spin of a dolphin signaled the end of the first lap, and both Hierocles and Celer maneuvered to avoid impact with the fallen chariots on the track. It seemed as if the slaves were too slow doing their job. Hierocles glanced around the stands and basked in the wild adoration of the crowd. No one dared cheer for anyone other than the one-man purple team that day.

Two more drivers outflanked Celer as he lost speed while avoiding the fallen cars. A few other chariots crashed and fell. The teams had sent their less experienced charioteers to the race because they intuited the empress's wishes and didn't want to risk losing their best men in a race lost by decree. However, these young drivers were hungry for recognition and, with hatred and jealousy for Caesar burning in their chests, they were taking unnecessary risks trying to catch up with him.

Antoninus gazed at the racecourse, but her mind was somewhere else. She had locked hands with Zoticus, and from time to time she turned her head to revel in his boyish beauty. The love of her life—or so she had thought so far—

was running that race, risking his life for his honor, but somehow she didn't care about the outcome. Everything had been arranged, so there was really nothing to be excited about. She had a different, special feeling that day. In the few days since they had met, she had developed real feelings for that Greek boy. He was totally different from her husband: maybe not as handsome, surely more athletic, but the physique wasn't all that matter to her. It was the way he treated her. With Zoticus she truly felt like a lady, even though it had been Hierocles who had led her into a more feminine role. To Hierocles she was a wife, but with Zoticus she could be a girl and indulge in all the girliness she wanted without fear of being ridiculed or criticized. Zoticus was about the same age as her husband, but his spirit was much younger. Yes, he made her feel very comfortable. *If he could only stay longer…*

On the sixth lap, Celer was back in fourth position, just behind one green car and one blue, with Hierocles still leading the race. A strange series of jerky movements by the green charioteer—as if protecting Hierocles—caught his attention. *Traitor.* Indeed, although Caesar knew he had the support of his powerful wife, he had also convinced his former colleagues—with monetary benefits—to form a guard in his favor against Celer.

The blue car accelerated, chasing Hierocles before the end of the sixth lap. Caesar's green escort steered his car to block his opponent's path. The blue charioteer was undeterred and continued his pursuit. At the end of the last lap, his horses got too close to the central column and his chariot crashed spectacularly, debris flying through the air. Pieces of wood and metal hit the driver of the Greens, whose car also crashed and was left in pieces on the field. A huge gasp came from the crowd, followed by the loudest cheers. Only two charioteers remained at the head of the race, Celer and Hierocles.

Hierocles passed by the imperial box with more than thirty paces ahead of his red pursuer. He gritted his teeth and lashed the whip furiously, determined not to lose by overconfidence a race that had been fixed from the start. All he had to do was keep up the pace and make sure he circumvented any remains he might find in his path.

Celer, on the contrary, had to increase speed considerably if he wanted to reach Hierocles. An opportunity came. The slaves were removing the remains of one of the broken cars, so Hierocles had to decelerate, steering slightly toward the center of the loop. He would run to the outer edge of the track and force Caesar against the center wall to slow him further. He calculated that by the time he reached that position, the slaves would have removed the debris. His horses were breathing hard amid a jumble of mucus and saliva, blood gushing from the animals' backs under his whips. As he neared the crash site, he watched in astonishment how the slaves ran off the track, leaving the pieces of wood and metal behind. With no time to brake or change direction, he darted uncontrollably against the pile of debris and the impact sent his body flying off the seat with such momentum that he landed in front of his horses, which trampled him mercilessly, turning his body into a pulpy mess.

Hierocles crossed the final line victorious, to the ecstatic cheers of the crowd.

"He won! He won!" Zoticus exclaimed, thrilled to tears.

"Indeed," Antoninus said, clapping graciously but with little emotion. He took Zoticus by the hand. "Come on, dear. The show is over. Let's go back to the palace."

In the stalls, Hierocles was being congratulated by Gordius—whose kiss was not rejected this time—the other charioteers and several of his friends. A man stood behind him, with a martial bearing that silenced all present. Hierocles turned around.

"So, here you are, my friend," he said, welcoming Comazon with an unrequited hug. "I hope you enjoyed the race."

Comazon signaled everyone to leave. "You cheated, did you not?"

"Do you really think so little of my abilities?"

"Do not lie."

"It was my wife," Hierocles said with a grin. "She wouldn't have stood to see me lose, so she had to make sure… But I would have won anyway, so it doesn't really matter."

"A man died."

"Several men died. It's part of the game. But I guess you mean that dirtbag, Celer. He ran against the broken chariots; he got what he sought."

"Did you order the slaves to clean the track just for you?"

"You have a very active mind, my dear *domine*," Hierocles said, poking Comazon's breastplate. "You should put it to use to protect the empress… and me."

Comazon leaned toward him, grabbing him by the wrists. He pushed him against one of his horses, which whined loudly.

"I am getting tired of your games," Comazon growled. "This race was supposed to be to salvage your honor, but I see that you have no honor to save."

The bodies of the two men got close to one another. Close enough to give each an erection.

"Get off me," Hierocles said, faking to struggle. "I won't stand your harassment any longer, General. I may have to talk to my wife about having you removed. A man with such a nasty temperament is unfit for your office."

"If I am gone," Comazon muttered, touching Hierocles's nose with his, "you will be gone too. Only my presence sustains this government. Get that into your head." With a jerk, he let go of Hierocles, who caressed his sore wrists. "This is what happens when a charioteer is named Caesar," Comazon said, as he left the stalls.

"At least I am a charioteer and not a mime."

Comazon turned around in shock. "How the hell do you know that?"

"I've been doing my research, General. Between what my wife has told me and what I've found out myself, I know all about you. You're not who you pretend to be. In your youth you were a clown, an actor, and to be honest, you still are. In front of the people and the senators you pretend to be a manly man but woo-hoo..! Those parties with the Third Legion must have been really fun."

Comazon's right hand clenched into a fist. His face was incandescent steel. He was instants away from beating that beautiful face to a pulp.

His emotions didn't go unnoticed. "You won't do that," Hierocles said, petting and kissing his horse. "I doubt you'd like your dirty laundry aired before all of Rome... Can you imagine the looks you'll get in the streets and in the Senate?" He smiled. "Besides, there's a more important reason. You have a weakness for beauty, don't you? In all its forms. The good... and the evil." He walked slowly toward the general. "You know what's beautiful? Me and my wife making love. That's what I would call... the 'definition of beauty.' Beauty in action. Wanna watch sometime?"

Comazon threw a punch, but Hierocles caught it. He laughed. "It's alright, Comazon. Calm down now. No hard feelings, I promise. I'll see you around," he said, walking away and leaving the stunned general in the stalls.

Δ

Antoninus led Zoticus directly to the baths as soon as they reached the palace through the tunnel that connected it to the circus. They both took off their clothes. Antoninus took a dive into the water and, when she emerged, asked Zoticus to sit on one of the edges with his legs in the pool. She came over and leaned against his legs, looking up at him with a mischievous smile, before taking his still flaccid penis into her mouth. She sucked the whole of it, slurping with gusto, savoring its salty taste, then focused on the dripping head, pulling the skin back and licking the lubricated glans. Zoticus lifted his head and sighed. She continued to rock up and down, feeling the increasing hardness of the Greek athlete's manhood. He moaned louder and, after a while, asked her to stop, warning that he was about to cum. She took the cock out of her mouth and pulled him into the pool, where he fell in with a loud splash, making her squeal. The lovers kissed passionately, feeling the smooth sliding of their bodies.

They played, swam, and threw water on each other for hours. When they had enough, Antoninus held onto the wall of the pool, Zoticus hugging her from behind, his cock tip teasing her hole. Antoninus closed her eyes in anticipation of the pleasure to come.

A loud sound of footsteps abruptly snapped the couple out of their bliss. Hierocles appeared in front of them. The lovers stared at him, trembling, with wild eyes.

"Hello, husband. Congratulations!" Antoninus said, trying to regain her composure. "Do you want to join? The water is delicious."

Hierocles glared at the pair with icy eyes. He turned around intemperately and walked out. Antoninus shrugged and turned to her friend for a kiss.

Comazon walked through the streets in the direction of the Senate House, still shaken from his encounter with Hierocles. He had been summoned by Julius Paulus, so it couldn't be a trivial matter.

"You don't look well," Paulus said upon his arrival. "Has anything happened?"

"Nothing important. I understand you have serious business to discuss. What is it?"

The senator led the general into the main hall. As they walked, Paulus glanced at the picture of Antoninus hanging above the precious statue of Victoria and looked back at Comazon, finding only an absentminded man. Paulus invited Comazon to sit next to him in the first of the senatorial rows.

"You are a man of principle, General Comazon. You have fought for Rome on innumerable occasions, saving her from terrible enemies. Therefore you must understand that our current problem is not the enemy without, but the enemy within."

Comazon gazed at him impatiently. He was not in the mood for flattery.

"I'll get straight to the point. You witnessed what happened in this house a few days ago."

Comazon nodded.

"As you surely understand," the old man continued, "we, the Senate, cannot allow this situation to continue. Rome will be ruined if we do." He paused. "Did you know that that was only the second Senate session that the barbarian has attended since his appointment? At the first one he remained silent, which is only natural, not being used to being among civilized men. I think he was seriously intoxicated at that time. He cares more for his sleek chariots than for the state of the empire. And he won't decline an invitation to a race, that's for sure."

"Why are you complaining? It is probably better to hold the sessions without his presence."

"The only reason we need him is because he will not pass our measures unless he's briefed on them. As if that illiterate man understood anything about law and politics. Our initiatives have lagged because of his incompetence. I wouldn't mind his absences if he would only let us act freely. It's a disgrace that a man of his kind should even enter this hall."

"I know the situation is not optimal, but radical measures at this time will only cause instability. You must recognize that the empire is at peace. There are no revolts in the provinces. Our legions on the frontier were able to keep the Goths at bay. People are happy."

"Yes, but for how long? Things were fine when Maesa ran the empire. But they will deteriorate rapidly in her absence. You have seen in your career how unstable the political situation can get when the person in charge is incompetent."

"I do not see what can be done about it. He is the consort of the emperor."

"That can change. You have seen how easily the emperor has disposed of two wives," Paulus said bitterly. "It shouldn't be difficult to get rid of a third spouse in the same way."

Paulus had planned to marry Julia Paula to Comazon to bring him closer to the family, but for some incomprehensible reason, Comazon had shown no interest in courting her. The strangest thing, however, was that Julia

Paula, after her initial enthusiasm, had stopped talking about the general from one day to the next.

"I am afraid it is not the same. This time there are feelings involved, not only, if you will pardon the impertinence, convenience. The emperor will not let go of that man so easily."

"There are other ways."

Comazon stood up and stared at him. "I am not the man for that job, Your Honor."

Paulus also stood up. He paused for a moment, mustering courage for what he was about to say. Then he looked Comazon straight in the eye. "What is your price, general?"

"I am not a mercenary. Now, with all due respect," Comazon said, saluting and walking toward the exit.

"Is it the throne?" Paulus voice echoed in the empty chamber like in a cave. "Is the throne your price?"

Comazon turned around and walked back to the old man. "It is one thing, honorable *domine*, to depose an opportunist, and another…" He stood still, his chest heaving. "I will not follow Macrinus's example—a prefect who betrays the emperor. That will never happen. All I can promise you is that I will try to make him see the truth. But I will never act against him," he said before leaving the *curia*.

After the meeting, Comazon could resume his ruminations about the unsettling encounter with Hierocles. *Blackmail.* So now he was about to become a victim of blackmail? How did he get caught in this imbroglio? How did things get out of hand so quickly? Hierocles was threatening to expose him publicly as a man lover. What would that mean for a commander in his position? Ruin. Such things could be let slide for an emperor, but not for a man who was supposed to be the epitome of masculinity for the entire Roman Empire. He would become the laughingstock of senators and common people alike. What if Hierocles also aired his sexual adventures with legionaries in the camp? That would earn him and his boys the death penalty. And without him, Antoninus would fall.

Yet, this situation was not new. Maesa had also been aware of his preferences, and she had always had the power to expose him that Hierocles now had. She wouldn't hesitate to use it if he ever refused to serve and protect Antoninus. But that was not the reason he was still there. He was there because he cared; he sincerely wanted to protect his boy, even though she had made it very clear that there was nothing between them. So Hierocles was lucky. And so was Maesa. He would stay and keep doing his job, not out of fear, but out of love.

Δ

Later that day, Antoninus took Zoticus to the colossal palace kitchen.

"A promise is a promise: now you'll have to show me those culinary skills you've been bragging so much about," Antoninus said, in a jovial mood she hadn't been in for months.

"I'm not the only one here for the first time, am I?" Zoticus asked with a wink.

"You are not. I have full confidence in my cooks to always prepare what I want, and how I want it. Unfortunately, I can't say the same about you," she said, poking Zoticus. "Now, where's everything? Where are the ingredients?" she said, clapping her hands.

"Here they are, Lady," the oldest cook said. "We have acquired everything this morning, fresh as you requested."

"Well, here we have the... flour," Antoninus said, throwing a handful at Zoticus.

He grabbed another and did the same to her. They both laughed, throwing flour at each other and at the helpers, who weren't sure if they should take part in the food war.

Hierocles sneaked in. What he saw appalled him. All that joy, all that fun. He motioned for a slave with pierced ears to follow him outside.

"Alright, alright, you win!" Zoticus said. "Please let me start, otherwise we're never going to finish."

Antoninus agreed and watched him prepare the dough and ball it. She took two of the balls, put them together, and gave them a slow lick.

"Don't eat them yet. First we have to fry them," Zoticus said, pretending not to notice the lecherous reference.

In small batches, Zoticus fried the dough balls to a crisp, let them dry and sprinkled them with sesame seeds, nuts, and honey.

"Here you are, Greek *loukoumades*!" he said after a while, offering a plate to the empress.

"They look like *globi*," she said, unimpressed.

"Wait until you taste them."

"Mmm," Antoninus said, biting into one with a delighted expression. With the pastry still in her mouth, she drew near Zoticus and tongue-kissed him. "This really tastes good," she declared, to the applause of cooks and slaves.

The couple carried the dessert plates to the main *triclinium*, where a romantic setting with roses and candles had already been arranged by Stephanus.

"We need wine!" Antoninus shouted as they lay down on the divan. "Bring some rosé!"

The cupbearer—none other than the slave with the pierced ears—entered and offered a cup to his mistress and another to her friend. He stood watching for a while in silence.

"What are you standing there for? Go!" Antoninus said with two claps. She turned to look at her lover and kissed him on the lips. Then she proposed a toast. "To love!"

They both quaffed their goblets. Zoticus plummeted on the divan, the gold goblet tumbling noisily from his hand.

"Zoticus? Zoticus!" Antoninus cried in despair.

They were immediately surrounded by all the slaves and cooks. By all, except by the one with the piercings. He had fled. Antoninus shook her friend vehemently but got no response.

CHAPTER 7

GOING SOUTH

Antoninus ordered the funeral rites of Zoticus to be performed according to the Greek tradition, per the wishes of his family. The body was washed, anointed with oriental oils and perfumes, dressed in a thin shroud, and placed on a high bed inside the house of Zoticus's aunt. Not only her relatives and friends, but also the most prominent families of Rome came to mourn and pay their respects, having learned that the young man had attained the status of favorite of the empress during the brief time of his visit.

Antoninus had led the procession—which began before dawn—surrounded by her family and the Praetorian Guard, with the notable absence of Caesar. The loud and constant sobbing of the empress could he heard many *passūs* away. At one point, she could not take it any longer and fainted. Comazon hurried to keep her from falling and carried her in his arms the remainder of the procession. The feeble body, long and weak as a leaf of grass, had not weight enough to tire the powerful arms of the general, who felt himself in a sort of mournful transcendence. Although the young man had been his rival, he had not wished his death.

About an hour later, they arrived at the Greek cemetery. The sarcophagus was placed inside his aunt's family tomb, which was rectangular in plan and surrounded by elaborate, brightly painted marble columns and funerary statues. Antoninus, who had come back to his senses, was able to stand with the help of Comazon. Two slaves carried the tombstone, which bore a carving in Greek commemorating the many feats the athlete had accomplished at his young age. The empress uttered a sigh as the tombstone was placed, as if part of her spirit had also departed.

Back in the palace, Antoninus excused herself to go to her room, saying she needed to sleep. She found Hierocles lying in bed, dressed in a silk purple robe, loosely tied by a golden ribbon.

"Are you done with your mourning?"

Antoninus did not answer. She changed her clothes to a light tunic and lay down without saying a word, two cubits away from her husband, facing the opposite side of the bed.

"I know you're angry that I didn't attend. Why should I? I know he was your friend, but I never met the guy." He paused briefly. "Besides, you had developed a certain closeness with him. I didn't like that."

Antoninus turned furiously on the bed to look at Hierocles. "So, I'm not allowed to have friends? Is that what Caesar wants?"

"It is not appropriate for a married woman to have male friends. She should devote herself to her husband."

"Just as her husband should be devoted to her as well."

"I got other things to do. I must take care of the Romans. I can't leave important matters in the hands of the senators, who are nothing but a brute, incompetent lot."

Antoninus knew that she would not win the argument. She changed her mind about trying to sleep and got out of bed.

"Where are you going?"

"To where I should be right now. To the temple to pray."

"You're going to pray to that silly rock?"

Antoninus ignored the vitriol and changed back into her day clothes.

"Come back," Hierocles said in a commanding tone.

The empress turned around. Her husband had removed his robe and lay naked with a huge erection.

"This is the only rock you ought to worship."

A torrent of mixed emotions crawled inside Antoninus. On the one hand, rage, hatred, disgust at how her husband could be such a vile, unfeeling beast. On the other hand, the cruel reins of a religious-like devotion pulling her hopelessly to that bed. The moments she had lived with Zoticus were swept away by a raging storm and flushed down the Tiber in An instant.

She climbed onto the bed and bent down in front of the mighty cock that had so many times penetrated her. She took her time to smell it, as if she wanted to become intoxicated with its aroma. She rested her arms on her husband's potent legs and licked the bull balls, savoring the salt, finally taking the monolith into her mouth. She focused only on giving pleasure—since at that moment she couldn't feel it herself—

and her husband moaned in that sweet voice that melted her force of will. She glanced at him and saw him with open arms resting on the pillows, eyes closed in delight. In a moment she forgot Zoticus, the procession and the funeral rites; she forgot her god Elagabal, who was left waiting to console her in the temple; she forgot Comazon's loving support throughout the mourning; she forgot all and everything that made her human, apart from being a source of pleasure for her husband. When he was done, she lost herself in the taste and smell of his cum, swallowing it as if it was a cure for her sorrows. Tears flowed from her eyes: warm, salty tears of gratitude to her husband, gratitude for giving her a reason to go on living. She moved closer to him and snuggled into his arms. Hierocles petted her lightly.

He rose when she was just beginning to drift off to sleep, placing her carefully on the bed, and paced the room in search of wine. In the gloom, she observed the magnificent features of the man who was her husband and master: the curves of his muscles—grown after years of chariot-driving—the smooth hair of his huge, round buttocks, and most importantly, his giant penis, which even in a shriveled state retained its godly magnificence. She rejoiced in the tanned tone of his skin—which she adored so much—in the sparse but arousing chest hair, and in his scruffy beard. His thick lips sipped from a cup and he wiped them with the back of his hand. Everything she had experienced with the young Greek had been nothing more than a foolish illusion. This was her man. This was her universe.

Hierocles returned to the bed bringing the cup with him and noticed that she was awake. He took another sip. A few minutes passed in silence.

"I killed Zoticus."

His voice resonated in her ears like the stomp of an elephant. She rose and rubbed her red, puffy eyes.

"What did you say?" she said in a trembling voice.

"I killed Zoticus. I had him poisoned. I think you should know."

The empress's lips curled into a stark snarl. She snatched the cup from his hand and threw it against the wall, splashing the wine all over the bed and carpet. Beating his chest as hard as she could, she shrieked until Hierocles grabbed her from behind and clamped a hand over her mouth.

"Hush. Hush!" he hissed into her ear, causing her eyes to widen in horror. "You, *domina*, were getting too close to that man. You took him to the races and showed yourself like a whore. I, Caesar, will never allow my wife to make such a spectacle. By Hades, I won't, you, filthy bitch!" He let go of the grip, made her face him and slapped her with an iron hand.

Her jaw locked, and a sharp pain shot through her chest. She threw herself on the bed and, panting, desperately tried to pull the sheets over herself in a puerile act of self-preservation.

He stood up and put on his silk robe. "From now on, you will speak only to those whom I approve of. No more parties, no more fooling around with young athletes. You will behave like a wife. Did you hear me?" he thundered.

She didn't respond. Her body was shaking uncontrollably.
"I asked: Did you hear me?"
"Yes," she replied breathlessly.
"Good." He left the room.

Δ

After Hierocles left, Antoninus acted on her intentions to visit the temple. The empress looked tired and weak; she had hardly worn any makeup and, for a moment, looked like a boy again. Comazon offered her company. How smitten he had been since he first saw her perform in the temple, still as a he, with those sideburns and that fashion statement of a boyish mustache. It wasn't only the striking attire and sinuous moves that had enchanted him, but, above all, her engrossing self-confidence—a confidence that was now but a faint memory.

The general opened the door to the temple. The filthy surfaces and unwashed carpets of the *cella* would have been unthinkable in the first months of her reign. They stood in front of the altar for a moment. Antoninus climbed the steps to it and opened the dusty black and gold velvet curtains that covered the black stone. She returned to Comazon and knelt in front of the god with hands held high, a position he had never seen her in before. Comazon, despite not practicing the curious oriental faith, felt compelled to kneel beside her. Although out of respect for the empress he had never expressed it, he found the cult absurd; true, the Roman gods were also made of stone, but at least they had a human form.

This worship of a formless, igneous rock neither appealed nor made sense to him.

Antoninus prostrated herself, her tears hitting the marble floor. They were a mixture of sincere repentance for having abandoned the god for so long, and for the death of Zoticus, which in her mind could be nothing more than a punishment for her infidelity, even if carried out by the hand of her husband.

Was there something else, something sinister, driving Antoninus to the temple that morning? Did Hierocles have anything to do with it? Certainly, it was only after meeting him that she had started to disregard her religious duties.

After hours of whispered prayers, tears, prostrations, and long periods with her hands in the air, Antoninus tapped on Comazon's arm, signaling that they should leave. Comazon had closed his eyes and had almost dozed; his knees ached to get up. Antoninus closed the altar curtains, and they left the temple. There had been no dance this time. While it was certainly more entertaining when the temple service took the form of a musical performance, this seemed a more traditional form of religious worship; something that could perhaps make the cult of Elagabal more enduring. How could large masses of people from future generations dance around a rock as part of a religious service?

"I miss this, you know, going out in the street without a bunch of bodyguards following me everywhere. Walking outside just with a friend," she said, taking the general's arm on the way back to the palace.

A friend. Just a friend. She had made that very clear that day outside the Senate. Yet how could Comazon's feelings change? They hadn't since the battle in Syria, when he saw the emperor riding with the sun on his back. Since that moment he had been sure that Antoninus was meant to be his boy. Was what he saw reality or just a vision? He could never be sure. But he would never ask. He would never dare touch such a sacred moment in his life.

"You do not come to fulfill your religious duties as often as you used to, Excellency" Comazon said.

"That is true," Antoninus said with a sigh. "I should do it again. It's just that, you know, a wife's duties and obligations get in the way sometimes... And my husband..." She hesitated for a moment. "Well, someone who loves you doesn't want to see you on a stage... They want you only for themselves."

How false and empty those words sound, Comazon thought.

"You know, Comazon, all my life I've dedicated myself to serving a god, but now I know that in reality, all I ever wanted was to serve a man."

But it should be the right man, Comazon thought. *If you only gave me the chance, I would always be there for you and, unlike that vile man, you wouldn't have to serve me...*

Δ

They arrived at the palace in the cool of the evening.

"Thank you for accompanying me on my visit to the temple, Comazon. I thank you sincerely," Antoninus said, taking his hand.

"Are you feeling better, Excellency?"

"Yes, I just need to rest. I hardly slept last night."

Comazon was about to walk out into the street when he was stopped by Maesa.

"Comazon! May I have a word with you?"

"Of course, *domina*."

"Let's go to the library."

The library was one of the rooms of the palace that interested Comazon the least. He was a man of action, not of papyri. Ironically, there seemed to be no one left in the palace who cared about books, except Maesa. She was an avid reader and had made sure that the imperial library contained copies of the best scrolls from Alexandria and other centers of knowledge.

Maesa ordered a slave to bring warm milk with honey for two. "Please, have a sit, General."

The slave returned promptly with the drinks.

Maesa took a slurp. She stared at Comazon for a very long time. A stabbing pain hit Comazon's head.

"Comazon, you have been with us from the beginning. Without you, my dear Antoninus would have never sat on the throne. It was you, with your love and your courage, who won the battle, while all the others fled. You're the sole protector of the emperor among a pack of wolves. And recently, you have watched this terrible situation unfold before our eyes. Time and again, we have left things in the hands of destiny, but now I am convinced that it will never end unless we take action."

"What is it that you need?"

"We have to remove the source of all our problems, once and for all."

Comazon's eyes widened. "Remove Caesar?"

"Don't call him Caesar, for Elagabal's sake. That beast is not worthy of such a noble title. And yes, we must eliminate him. It's the only solution. It's in everybody's mind that the empire has become a headless state. I know we've had this conversation before. Back then, you asked me to trust fortune, but fortune is against us."

"You can be sure that I do not like him, *domina*. I do not like him at all. But to remove him by illegal means would be treason. It is the emperor himself who must act."

"If you're not convinced that this is the only way, I have one more thing to tell you."

Comazon looked at her attentively.

"He killed Zoticus."

Comazon frowned. "How do you know?"

"He ordered a slave to poison his drink. The poor thing confessed everything to me and begged me not to execute him. He said he could not refuse an order from Caesar. I saved his life by sending him away immediately."

"You were very gracious. Does the emperor know what happened?"

"He knows. And he won't do anything. We talked about it at great length this morning, before you and he went to the temple. He used all kinds of excuses to justify him, even saying that it was his own fault for not being a faithful wife. See what I am talking about, Comazon? Hierocles, that monster, has become his god, replacing the almighty Elagabal."

Comazon understood Maesa's point of view. Yes, Hierocles was the emperor's legal husband, but he had betrayed his position as consort and seized power by persuasion. This murder gave him a valid reason to proceed. Homicide was something that even Caesar should not be able to get away with. Law and order were what kept the empire in one piece.

"Leave it to me, *Augusta*," he said standing up, leaving his cup of milk on the desk.

Maesa nodded with a smile. When Comazon left, she sat still, thinking. As soon as the general got rid of the pig, she would have to get back to work immediately. Antoninus would be devastated, and even more incapable of playing the role of emperor. She could then rule more openly and bring Rome the stability she so desperately needed. But for now, she just had to wait and be ready.

Δ

That night, Hierocles had gone out partying with his friends at the usual brewery. He didn't mind leaving a lonely wife at home: having unlimited drinks with his old buddies was infinitely more appealing that listening to the sobbing of an unbalanced woman. Comazon had followed him and sat down in a corner of the bar. Since it was unusual for a full-blooded Roman—let alone the praetorian prefect—to visit a brewery, the bartender assumed he was on duty looking after Caesar's safety and offered him free drinks for the night. Besides, he enjoyed having the legendary general around.

"I like this Caesar," the barman said as he served him one of his finest brews. "He's a man of the people, he's one of us. He hasn't changed a bit since he came to power. Besides, he's so generous. At every game there are gifts for the people and distribution of grain and meat. He even started a lottery. I know of some lucky ones who have gotten gold coins with his effigy. Most of them don't even want to spend them, so they can keep a souvenir of his pretty face. It's wild, don't you think?"

Comazon looked at the man and took a sip of his beer—which he found disgusting—and said nothing. The brewer, like most people, was unaware that the generosity actually came from the emperor himself, not from this clown. Hierocles just took credit for it.

Comazon continued to examine Hierocles's behavior during the night. The charioteer laughed obstreperously, sang stupid circus songs, hugged and kissed his friends; he was really having a good time, while Antoninus was lonely at home, crying, thinking of him. Maesa was right: someone so utterly despicable had to go. And yet… there was something about him, an aura of irresistibility that made Comazon wish he would stay around. But why? After all, he was fucking the emperor in more ways than just the literal one. He was a true disgrace to Rome and her people. Comazon wanted him out of power, but not gone. He had a second drink. And a third.

He lost count of how many goblets of beer he washed down through the night. Somehow, the taste got better with each tipple. Finally, after some time, he noticed with a blurry sight that Hierocles had stood up and was apparently saying goodbye to his comrades. He rose and followed him from a safe distance. Outside, as Hierocles was about to get into his chariot, the general came up behind him and laid a hand on his shoulder.

"Comazon", a startled Hierocles said, who had also had too much to drink. "What are you doing here?"

"Watching over you, Highness."

"You don't have to do that, my man. I was among friends. No one would dare hurt me here."

Comazon leaned heavily on Hierocles, putting his arm around his shoulder, and clumsily dragged him away from the beerhouse.

"What are you doing? We need to go back to the palace. Come on, Comazon, you can ride with me."

Comazon continued to pull him until both men entered a cavernous alleyway, lit only by a distant torch. Comazon pushed Hierocles against the wall, pinning him by the shoulders, and stood an inch away from his face, his alcoholic breath mixing with the consort's. He looked deep into the clear green eyes.

"Why did you kill Zoticus?" he said in his husky voice.

Hierocles's mouth drew into a snarl. He frowned nervously. "What are you talking about?"

"You do not have to deny it. You just have to tell me why you did it."

Hierocles looked to the side. His chest heaved up and down, convulsed by agitated breathing, and his heartbeat thundered with the force of an earthquake. He looked at Comazon again with terror in his eyes. "He had to die! My wife was cheating on me with him. Any man with a jot of honor would have done as I did."

"Men do not poison. That is for cowards. Men kill with their swords," Comazon said, unsheathing his *gladius*, the polished steel glinting in the torchlight.

"Put that down, General. What do you think you're doing? If… you put it down and release me, maybe I can explain it to you."

Comazon sheathed his sword again.

"I… I love my wife; I couldn't bear to see her with that man. I discovered them in the baths, so close to one another… it hurt me. It hurt me so bad I couldn't handle it."

"Still not enough motive to commit murder."

"Comazon, be reasonable. Besides…"

"Besides, what?"

"I've done you a favor too."

Comazon stood back, frowning. "You did me a favor?" he said, pointing to himself.

"If you say it's the hour of truth, then it should be for both of us. Don't think that I'm not aware of your feelings for the empress. You love her, you always have. Overprotective, always jealous; my presence bothered you from day one, don't deny it. You wanted her all for yourself, didn't you? That's why you installed her on the throne, so you could be near her." He smiled. "See how good I am at tying

243

things up? Now at least things are back to where they were: I removed a rival for both of us."

Comazon shook his head, as if trying to check that he wasn't having a bad dream.

"As a sign of goodwill, I make you an offer," Hierocles continued. "I can share her with you. Take her anytime you want. I couldn't share her with that guy, but with you... with you it's different."

"Do not try to make fun of me, you fool," Comazon roared. "A murderer must pay for his crime," he said, putting his hand back on the hilt of his sword.

"Wait. Wait! There's something else you want. I know it. Something you want really bad." Hierocles turned around, untied his toga, lifted up his tunic, dropped his *subligaculum*, and bared his bulky, hairy butt to Comazon. "You wanna fuck me? That's what you want, right? Then, fuck me. Do it now!"

Comazon froze, stunned, losing his balance to the point of dropping his sword. He touched his crotch and felt a massive boner, his heart was pumping out blood at a dizzying rate. His body was screaming for him not to miss this now-or-never opportunity. He hated that jackass, but a tantalizing force, impossible to resist, pulled him toward the charioteer. He couldn't back off. His flesh was burning. He had to take that ass.

Comazon pulled down his *subligaculum*, lifted up his tunic and, after a careless spit, shoved himself mercilessly inside the manhole in a single stroke.

"Arghhh! Easy, idiot! It's my first time!"

But Comazon didn't care. He kept thrusting inside the wanting hole, freeing himself not only from all the hate and contempt, but also from the desire, from that crushing yearning that had oppressed his guts for so long. He didn't care about Hierocles's pretty face or his huge dick; at that moment all he wanted was to destroy his rear. To make him pay for his crime, somehow.

Hierocles, for his part, had been wanting cock for quite some time—ever since he had arrived in Rome—but hadn't found a guy worthy of sticking it in him. He too had felt a strong desire for the general since that first meeting at the pool; they could have fucked like bulls that day, had he not already had an appointment with the emperor. However, at that moment, regardless of the circumstances, he was finally experiencing a fat cock inside, and it couldn't have felt more amazing. He loved the sensation of fullness, and he doubted that any other cock could satisfy him like this.

Comazon was still pounding non-stop: panting, sweating, momentarily regaining consciousness after the beer binge. With no love in question, he was finally screwing the golden-hair ass, riding the unicorn. He cupped Hierocles's balls and then smelled his hand. The arousal boost made his cock harder than steel and made the feeling of fucking even more heavenly.

When the moment of release came, he pulled his cock out and jerked it off vigorously. He spilled the seed over the hair bush above the ass crack, staining him as the cheap prostitute he was. Grunting and trying to catch his breath, Comazon hastily tied his *subligaculum* and picked up the sword from the ground before walking away. He didn't care if a thug came along now and killed the consort; he would do everyone a favor.

Hierocles was left shaking, leaning against the dirty wall. He slowly slid down until he hit the ground, smearing mud on his face. His hole was pounding with a mixture of pleasure and pain he had never imagined possible. Suddenly, a wave of fear flashed through his body like a bolt of lightning. He remembered where he was; he had to get out of there as soon as possible.

Δ

In the wee hours of the morning, a restless Antoninus paced nervously through the halls and corridors of the palace. In his wanderings he bumped into his grandmother.

"Have you seen my husband today? He didn't come to sleep."

Maesa struggled to contain a smile. "No, I haven't seen him since… well, actually it's been a while since I last saw him. You know that he and I don't talk much, right?"

"I'm worried, Grandma! Where's Comazon? He should go look for him."

"I haven't seen him either. You know he's usually up at this hour."

"In that case, I'll go out and look for him myself."

"I don't recommend you do that. You know your husband better than me. Surely he went out partying and now he's passed out somewhere. I wouldn't worry about it. Why don't you join me in the knitting?"

Antoninus rolled her eyes and walked away.

Maesa was going to get something to drink in the kitchen when the guards announced the arrival of a messenger. She instructed them to let him in. The little man delivered a small note, which she read with interest, after which she rushed back to her room.

At the most famous brothel in the city, a scared Lucia went to the reception to talk to Lucretia, the owner of the establishment.

"How is he," Lucretia asked.

"He's still sleeping. He hasn't woken up since last night."

Hierocles had arrived at the brothel in a deranged frenzy before dawn, barely conscious, due to exhaustion and drunkenness. Lucretia had led him as usual to Lucia's room, but this time he was not down for sex and passed out as soon as he hit the bed.

"There's one thing that worries me," the young woman continued. "He's been tossing and turning in his sleep, and he's left blood on the sheets."

"Is he hurt? Someone may have attacked him."

"I didn't see any wounds. In fact, it seems like the blood is coming from his behind," the girl said, a little embarrassed.

Lucretia frowned. She was silent for a minute. "Keep watching him. Don't wake him up but stay alert in case he needs help."

"Will do, mistress."

Δ

A couple of hours later, Maesa had complied with Senator Julius Paulus's request to meet him at his *domus*. She arrived just in time for the *ientaculum*.

"*Clarissima*, thank you for honoring us with your presence," the senator said with a kiss. His wife also approached to greet her. "Please, join us, I hope you haven't had breakfast yet."

"I have not; I came in the greatest of haste as soon as I received your notice."

"And I certainly appreciate it," Paulus said.

They began by discussing the various problems facing the empire, but the real topic of conversation soon followed.

"And regarding the charioteer…" Paulus said with disgust. "Have you thought of a strategy with which we could… put him out of combat, so to speak?"

"I have, indeed," Maesa said, spreading her bread with fruit preserves. "In fact, we may receive favorable news during the day. He did not sleep in the palace last night," she said with a wink.

Paulus nodded with a frown. "Interesting. But maybe it could have been one of his party nights, don't you think?"

"It's possible. But Comazon hasn't reported to work yet either. And that could be a very good indication that my suspicions are true."

"Comazon… What does he have to do with this?"

"I asked Comazon to… take matters into his own hands."

Paulus wiped his mouth with a napkin. "But that man is a true believer in the rule of law. I had already made that request to him, in fact, with an offer I thought would be irresistible… but he flat-out refused. He would never do anything he deems illegal."

"Believe me, he would, and he has," Maesa said chuckling, remembering the bribe in Emesa. "He's a special type. You have to know how to approach him. And this time I gave him more than enough reasons to act."

"There's one thing I think you should know about Comazon, dear Maesa."

She gazed at him intently.

"I don't really know how to say this. It's an embarrassing matter for our family… I'll try to keep it short. We wanted the general to court our daughter with a view to marriage, but… she found out, under the most horrid circumstances, that the general prefers…"

"Prefers…"

"Prefers the company of men," Paulus said, almost out of breath.

"Oh," Maesa said, faking surprise, "well… I am sorry for what your daughter had to go through, but… well, I don't think that has anything to do with what I asked him to do." *Though, thinking about it, it did.*

"I really hope so. But do you have a second plan, in case things don't go as expected?"

"Let's see. Suppose that, for whatever reason, Comazon is unwilling or unable to take the charioteer down… in what other way can we kick Hierocles out of the way?"

"Maybe we could try poison?"

"That has been done so many times before. Besides, we just had a poisoning in the palace, so I really don't think it would be wise to have another one, but…" Maesa's eyes sparkled.

"What's on your mind, *Augusta*?"

"Something has just occurred to me… It's so silly that this hadn't come to my mind before."

"You leave me guessing, dear friend."

"Never mind. I must still work out the details. But this is a brilliant idea that would solve everything."

Her idea, if executed correctly, would indeed solve everything. To begin with, she had to write a letter. A very important letter to a place far away. And then, she had to work with Comazon. Or rather, *on* Comazon.

Δ

The whole day had passed and, at dusk, Hierocles had finally opened his eyes, feeling ran over by an elephant. His head was an erupting volcano, his muscles and bones were sore, and he had a strange throbbing pain in his ass. Then he remembered. Comazon. That son of a bitch had taken what he wanted and had left him to die. But what a good fuck it had been. He licked his lips but felt them dry.

"Water!" he yelled as soon as he realized where he was.

A scared Lucia entered the room.

"My Lord! I'm so glad that you have awakened. I was afraid you might die."

"Why didn't you call the doctor, if you were so afraid," Hierocles said, slowly regaining his cockiness.

"The mistress asked me to wait."

Hierocles patted the bed. She sat down and he rose slightly to stroke her long black hair.

"You're such a sweet and beautiful woman. I'm sorry I wasn't in a position to please you last night."

She smiled and began to play coquettishly with her hair. "You can still do it tonight, if you want to."

"I doubt it. I feel terrible. I'm surprised I'm not dead."

"Were you attacked by someone last night, Caesar?"

Hierocles was startled by the question. "What do you mean?"

She showed him the stained sheets.

"By Bacchus!" he exclaimed, trying to come up with a quick answer. "Yes… yes! I was! I almost didn't remember it. Some thug attacked me while I was trying to get back to the palace. But I defended myself and gave the motherfucker the beating he deserved."

"May I see your wounds? I can wash them and—"

"No!" Hierocles said, instantly changing his frightened expression to a smile. "I'm alright. I'm sure it's healed by now. It was just something superficial."

The woman smiled and caressed his shaggy beard.

"You've totally changed my mood. We may have a little fun tonight if you still have time."

"I have all the time in the world for Caesar. Tonight, I'll be your empress!"

Hierocles laughed out loud and kissed her. "Alright, queen, but where's my water?"

A couple of hours later, a surprise visitor arrived at the brothel.

"Excellency!" a shocked Lucretia said. "We're most honored by your presence, but I wish you would have notified us in advance to make preparations befitting your Grace."

"Is my husband here?"

"Caesar? Uh… uhm…"

One of the younger girls looked at the floor and gave away the answer.

"Where is he? I want to see him right now!" Antoninus said, rushing inside.

"Empress! Please, wait!" Lucretia cried, running after her.

Antoninus scurried down the halls looking in every *cubiculum*, noisily opening the beaded curtains, frightening the women inside. Then he heard noises. The shrill moans of a woman and the deep grunts of a man. He opened the curtains. Caesar was lying on the bed with a voluptuous woman riding his cock. Their hands were locked, and she moved with a rhythm of cadence that Antoninus wished she had learned during her stay at Plautina's brothel. The prostitute looked back and covered her breasts with a terrified shriek. Caesar looked at the intruder too. His smile didn't even fade. Antoninus slammed the beaded curtains against the wall and ran away as fast as she could.

"She'll get over it," Hierocles said. "Let's not spoil the fun."

Lucia slowly resumed her movements. Hierocles's cock had not lost any of its stiffness.

Antoninus wandered aimlessly through the deserted streets. She had escaped from the palace without guards, especially since Comazon was nowhere to be found. She didn't seek shelter in the midst of the raging storm. Stopping at a corner, she wailed like a banshee, with the cry of Rome herself—a woman stabbed in the back. She ran, then stopped and sat on the dirty sidewalks, letting her white robe become a muddy rag, and the rain wash the makeup off her face. When her eyes were swollen and empty, she returned to the palace. There was only one thing to do.

Lying in his bed, Comazon woke up naked and with a strong headache. He got up, looked out of the window, and watched the raging storm outside. He was confused. Was it the same night or had he slept an entire day?

He lit a candle and saw his uniform tossed on the floor and his sword beside it. He picked it up. There was no blood on it; at least he hadn't killed anyone. He recalled an altercation of some sort. Touching his balls, he felt a slight pain. He smelled his other hand, which still emanated a powerful, sweet, lascivious scent. Hierocles. Damn. He reveled in the thought of the feel of penetrating that virgin ass. *Wow.* It had been a while since he'd last deflowered an asshole. Those army boys weren't exactly virgins when they joined the legion, let alone the prostitutes he procured on the street. He must have gotten totally wasted at the brewery the previous night. But if he had slept all day, why hadn't anyone looked for him? Now was not the time to report to the palace; surely his men were mounting guard already. *This is totally unlike you, Comazon. What the fuck is happening to you*!

In the meantime, Antoninus was back in the palace. She headed straight to the imperial baths, shed her soaked tunic, and plunged into the cold water. She hugged herself, trying to evoke the sensation of the smoothness of Zoticus's skin. How wonderful it had felt when he teased her hole with his cock!

In her room, she chose to dress in a beautiful yellow *stola* she had not worn in a long time. She put on some make-up. Then a little more. And more still. She applied ruby red lipstick and licked her lips. She put on a big yellow wig and flower garland on her head. When she was ready, she walked out of the palace through the front door. If the guards were startled by her appearance, they did not show it.

She went down the stairs gaily, jumping and dancing like in the good old days, when she used to praise Elagabal. A crowd of curious onlookers, mostly thugs and criminals, gathered around to watch. For some, Rome was truly a city that never slept.

"How much for a night?" one of them shouted.

Antoninus approached him and tugged at the collar of his tunic. "How much have you got on you?"

Wows and oohs were heard.

"I have this much," the man said, showing her a few *denarii*.

Antoninus snatched the money, took him by the hand and led him upstairs to the palace, ordering the guards to open the doors.

The onlookers stayed outside, waiting to see what would happen. Half an hour or so later, the doors opened again. The man came out in a triumphant attitude with his fists up, rocking his pelvis obscenely, with Antoninus behind him, blowing a kiss in the wind. The onlookers burst into cheers.

"I have ten *sesterces*," another man said.

Antoninus motioned with her index finger for him to come in. Twenty minutes later, he was out. A few more men came and went before another man arrived wearing a dirty, disheveled toga and smelled of sweat and cheap perfume.

"What the hell is going on here?" Caesar shouted. "Go, before I have you all killed!"

The men scattered, expressing their disappointment. Hierocles ordered the guards to open the gates and walked determinedly down the hallway to the imperial *cubiculum*. What he saw nearly made him choke. A man was standing and penetrating Antoninus, who was naked, lying on the edge of the bed with his legs spread wide.

With a grimace of rage, Hierocles pulled a dagger from a chest and stabbed the panicked man—who had barely tied his *subligaculum*—in the heart.

Hierocles walked a few steps toward Antoninus, tossing the dagger on the bed. He glared at her for an instant before punching her face. He grabbed her by the neck and threw her to the floor. Then he hit her again. And again. The wails of pain could be heard all the way to the main entrance, but none of the guards moved a finger. He punched her stomach, and kicked her when she tried to curl into a ball.

"I'm going to kill you, you miserable bitch! I can't believe you had the nerve to bring scum from the streets into this bed, my bed! I should break every bone in your body!" He pulled her harshly by the arm, causing her sharp pain, and threw her on the bed.

"You did it first!" she shrieked, as she rose, saliva hanging from her teeth and tears flooding her eyes. "You went to that filthy place to fuck another woman. A woman!" She grabbed the dagger and pointed it at his heart. He gripped her hand tightly, making her drop the weapon.

Hierocles nodded, his face shaking and his eyes wide. "Yes, I did it. And you know why? Because I'm a man. I've got the needs of a man. You're not woman enough for me, you freak!" he said, slapping her face. He gripped her flaccid penis and balls tightly. "See this? I don't like it. I crave real pussy. You should have it cut off, or one of these days I'll do it myself!" He threw her on the bed once more and stormed out of the room.

Antoninus remained lying still, her nose and mouth bleeding, unable to control the trembling of her body. The words *not woman enough* resonated incessantly in her brain, like the echo of a cavern. She covered her ears to try to make them go away.

She remained huddled inside the quilt until dawn, shivering, although the room was not cold. She rose with the first songs of the birds and put on the first robe she could find. Leaving the palace in the direction of the Temple of Elagabal, she kept her gaze fixed on its column, from where a few years before she had distributed gifts to her people, amid the ecstasy of the temple's dedication. She could climb it and throw herself from it, diving into the beauty and magnificence of Rome's triumphal arches, imperial dwellings, vast porticoes, and winding streets, and procure herself an end worthy of her artistic sensibility.

While she brooded over the possibility, shocked merchants and forum shoppers gathered around her. She changed course and walked through them, pushing them aside, toward one of the houses in the city center, and slammed the door with the hammer. A slave appeared.

"I want to see the doctor."

"At once, Highness." The slave led her inside.

The doctor arrived a few minutes later, dressed in a simple tunic. "By Venus, my Lady, what has happened to you?"

"I just have one question for you, doctor."

The doctor stared at her.

"Can you make me a vagina?"

Δ

A few hours later, an enraged Maesa stormed into Antoninus's bedroom. The empress was curled up in bed, her hands clutching the sheets that barely covered her body.

"You're a disgrace! Are you really going to allow that man to treat you this way?"

Antoninus sobbed without uttering a word.

"You are the empress of Rome. Look at yourself!" She held a mirror up to her face so Antoninus could see her black eyes. "Look what that man you call a husband has done to you! Is this how you want to show yourself in public? As a battered…" she struggled to utter the word, "'wife'?"

"As a devoted wife, which is what I am!" Antoninus cried. "As a woman in love, reprimanded by her husband whenever she needs it. Besides, he's from Caria, all Carians are wife-beaters."

Maesa shook her head in disbelief. "You've gone insane. Totally insane! The doctor has already told me what you went to see him for. I should have you locked up for the rest of your life!"

"Try it! My husband will never allow it!"

"We'll see about that," she said, leaving the room. She stopped and faced her again. "If you still have a little respect for yourself and for Rome, leave him! Divorce him!"

"I'll never leave my husband. Go! Go away now and leave me alone!"

Outside, she ran into Comazon. "Oh, you? Finally! Where have you been? I need to talk to you immediately!"

Soaemias appeared running, slightly out of breath. She looked at Maesa and Comazon with worried eyes but didn't say a word. She entered her daughter's room, finding her sad and helpless, and sat down beside her, running her fingers through her hair.

"Did the doctor rush to you to snitch on me too?" Antoninus said, without looking at her.

"Yes, my dear. It was only natural for him to do so."

"Why can't anyone treat me like an adult? I'm capable of making my own decisions! Am I not the commander of the world?"

"You are the empress of Rome, but you are also very young, and there are certain things you should ask your elders for advice on."

"I don't need advice to know what I am." Antoninus rose and looked at her mother. "I am a woman, and as a woman I want to live!"

"Haven't I supported you since you made that decision?" Soaemias said calmly. "I can't say I fully understand you, but I'm here for you, darling. Why didn't you tell me what you wanted to do?"

"Because you'd think I'm crazy," Antoninus said, sobbing.

"I don't believe that at all. But the doctor has already told you: such procedure is not possible; you would only injure yourself and die... No one has ever done anything like that before."

"Men get their balls chopped off all the time. You know that very well."

Soaemias took a deep breath. "Losing his balls didn't make Gannys a woman, right?"

Antoninus gave her mother a pleading look.

"Listen to me, dear. Being a woman is much more that having a vagina; being a woman is a state of the spirit, of the soul… is a way of seeing and experiencing life. You don't need to have surgery to live as a woman, to be a woman… Simply follow your desires and do the things you want to do; free yourself, darling… and your spirit will know the way."

Antoninus hugged her mother tightly.

"And I wish you would free yourself from that man too."

She let go of her and gazed at her intensely. "I can't let him go. I can't, Mother! I love him too much; I love him to the bone… If he'd leave I would no longer have a reason to live."

"You have me, you have your grandmother, who, stern as she is, loves you deeply… you have an empire with millions of souls to care for, but most importantly… you have yourself, dear, you should live first of all for yourself…"

"What's wrong with a little beating? My father used to beat you too and you never complained."

Soaemias remained silent for a minute. What a bad example she had set for her daughter. "Listen, honey, it's different—"

"How is it different? Because you're a real woman, and I'm not? That's what you think, isn't it?"

"No, dear, I assure you that—"

"Please go away, Mother. Don't lie to me. Don't pretend you understand, because you don't." She stood up and looked away. "Leave me alone! I need to be alone!"

With a devastated face, Soaemias left the room.

Maesa and Comazon entered the *tablinum*.

"Yesterday I ran into some trouble," Comazon said, in an apologetic tone, "and I just came to check if the emperor is well."

"He's not well… of course, he's not well," Maesa said, showing him a chair.

"Obviously you did not obey my orders. What did I tell you, Comazon?"

The general looked down.

"The incompetence in this palace is unbelievable. Where were you last night instead of fulfilling your duties? In fact, where have you been since I last saw you?"

Comazon tried to speak, but the words wouldn't come. He was not prepared to face an angry Maesa that morning.

"Yes, I know. Surely you were drinking. You have a problem with wine and you need to curb it. It's seriously impairing your work."

"I did go to a brewery; I will not deny it. But not for what you think. Hierocles was there, and I was watching him, but…"

"But…?"

"But it is true, I got too much to drink, and I am not really used to drinking beer. I lost track of him afterward. I thought he had gone back to the palace, so I went home."

"Well, he didn't! He didn't show up all day yesterday, so I thought you'd done your job. How wrong was I. He was in a whorehouse while you were curing your damn hangover!"

In a whorehouse? How did he have the stamina for sex after what had happened? Blessed youth! A smile broke out on his face upon the memory of their encounter.

"What's so funny, General?"

"Nothing, *Augusta*. I was just thinking about how he managed to have vitality for that kind of activity after a binge like that."

"And that's not the worst part. Sit back and I'll tell you."

She told him all about how Antoninus had discovered him and what had happened afterward.

Comazon rose from his chair. "I will kill that bastard now."

"You've already failed. There's something better you can do." She clasped her hands and stared at him. "Why don't you… demonstrate the emperor that you really love him?"

Comazon's heart leapt. He had already given up the possibility of ever getting close to Antoninus. He had tried to bury his love, but deep inside, a small candle of hope remained, fighting for some air to stay alive.

"Right now, he needs all the support he can get, and who better than someone who has loved him in silence for all these years?" She rose and approached him from behind, putting her hands on his shoulders. "Maybe now it's time for you to take one more step, and…"

"And…"

"Take Antoninus away."

Comazon paced nervously around the room.

"Where to? There is nowhere to go."

"I guarantee no one will bother you." She walked toward him. "The Senate will be more than happy to see him go. I will get rid of Hierocles, and I will see that you will never have to work another day in your life."

"But who will be emperor now?"

"Leave that to me."

Comazon shook his head. "What you are proposing to me is too much. I cannot do it."

"Don't you love Antoninus more than yourself?"

"Yes. Yes!"

"Then, take him, run away, and forget everything. You've already done your service to the fatherland. It's time for you, for both of you, to be happy. Soon he will realize that Hierocles was a terrible choice and forget him. Your love will help him do that."

Comazon was breathing hard, unable to hear anymore. He left the *tablinum* without waiting to be dismissed.

Maesa was left alone, thinking. Would he do it? At least he didn't say no outright. His heart would fight against his mind and win. Regardless of how brave or intelligent men were, they were always slaves to their desires.

Now, on to more practical matters... Where could they go? They could flee to Greece, Syria, or anywhere along the frontiers; they could get there quickly and above all, never return. A possibility existed that Paulus and the other senators would arrange for them to be assassinated on the way, but she didn't really care. With Antoninus out of the way, Hierocles would fall like ripe fruit. She then would be able to install her new pawn, who, incidentally, was already on his way to Rome.

Her thoughts were interrupted by her daughter, who entered the studio unannounced.

"I've talked to the doctor—" Soaemias said, sitting in the chair that Comazon had just left.

"Dear, I have the most terrible headache; would you mind if we talked later?"

"I need to have this conversation with you right now."

Maesa took a breath.

"The doctor told me about his conversation with Antoninus. Why didn't you tell me about it yourself?"

"I didn't want to worry you unnecessarily. What would you have done anyway?"

"What I did just now. At least try to talk to her. Or rather, listen to her. Understand her reasons…" She paused. "Do you think we could seek another medical opinion about the procedure?"

Maesa gave her daughter a condescending look. "Of course not. Besides, the removal of the genitals does not turn any man into a woman. Gannys certainly didn't lose any of his masculinity when his balls were cut off. At least, not with you in bed."

Soaemias did not hear her mother's scathing comment. She was lost in thought. "But, what if Antoninus is actually a woman? A woman born in the wrong body. She has certainly never showed any traits of manliness… What if performing that operation would actually make things right for her?"

"Enough of this nonsense. You excuse her for everything. When will you start being a good mother?"

"At least I try to understand her. No one else seems to. She needs to know that there will always be someone by her side, whatever the circumstances."

"It would be better if that person was you and not that hideous man."

"She doesn't want to leave him…"

"Not yet, child. But, no worries, things will be over soon, very soon…"

CHAPTER 8

THE TIBER

Two months later, tired and disheveled, a woman and a young man arrived at the palace gates.

"*Domina*, visitors from Emesa have arrived and are asking for you," a slave announced to Maesa in her quarters, while she was accompanied by Soaemias.

Maesa smiled. "Have one of the slave girls take them to the guest quarters. Tell them to freshen up in the baths and make sure they are provided with new clothes. We'll meet in the main *triclinium* for dinner when they're ready."

Soaemias looked at her, puzzled.

"Oh, your sister is here. And her son," Maesa said, her face brightening.

"Mamaea and Alexianus? What are they doing here?"

"I invited them."

Soaemias's jaw dropped. "Why didn't you inform me? Or Antoninus, for that matter. I don't think she knows, and—"

"I wanted to give you both a surprise. And from what I can see, I succeeded."

Hours later, Maesa, Soaemias and the newly arrived Mamaea and her son Alexianus were dining in the main *triclinium*.

"Thank you for all your attentions, Mother. We feel so refreshed now, after such a long trip," Mamaea said.

"It's the least I can do for my precious little daughter," Maesa said, smiling. "Was everything alright on the trip?"

"Yes it was, despite the rush. Don't you think so, dear?" Mamaea said, nudging her son.

"Yes, Mother," Alexianus replied, yawning.

"I can imagine how tired you must be, but you'll have a great night's sleep tonight. And tomorrow, you'll convene with the empress."

Mamaea had been warned by letter of Antoninus's sex change. "Is… the empress indisposed today? We would have loved to talk to her tonight. Wouldn't you like to see your cousin again, dear? You haven't seen him… I mean, her… since, well, since she was still a boy…"

Alexianus looked at his mother and then back down at his plate. Soaemias ate her olives in silence. She hadn't spoken a word during the whole dinner and still didn't know what to think of this crazy idea of her mother. Why would she bring Mamaea and Alexianus to the palace in such a hurry?

In the palace gardens, Antoninus strolled with Comazon along a walkway surrounded by daffodils in bloom. She plucked one and smelled it, giving it to him to smell too.

"Thank you for keeping me company, Comazon. You've been very kind to me lately, especially since—"

Comazon put a finger to her lips. "You do not have to say it. It is over. Besides it has not happened again."

"It hasn't happened because I've been a good wife. I haven't given my husband any motive to give me another beating."

"If he threatens you, I will be there to defend you, *Auguste.*"

"You weren't there the last time. Where were you, by the way? You never told me."

That was something best kept in the dark.

"Drinking. I am sorry, Excellency. It will not happen again."

"You've said that a thousand times," she said, smiling. "I'm not worried about it. You like your wine, there's nothing wrong with that. It's not like you have to keep an eye on me the whole day."

But I would like to. I would love to watch you every hour of the day, thought Comazon. "His Majesty is most kind."

They walked a few more minutes before returning to the palace. Antoninus's mood was calm and bright that evening.

"Majesty, may I ask you a question?"

"Yes, you may."

"Is Hierocles forcing you to… become a woman?"

Antoninus smiled. "No, Comazon, of course not. He did suggest that I adopt a more feminine role, but as far as forcing me… You wouldn't understand. I am a woman. I've always been. I do not identify with the male body at all. Dressing and acting like a woman has been… liberating."

Comazon looked at her, confused.

"Don't make that face, please. Let's do something fun. I'd like to take a bath after this long walk. Would you like to join me?"

The naturalness with which Antoninus spoke made Comazon's heart race. He gulped. "Sure thing, Majesty. So, I do not suppose you will be joining your aunt and cousin for dinner?"

"Of course not. I won't let my grandmother impose her whims on me. I'll see them tomorrow."

Once in the baths, Antoninus tested the water with her foot. "The slaves didn't forget to keep the water warm. One of the things my husband's authority is good for."

Antoninus shrugged off her cape and allowed Comazon to pull her tunic over her head. She dropped off her *subligaculum* and jumped into the water, not without inadvertently providing Comazon with a few instants to admire her slender but very toned pale body. Comazon sighed, trying hard to repress his thoughts.

"The water is delicious, you should join me," Antoninus said squeezing the water out of her hair.

"I am alright."

"Come on, Comazon! Don't be a killjoy."

A perfect time to be an obedient soldier. He untied his sandals, removed the heavy breastplate and helmet, and shrugged out of his tunic and *subligaculum*. His bear body was fully exposed, but Antoninus did not seem to notice.

"Come on, jump!"

Comazon jumped in with a big splash. As soon as he emerged, he was met by Antoninus with a splash war. The general drew closer and embraced her to make her stop. The empress fought back and tried to escape from the grip, but Comazon reached her again and locked her from behind. Antoninus pulled forward and dragged him to the edge of the pool. She grabbed the wall, but Comazon did not let go of the grip. His hard cock had hopelessly found its way toward Antoninus's hole.

Antoninus turned to look at the general, staring into his intense turquoise eyes. He saw the soul within the empress's eyes, that soul he had wanted to possess from the very first day. Now he had her just as he had always wished, alone and all to himself. Letting go of his inhibitions, he brought his mouth closer, unleashing the passion that for so long had consumed his body. Closing his eyes, he possessed her with his tongue, losing himself in the heavenly moment. He pressed the empress's cock with his own against her abdomen and did not stop kissing her until he was almost out of breath.

"I have waited so long for this."

Antoninus understood the general's urge. To have been by her side for so long, loving her while she had married another man, must not have been easy. He had done his duty, protecting the couple in spite of his feelings, offering his friendship in times of pain. He deserved a real reward. She turned around, giving her back to the general. He held on to the edge of the pool with one hand and with the other placed his cock where it belonged.

"No, wait, wait a little. Let's go to the room."

In the brewery, a drunk Hierocles shared the evening with his friend Gordius.

"Hey man, what's wrong with you? You don't look good at all," Gordius said, patting him on the shoulder.

"Nothing. The affairs of the empire wear me out. That's why I'm here trying to enjoy an evening with you."

"And I surely appreciate that, dear friend. What about your wife? Still giving you trouble?"

"Nah, she's learned her position." Hierocles took a sip of his beer. "She's in her room right now, probably sleeping. I really don't give a shit."

"What about those visitors you said arrived today?"

"Ugh, I don't know. More trouble, I guess. It's my mother-in-law's sister and her son."

"Didn't you care to meet them?"

"I know I will, eventually. It didn't have to be today. They'll be staying a long time, I suppose. One doesn't make a trip all the way from Syria for nothing."

"It's interesting you should say that. Have you thought about what the reason for their visit might be?"

"I don't know, Gordius. But I will find out."

"Don't you hate that in spite of being Caesar, and the *de facto* ruler of the empire, you still have to deal with in-laws and your wife's hogwash? I know you're the heir to the throne, but your wife is younger than you."

"Who knows, many things can happen."

"Do you have something in mind? Oh, do tell! Your secrets are safe with me."

"Don't be so curious, Gordius. I mean… things happen. You know, accidents…"

"Accidents… you smart son of a bitch! You haven't changed a bit since your days in the stables."

"Believe me, I have. And now I'm very close to fulfilling all my wishes. No one will stop me."

"Cheers to that!"

The men clinked their goblets.

"By the way," Gordius whispered, drawing closer to Caesar. "What are you doing after this? We could still, you know…"

"You're the one who hasn't changed, you slut. You're still fucking crazy!"

Antoninus and Comazon emerged from the water and dried themselves with sheepskins. They walked barefoot through the corridors leading to the imperial chamber under the candlelight.

Antoninus led Comazon to the bed, where the general was all over her, enjoying the delicious feel of her smooth skin with his rough hands. The empress lay on her back, resting on the pillows against the headboard. Comazon kissed her body from the nipples down to the navel, rubbing his stubble on her abdomen until he reached the cock, which stood straight and tall like an obelisk. He licked the circumcised head and sucked it delicately, applying just a gentle, pleasurable amount of pressure. Antoninus moaned softly.

Comazon reached out and blew out one of the candles, leaving the room in a comfortable dimness. He took a bottle of rose-scented oil, rubbed some on his hands, and poured a few drops on Antoninus's throbbing hole. Pushing Antoninus's legs back with his body, he leaned in to kiss her. The empress caressed the general's broad back, letting his chest hair tickle her smooth pecs. Comazon rose, rubbed his cock with his oiled hand, feeling an intense but pleasurable heat, and made the first insertion, the wanting ass sucking the thick cock head in.

"Ohh," Antoninus moaned, her breathing getting faster.

Comazon kept pushing gently, his cock sliding its way like a hot knife through butter. He stayed inside for a few minutes, silent and unmoving, enjoying the perfect, glove-like fit, letting the young hole grow accustomed to his girth. Antoninus welcomed the pressure and closed his legs tight to better feel the general's weapon of choice.

Comazon leaned forward again and kissed his boy—for she was still a boy to him—his tongue moving as deeply as possible inside her mouth, almost making her choke. Antoninus reciprocated with the same intensity, being possessed by a real man for the first time in her life.

What had started as a slow fuck quickly grew in passion, Comazon inserting the full length of his cock with each thrust and feeling the welcoming warmth and smoothness of the empress's passage. Antoninus continued to play with the general's heavy fur, giving him her delicate neck to kiss, letting him breathe on her ear, begging him in whispers to fuck her more.

After a good while, Comazon was getting close, and he would not be able to hold his gush much longer. His seed— that seed that would never yield him a son—escaped his body in rhythmic bursts of ecstatic bliss. He moaned loudly. Many times he had cum inside the guts of another man, but never while being truly in love.

When he was done, the general lay on his back, placing his forearm on his forehead, exposing his hairy armpit soaked with sweat. An intoxicating heat invaded his head and carried him to Olympus. Now his life was complete. Nothing more sublime could be experienced in this world. However, as he was beginning to come down from the orgasmic high, a thought came to his mind… Perhaps there could be even greater happiness in this life, after all? A peaceful, blissful, lasting kind of happiness?

Antoninus lay on the velvety chest of his lover, the rhythm of their breathing in perfect synchrony. And so they remained, lying still for hours, in perfect peace.

Moments earlier, Mamaea and Alexianus were walking through the palace corridors on their way to their quarters when they passed by the empress's chamber.

"What are those sounds?" Alexianus asked.

"Sounds?" his mother asked, sticking an ear to the door. The moaning of two voices, one high-pitched and one masculine, came to her ear. She gasped. "Nothing. Keep walking!"

"But Mother, I'm sure—"

"No, you're not! You've just had too much to drink tonight."

Mamaea left her son in his quarters, kissed him goodnight and blew out the candles on her way out. But she did not go to her room. She wandered looking for an exit to the garden. Once outside, she walked among the many bushes of roses, daffodils, and other flowers, down to a bench surrounded by two cupids. She waited.

Minutes later, a figure in a cloak arrived and sat down next to her. "We don't have much time," she whispered. "Did you make sure no one followed you?"

"Yes, Mother. But why all this secrecy? Why did you want to meet without Soaemias?"

"I didn't know you cared so much about your sister."

"I don't. But the curiosity about what you want to tell me is killing me!"

"I want to make your son emperor. I didn't want to risk it telling you by letter."

Mamaea was about to let out a scream of excitement.

"Hush! Don't ruin things!" Maesa said, covering her daughter's mouth. "Making Antoninus emperor was a disaster. I was aware of his 'peculiar' personality since he was a child, but I never thought it would be such a monumental hindrance to my plans. And things have gotten much worse since he installed that brute charioteer as Caesar. He's been running the government all by himself and hasn't even let me have a say. He's going to ruin everything. He even demanded a position for his mother. Can you believe it?"

"I do believe it. I told you in Emesa that you were making a mistake, mother. Alexianus has always been the wiser of the two boys."

"Yes, but he was fourteen at the time. Who would have taken him seriously? And besides, I had the excuse of inventing that Antoninus was Caracalla's son."

"So, he's not…? You spoke with such confidence that I came to believe that Soaemias had really slept with Caracalla."

"You know she's not that kind of woman. She's naive and good-hearted; she let me go on with the deception, but reluctantly. Now I see that I would have had a more active cooperation from you."

"Of course, Mother. I'm glad you at least accept it now. So, what's the plan?"

Loud moans of ecstasy came from the empress's chamber.

"It sounds like the first part is already underway."

"What?"

"It's Comazon's voice you hear. That man really loves Antoninus. If he could replace Hierocles in Antoninus's heart, the first part of the task would be done. Then you and me would have to work on the second part."

"The second part? Tell me what it is, Mother. I'm dying to know."

"We have to make sure Antoninus names Alexianus Caesar and heir."

Mamaea gasped. "But surely we won't be able to do that, Mother… From what you've told me, he's totally under the influence of that hideous charioteer."

"That's precisely what I expect to change tonight. And then…"

"Then…?"

"Then we have to keep an open eye, dear child; we have to look for the right moment to storm in. If Comazon takes Antoninus away, we must make sure that your boy is Caesar before they leave. I don't know exactly how things will turn out but remain vigilant… remain vigilant!"

Δ

Antoninus woke up the next morning, when the first rays of sunlight crawled through a crack in the curtains. She and Comazon were still lying in the same position as when they fell asleep.

"Comazon, Comazon wake up," she said, carefully patting his face.

The general woke up, and after an instant of confusion, he saw his beloved's face and smiled. "Why did you wake me up so early? I was having the most beautiful dream."

"What was it?"

"I was dreaming that we lived together in a small villa and that… we had a little family."

Antoninus dropped onto her back and let out a sigh. "This was a mistake. We shouldn't have done this."

Comazon looked at her confused but did not drop his smile. "What do you mean? These have been the best moments of my life."

"Yes, but… it wasn't right. It wasn't right! What time is it? My husband will be here any minute and I—"

"So what? He will have to face me if he has anything to say."

"Please leave now, Comazon. Leave and forget all this. Go back to your duties and never return to this part of the palace again. I'm sorry. I'm sorry!"

"Antoninus, my love! How can you say this after the magical night we just had together? How can you…?"

Antoninus got up abruptly from the bed and awkwardly threw a sheet over her shoulders.

"Please, Comazon. Don't make things more difficult. I was confused, I didn't know what I was doing. Hierocles… Hierocles will be here any minute. You have to leave. You must leave now, please!"

Comazon couldn't understand a thing but didn't want to make a scene. Not after the love they had shared the night before. Surely she was experiencing regret—something normal for a married woman who had cheated on her husband. They would have time to talk later. He picked up his clothes, got dressed hastily and left the room.

Antoninus leaned against the door and slid to the floor, tears running down her face.

When Hierocles arrived a few moments later, Antoninus was in her bed, and appeared to be asleep. He stripped off his toga and lay down beside his wife wearing only his tunic. She sensed his presence and turned to him.

"Oh husband, you're here," she said, caressing his chest. "I didn't notice you coming in."

He didn't answer. There was something different in the room, but at first glance he couldn't tell what it was. Then he noticed a smell. A very familiar smell. Comazon. His heart skipped a beat. So, he had taken his word of sharing his wife, after all.

"Do you want to have breakfast in bed? I can order the slaves to—"

"No. You can have it if you want. I have to go."

"But you've just arrived. Come on, please, stay just a little longer," Antoninus said, rubbing his chest harder and looking for his mouth.

Hierocles pulled her hand away, stood up and put his toga back on. He left the room.

A few minutes later, Stephanus arrived with a basket. "My Lady, here's your breakfast."

Antoninus, leaning against the headboard, motioned with his hand for him to put the basket on the bedside table. "Do you know where my husband went?"

"No idea, *domina*. He seemed to be in a bit of a hurry."

"He must have remembered a meeting in the Senate or something." She rose. "I'm going to take a bath. You can have this if you want. I'm not hungry."

Comazon arrived back in his house and sat down on the bed. He rested his head on his hand and, for the first time since the dissolution of the *Legio III Gallica*, he wept. He wept desperately, releasing all the sorrow of his broken heart. He tried to find solace in the moments of ecstasy when his spill filled Antoninus's insides; in the sweet, sliding movements that preceded that moment; in the deep, passionate kisses in the pool… all for what? Had it really been all for nothing?

Antoninus's marriage to Hierocles was falling apart; he wanted to drive her away from Hierocles, to cut the emotional ties with that abusive man, to remove the blindfold from her eyes. Then he could take her away, even as far as the land of the Greeks—where living their life as a couple publicly would be easier—and forget about Rome. What a dream! But the reality was that, even with all his care, his love and tenderness, the loathed charioteer was still there, obscuring his future like an evil shadow. The dream he had had while on Antoninus's bed haunted him: he and Antoninus, as a man or a woman—he couldn't quite remember—together in the countryside, raising a family of adopted children, living a life of beautiful simplicity. But it had been just that. A dream. Something illogical. Something impossible.

There was a knock on the door. He rose and went to open it. What he saw shocked him.

"May I… come in?" Hierocles said.

Comazon welcomed him in with a wave of his hand. Hierocles admired the lush green myrtle and ivy that decked walls and doors. The columns were wreathed with vines. The atrium had colored glass windows and lamps in the shapes of animals, covered above by a purple woolen cloth. A soft scent of nard hung in the air. An austere *domus*, with the martiality of a soldier, and far from the luxuries of the palace, but not a bad place to live. At least much better than the dumpster where he used to live during his time as a charioteer.

"You still have a passion for the Orient, don't you? I don't know many Romans who procure this fabulous incense. They find it too exotic."

"I was stationed there for a long time. There are certain things that I took a liking to," Comazon said, while pulling up a chair for the uninvited guest. "Something to drink?"

"Wine, please."

Comazon took an amphora from his cabinet and poured a goblet for the consort and another for himself.

"I shouldn't be here after the way you left me to die in the street," Hierocles said taking a sip. "In fact, I haven't forgiven you."

"You said it better than I could. There is no need for you to be here, Highness."

"Cut the hogwash, Comazon. Your dick has already been in my ass. Call me by my name: Hierocles."

Comazon sighed at the memory. He also took a sip of wine. He had fucked Rome's most precious virgin ass, but now, in light of what had just happened, it didn't matter all that much to him. In fact, it didn't matter at all.

"Why are you here, Hierocles?"

"You look rough. Have you been crying? Am I wrong, or the big tough general has a heart after all?"

"My personal life is none of your business. Now, if you will excuse me, I have things to do— "

"Actually, I think it is." He paused. "I know you slept with my wife."

A sepulchral silence filled the room. For a few minutes, neither man drank from their cups.

What could Comazon say as an excuse? A certain promise made in the dark came to his mind. "You said I could have her anytime I wanted."

Hierocles nodded with a smile. "I see you weren't that drunk the night you fucked me. You were perfectly aware of what you were doing."

"So were you."

"Yes, I admit it. It was consensual. I wanted you. And you wanted me too. Let's get over it."

Comazon considered for a minute. Then he held out his hand. Hierocles shook it.

"Thank you. That's what I expected. I have one more question for you, though."

"What is it?"

"Does this friendship mean that you will be loyal to me under any, and I mean any circumstances?"

"I will always be loyal to Rome and her institutions."

"No, but I mean, loyal to me. To me personally."

"I will be loyal to Rome and her institutions," the general repeated. "And I will give you a piece of advice, young man. Power and gold are not the most important things in life. There are such things as honor, respect—"

"And love?" Hierocles said, raising his goblet. Seeing from Comazon's unsmiling face that there was nothing more to say, he rose from his chair.

"One thing, though," Comazon said.

Hierocles pricked up his ears.

"I do not want to hear of you hitting the emperor ever again."

Hierocles smiled and headed for the door. Outside, he had the chance to admire the man who had been his only taker. He looked him up and down. "Damn, man. You're hot. You sure were a good fuck."

When Antoninus returned to the room, she discovered Stephanus lying on the floor, with the basket in disarray and food spilled beside him. She leaned forward and, holding his head, saw two sharp bleeding holes in his neck. She let go quickly, shrieking in terror. A loud hissing sound came from under the bed. Antoninus peeked in and a cobra bared its fangs menacingly at her. She ran out of the bedroom, crying for help.

A few minutes later, two slaves surreptitiously entered with nets to catch the reptile. Antoninus, Soaemias and Maesa remained outside. Soaemias hugged her inconsolable daughter.

"A snake was in my food, yes!" a sobbing Antoninus said. "Someone tried to kill me! We will have all the slaves in the household interrogated immediately!"

"Do you think it might have been Stephanus himself? He's the one who brought you the food, right?" Soaemias said.

"Of course not, Mother. If he knew the snake was there, then why is he dead?"

"Well, maybe it got out of his control and turned on him… You can't really train serpents."

"Don't waste your time with stupid reasonings. I know very well who did it," Maesa said.

"Who?" Antoninus yelled.

"Isn't it obvious, child? Your husband! He has poisoned before, now he tried it again."

"You're lying, you're lying, it can't be him! He's not even in the palace right now."

"He could very well have sent the basket with Stephanus. Unfortunately, the poor slave cannot tell us now."

"No! I refuse to believe it!"

"Don't jump to conclusions, Mother," Soaemias said. "You have no basis for your assertions."

"Of course I do," she said, gripping Antoninus's chin. "It's time for you to take that veil off your face. Your husband is a murderer! He killed your friend and now he tried to kill you. Are you really that stupid?"

The noise drew Mamaea and Alexianus into the room, still in their night robes.

"This is who you must name Caesar. This is the one who must be your heir!" Maesa exclaimed, pointing at Alexianus. "By Elagabal, wake up from the spell and for once be worthy of your title!"

Antoninus blinked with tear-filled eyes. The image of her cousin looked blurry and distant. After a few moments she was able to sharpen the focus. There he stood, a few years younger than her, the boy she used to play with as a child. The boy she hadn't seen in four years.

The slaves left the room with the snake hissing and writhing inside the net, jerking in all directions.

"Take it away and cut its head off, by Elagabal!" Maesa said. "And you, dear child, why don't you take the chance to talk to your cousin?" she took the hands of Soaemias and Mamaea. "Come, daughters, and let the boys have a private conversation."

Antoninus entered her messy *cubiculum*, followed by her cousin. She sat on the bed, while Alexianus remained standing in front of her.

"I'm sorry I didn't meet with you yesterday," Antoninus said. "I was… sincerely indisposed."

"You don't have to apologize, Majesty. Her Excellency is entitled to do as she wishes."

Antoninus was surprised at the ease with which her cousin had adapted to her pronouns. She looked up and observed him. He had transformed into the most handsome young man, with a slight mustache and youthful beard, which he had probably never shaved since it first appeared. His oval head and dreamy eyes gave him a semblance of wisdom. She lifted her hand and touched his chin.

"Looking at you is like looking at a mirror to the past," Antoninus said. "You look so much like me when I arrived in Rome, four years ago, full of dreams and illusions… And you are probably the age I was back then."

"I just turned eighteen this month, Majesty."

"Of course, forgive me for not remembering." She removed her hand from his chin and began to cry.

"Oh no, please don't cry, my Lady. I'm here to bring you happiness, not sorrow."

He sat down next to her and put his arm around her shoulder. She turned to look at him and rested her head on his neck. He wiped away her tears. She sighed and looked at him again.

"You'll be a great Caesar," she said in a calm voice.

Δ

The next morning, Antoninus requested the Senate to be in full session for a special announcement. The senators suspected something momentous, since Caesar was not present. Julius Paulus had received hints from Maesa but knew nothing for certain. She was also present at the session.

The empress appeared and ordered silence. "Fathers of Rome," she began her speech, in a moderate tone of voice that recalled her years as a boy, "I know that it is unusual for me to visit you in this most honorable house, but the matter that brings me is of the outmost importance and could only be handled by me personally."

The senators listened attentively.

"For some months now, I have delegated all government duties to my husband, who has also been appointed Caesar by me, with the right that I have to bestow titles according to my wishes. Well, it is my duty to inform you, that the affairs of state will continue to be handled by Caesar—"

Boos and hoots were heard in the stands. Some senators shushed their dissenting peers.

"The affairs of state will continue to be handled by Caesar, but Caesar will no longer be my husband," she said, extending her hand toward the entrance, where Alexianus, dressed in a manly toga, made his appearance. "Behold, the new Caesar of Rome."

The senators rose and applauded as Alexianus occupied the center of the *curia* with his cousin. Antoninus urged them to make silence.

"Now you may rest assured that in my heart there is nothing but the desire for the good of Rome. May Elagabal guide us on this new direction," she said, and she and her cousin left the hall.

Later, Hierocles stormed into the imperial bedroom while Antoninus was changing her clothes.

"What did you just do?" he roared, slamming the door.

"What I should have done from the beginning. Appoint my cousin as my rightful heir and Caesar!"

Hierocles slapped her. "How dare you try to disinherit me!? I'm gonna kill you!" he said, grabbing her tightly by the neck.

"Kill me! Kill me!" she hissed with eyes starting out of her head. "But you'll never be emperor!"

Hierocles's eyes widened with fury. He threw her to the floor.

"It's a pity you've already failed once," Antoninus said, touching her neck. "You won't get another chance. I will divorce you and throw you out of the palace!" she shouted, her mouth foaming.

Hierocles froze for a moment. Shivers ran down his spine. He drew closer to her and offered her a hand to get up. She took it. He tried to hug and kiss her, but she looked away.

"Listen, please listen to me. Things don't have to be this way… We can still make things work… You love me, I know you love me… and I love you too… but there are things, people who have come between us…"

She sobbed. He pulled back a little to look into her eyes.

"I found out… that you slept with the praetorian prefect."

Antoninus frowned and wiped away her tears. "How did you know?"

"You think a man can't smell the scent of another man who has slept in his lair?"

"Then why… why didn't you say anything? Why didn't you hit me?"

"I realized that hitting you wasn't the answer… It wouldn't have solved anything. I was hurt, deeply hurt; I wanted to kill you and then kill myself to join you in eternity," he said, sitting on the bed with his hands over his eyes, sobbing.

"Oh! No, husband, please don't cry…" Antoninus said, sitting beside him, "I… I was just being stupid, I felt abandoned and lonely and I… gave in to the moment… I don't feel anything for Comazon, I never have! I was weak… you know us women, we're fragile and give in to the slightest temptation… I swear to you, I felt nothing, and all the time he was inside me, I was only thinking of you."

"Do you swear it?"

"I do! By Elagabal Almighty, I swear!"

He turned to face her, and they melted into the most passionate kiss. A trickle of saliva joined their lips when they parted.

"Then, let's do things differently… Let's spend more time together, like in the old days. Let's make love every day, dine in bed, go hunting together. Fuck Rome, fuck the empire, fuck the senators! You are my wife and to you I will devote all of my time."

"Do you swear it?"

"I swear, by the almighty Elagabal."

She smiled and leaned on his shoulder. Hearing her husband proclaim his faith in her god convinced her that things had been resolved.

"One thing, though," Hierocles said.

Antoninus looked at him.

"For things to be completely right again between us, you must retract your decree and appoint me Caesar again."

"I will do that, love."

"When?"

"Right now, if you want."

Hierocles embraced her for long minutes. "Thank you, thank you, love," he said with tears in his eyes. "But you must also get rid of Comazon. He's a dangerous man; he's in love with you and wants to separate us."

She looked at him straight in the eye. "Don't worry about it, sunshine. I will ask him to leave today."

A couple of hours later, Antoninus, dressed in a sumptuous stole, and adorned with all the imperial insignia she could find and a little excess makeup, entered the main hall of the palace from her chamber, accompanied by her husband. Her grandmother, who had been waiting for her since she was alerted of Hierocles's return, lunged at her.

"Where are you going, my dear?"

"Back to the Senate."

"What for?" she said with a hand on her chest.

"To retract my decision and reappoint my husband as Caesar and my rightful heir."

"You will not do such thing."

"Get out of the way, Maesa," Hierocles said, stopping her with a gesture of his hand. "I will join my wife to ensure that her will is honored."

"You have no idea what you're doing," she said to Antoninus, ignoring Hierocles. "Alexianus has already introduced himself to the troops and they support him! A decision of that nature cannot be reversed just like that!"

"We'll see!" Hierocles said, pushing her aside.

Comazon, alerted by one of the guards, appeared through the main door.

"Get out of here, Comazon. Don't even think about interfering with my wife's decisions!"

"You are no longer in power. I take no orders from you," Comazon grunted, approaching Hierocles and showing him his fist.

"But you do take orders from me," Antoninus said, walking from behind. "And I say that you are relieved of your duties, Comazon. From now on, you will be the city prefect, but you will no longer have any authority over the army or the Praetorians."

Comazon stared at her in shock and disbelief. Furious, he made an about face and stormed out of the palace.

"Listen to me!" Maesa shrieked with her hands on her face. "At least let me talk to you before you do something you'll regret."

"It's me you need to talk to!" Soaemias shouted, making an entrance. "Daughter, there is something you should know. Something I have kept a secret for many years, but that it is time for it to come to light."

Antoninus looked at her with a contorted face.

"Don't do it!" Maesa shouted, lunging at her daughter.

Soaemias spoke before Maesa could stop her. "You're not Caracalla's child! Your real father is Gannys! Gannys! You should have never sat on the throne!"

The shock was too much for both Antoninus and Hierocles to bear, whose eyes seemed to bulge out of their sockets.

"Guards! Open the door!" Hierocles yelled in desperation.

The doors remained shut.

"My husband said, open the doors!" Antoninus said, harassing the guards.

"It's useless," Maesa said. "They have been warned to obey only me."

"This is ridiculous!" Hierocles shouted, out of his mind. "Open!" he yelled at the guards. "Open the doors immediately!"

As the guards remained motionless, Hierocles pulled his wife by her dress and dragged her back to her quarters.

"I have serious doubts that it is her free will to go there. Guards! Seize the charioteer! Free the empress!" Maesa shouted.

A group of guards rushed at the couple, who, followed by Soaemias, ran into the imperial *cubiculum*. Maesa arrived instants later and banged the door. "Antoninus! Open the door, child! We must talk! Please, be reasonable!"

A few moments passed and no sound could be heard inside.

"Guards, open the door! Kick it down if necessary!"

After several attempts, the guards managed to kick the door open. However, when they and Maesa entered the room, there was no one to be found.

Out in the streets, a panting soldier caught up with Comazon on the steps of the *curia*.

"General, General!" the man shouted, almost out of breath.

"What is the matter, Marcio?"

"An emergency has occurred. Hierocles, the empress, and her mother are on the run. Nobody knows where they are."

"What is all this nonsense you are saying?"

"You'd better come with me. I'll explain on the way."

Comazon walked hurriedly alongside the guard.

"I must warn you that this is a rebellion, General. The Praetorians have already learned of your dismissal, and they didn't take it lightly. Their bond of honor with you is stronger than any sexual pact they might have made with the empress before a foreign god. They've been loyal to her only because you've remained loyal. But now, everything has changed. As you know, Alexianus, the new Caesar, has already appeared before them, and they're not willing to submit again to that low life, Hierocles. They're out of control and ready to seize the empress and depose her. Now they want Alexianus not only to be Caesar, but also Emperor. And they want you back in office."

"I will talk to them," Comazon replied in a firm voice.

"And it also doesn't help that the emperor never fulfilled the promises of wealth he made to the men in Raphanea, something that Alexianus's mother already took advantage of, dispersing gold among the soldiers. If you had stayed a few minutes longer in the palace, you would have heard about the scandal, General! Antoninus's mother herself said that his father is not Caracalla, but Gannys! Can you believe it? And now Alexianus's mother bribed the soldiers to accept her son instead. I don't blame them for taking the money. They feel cheated, used, deprived not only of their fair monetary reward, but also of their sexual power, which they say Antoninus used to bewitch that charioteer and lure him to become her husband. It's obvious, since she abandoned the cult of Elagabal as soon as she married him."

"I will talk to them!" Comazon reiterated in exasperation at the soldier's verbosity.

Minutes later, Comazon and the soldiers arrived at the palace, where Maesa was still waiting with some of the guards.

"*Augusta*!"

"Oh Comazon, Comazon! If you would've been here, this wouldn't have happened." she said, throwing herself into his arms. "I wanted to buy time by talking to him in the palace, but now they've escaped, and we don't know where they are."

Comazon took her to the imperial bedroom and showed her the hidden passageway.

"No one but the emperor and the praetorian prefect knew about this place. This is how they escaped to the city."

"Do you know where it leads?"

"Yes. But by this time, they must be hiding somewhere else." He darted toward the exit. "Guards! Follow me! I want every man interrogated and every building searched. We must find them at all costs."

The men followed Comazon outside. "General!" one of them said. "You must know by now that the consensus of the Praetorian Guard is that the 'empress' must be deposed. This madness must stop! It's for the well-being of Rome. You must support us!"

"I will not support sedition against the emperor!"

One of the guards drew his sword.

Comazon signaled him to keep it in its sheath. "Let us find them first. Then we will all talk!"

They searched the city under a scorching heat, knocking down market tables, entering private homes, inspecting temples and palaces. After about one hour, the soldiers stopped at the foot of the statue of the Colossus a litter stealthily carried by four men.

"We must search the litter," one of the guards told the carriers.

"But, officer, a very prestigious senator is traveling inside and does not wish to—"

Comazon opened the curtain without giving the man a chance to finish his sentence. Hierocles jumped out of the vehicle through the other side and ran with the speed of a gazelle. Two Praetorians gave chase. Inside remained Antoninus, makeup smeared on her face, cuddling with her mother, both trembling with fear.

"Excellency, Excellency!" Comazon said breathlessly, sweat running down his temples. "Do not fear! You are under my protection. You need not worry; the guards respect me and will accept my solution. I will take you away from Rome. We can live a happy life in exile. Life in the campagna can be very pleasant… there are gorgeous villas, with orchards and vineyards, where we can live in peace… Or we can go even farther, to Greece. I want you to live with me, I want you to be my wife, my boy, whatever you want to be… I want to live the rest of my life loving you… Your mother can come with us too."

"And Hierocles?" Antoninus said, her eyes full of tears. "Take Hierocles too… Look for him, Comazon… Take him too…"

Stunned, Comazon took a step back. He looked around, but his vision had become blurred. He couldn't hear the sounds of the city, nor the murmur of the crowd of onlookers that had gathered around them. His tongue was dry, his lips parched. He felt faint, on the verge of staggering.

"Soaemias, come with me," he said with a grievous voice and a blank stare.

"No!" she said, clinging firmly to Antoninus. "I'm not going anywhere without my daughter!"

Comazon gazed at the guards and said nothing. Then he turned violently and trudged away with his hand on his *gladius*. The screams of Antoninus and her mother being ripped apart by the precise lunge of a Praetorian sword echoed in his ears, but the clamor soon grew weak and became confused with his own murderous thoughts.

"General! General!" two guards shouted, running toward him. "Hierocles escaped. We couldn't catch him."

At the same time, Maesa wailed in despair, like a siren, running toward the litter as fast as an old woman could. "No! Don't kill them! Not my Soaemias, no!" She looked inside the coach and fell unconscious to the ground before any of the guards could catch her.

Comazon didn't have to go very far. Only one place could serve as a hideout for the fugitive. He walked inside the *Cloaca Maxima*, his feet soaked to his ankles in sewage. His sense of smell had become oblivious to the filth; he walked like Hermes, stomping the ordure between the worlds of the living and the dead.

"Hierocles!" His voice echoed off the cavernous walls like the roar of Hades.

Running water was the only sound. He walked a few more steps and let out a second scream. After the third call, Hierocles emerged from a corner with his hands raised, his once immaculate garments stained with excreta, and with an anguish, never known before, disfiguring his face.

"The emperor is dead," Comazon said with a lump in his throat.

Hierocles's expression remained unchanged. Comazon drew closer, wielding his sword.

"Listen! Don't do anything before you listen to me!"

"Speak!"

"Comazon, you were right. You have always been right. Power and gold are not all that important. A simple life, a life away from trouble is what really matters. I regret the day I went to the palace. I regret falling victim to the whims of a stupid little boy. But you… you're a real man… you're someone who can be trusted… That's all I need, that's all I'm looking for… And I know that all you want is a boy for yourself… I can be that boy. Take me with you, oh mighty Comazon, take me with you! I'll do whatever you want! You can fuck me every day and every night, you—"

His words were interrupted by the solid impetus of the only weapon that Comazon should have used to penetrate him: his sword. The deep thrust drove the sharp blade across Hierocles's abdomen; Comazon pulled out the metal in a strong zigzag motion to inflict the greatest pain possible. Hierocles gasped, choked and, spitting blood, fell to his knees. He gazed into the blue eyes of the proud general one last time but found only contempt. The once heir to the throne collapsed face down with a loud splash, only a few curls of his golden hair remaining untouched by the soiled waters.

Δ

A cold sense of desolation emanated from the walls of the now former Temple of Elagabal. The altar was being dismantled, and the *baetyl* carried away to the palace, from where it would be sent back to Emesa to be worshipped by whoever still wanted to. The gods of old would return to Rome; Jupiter would once again take his rightful place in the temple.

Comazon entered the Senate house, where the painting of Antoninus was being dismounted from the prominent place it had occupied above the winged statue of Victoria. He ordered one of the slaves to bring it to him. He was so focused studying it that he didn't notice Alexianus, who had now taken the name of Alexander, walking behind him.

"He was beautiful, wasn't he?" the newly appointed emperor said.

Comazon turned his gaze briefly to the visitor, then returned it to the painting. Alexander put his hand on the general's shoulder.

"I'm sorry for what happened," Alexander continued. "It was too late to stop the frenzied crowd. He did not deserve to have his dead body desecrated in that way." Antoninus's body had been dragged through the streets, dismembered, and thrown into the Tiber. "None of us wanted that."

"I know."

"At least his mother had a proper funeral."

"How is Maesa?" Comazon asked, looking at the young man.

"Unwell. She just yelled incoherences when she came back to her senses. We had to lock her up in the palace. A doctor will be looking over her. I went to see her and…"

"And…?"

"She thinks I'm Antoninus. She threw herself on the floor asking for my forgiveness. I could not convince her otherwise."

Several slaves approached sweeping the floor with straw brooms.

"Comazon, I need to ask something from you."

"Whatever you wish, Excellency," Comazon said, dismissing the slaves with a hand gesture, and setting the picture aside.

"My mother has told me how attached you were to my cousin. She said you loved him like a son. I would be very happy if you could love me the same way."

Comazon smiled at the irony of fate. "Sure thing… Son."

Alexander hugged him. "Keep the picture. I'm sure you'll give it the best use possible."

Alone, Comazon picked up the painting, now only a crude token of the enthralling beauty of the Syrian boy, the pale emperor. He looked away for an instant and walked slowly toward the sacred fire of Victoria. He contemplated it one last time, the reddish light of the flames bringing out the undertones of the skin. He scorched one of its corners, letting the ashes fall. The flames reached the visage of the once most powerful human being on Earth, darkening it, staining it, razing it. He tossed the last remnants into the fire, watching them vanish in a sputtering cloud of sparks and smoke.

Printed in Great Britain
by Amazon